NanoStrike

Pete Barber

This book is a work of fiction. All characters, organizations, and locales, and all incidents and dialogue, are drawn from the author's imagination and not to be construed as real.

DEDICATION

Thank you, Joyce, for always believing.

1

In his makeshift laboratory in a bombed-out Israeli medical facility, Dawud dipped his hand into a small glass vivarium and selected a white rat with an orange stripe spray-painted on its back. He held the wriggling rodent by the tail, swung it away from the cage, and squirted two puffs from an asthma inhaler into its snout. When he was satisfied that the mist had dissipated, he returned the rat to the vivarium, setting it next to its brother. The rats touched noses and sniffed each other before recommencing their search for escape.

"Was that enough?" Firman asked. He spoke English with a slight French accent.

Dawud looked up at the tall, dark assassin—an infidel, yes, but also a useful tool for Allah. "Even a trace of inhibitor in the airway is sufficient to provide immunity from the weapon." Dawud took a puff from the inhaler and passed it to Firman, who sucked in a dose before moving to the end of the table, next to the rats.

Dawud sealed a lid on the vivarium, opened the valve on a straw-sized plastic tube connected to a compressed-air cylinder, and released the nanoweapon into the rats' habitat.

The untreated rat shuddered as if shot through with an electric current. Then it charged and slammed and bounced off the glass walls, legs pumping in a futile attempt to flee. Black-bead eyes sprung wide. Lips snarled back, baring pink gums and white teeth.

The rodent flipped on its side, jerked and spasmed for five seconds, and then became still.

The orange-marked rat edged forward and inspected a hard black column of charcoal that protruded one inch from the dead rat's throat, distending its jaws.

Firman's eyes stretched wide and a slow smile spread across his thin lips. "Damn! That was fast," he said.

Two weeks later, sixteen hundred strangers barreled through dark tunnels beneath London's nightly bustle. Brought together by chance and circumstance, homeward-bound workers, uneasy tourists, uniformed schoolchildren, and sated shoppers rocked and bobbed like marionettes with the motion of the train.

The tube train was well named: eight metal cylinders, each sixty feet long and eight feet wide, linked together in a chain.

At the center of the fifth car, holding a chrome rail, Firman peered between crammed bodies at the fortunate few with seats, lost in their books, smart phones, and tablet computers. His hands were damp with sweat inside thin, transparent latex gloves.

Firman pulled an inhaler from his inside pocket. Three times he sprayed the inhibitor, held, and then exhaled through his nose, coating his airways with immunity. His reserved English neighbors averted their eyes.

He lifted a black shoulder bag above his head and depressed a button embedded in the base. A high-pitched hiss signaled the release of compressed death from the canister within. Lethal molecules streamed into the car. Their unique, seeking nature found fuel in abundance: tongue and throat and lung.

It was a feeding frenzy.

Passengers, eyes stretched wide with terror, gasped and flailed before flopping to the ground, mouths gaped wide and crammed full of black charcoal.

In seconds, corpses surrounded him. A tragic barrier of unwitting protectors in case the car contained a hero.

It didn't.

Cheeks flushed with excitement, he pulled a video camera from his pocket and held it high, panning the scene.

When Firman's car burst into the stark light of Oxford Circus, central London's busiest Underground train station, he stayed below the window line, face hidden now in the shadow of a gray sweatshirt hood. Back pressed hard against the sliding doors, he knelt on a young woman's chest. The thin beat from her iPod was audible in the deathly silent carriage. Firman pulled an envelope from his side pocket, exposed an adhesive strip, and pressed the sticky message over the acne spots on her forehead, covering her stone-dead eyes.

At 5:09 p.m., rush-hour passengers stood six deep on the Central Line platform. They blinked away the rush of warm, stale air pushed from the tunnel by the slowing train. Tired eyes hunted for signs of space, and the death-car's windows showed empty. Hopefuls at the rear shuffled forward, sensing the possibility of an early escape.

The train stopped, doors hissed open, and Firman sprang backward, merging with the pressing crowd as it surged into the seemingly empty carriage.

A silent beat of awareness preceded screaming chaos when the potential riders nearest the train pushed and fought against the press of the crowd behind them, desperate to escape the macabre scene of bodies strewn like discarded laundry, frozen eyes crazed with terror and gaping mouths crammed with charcoal.

"They're all dead."

"Oh, my God!"

"What's happening?"

"Out of my way!"

Firman blended with the crowd, crouching low to avoid the station's closed-circuit TV cameras, digital witnesses to his work, the worst train disaster in London's storied history, the most callous terrorist act since that terrible September day in New York.

The crowd surged along the platform toward the exit stairs. In front of him, an elderly woman lost her footing. The frantic mob parted and washed around her prone body like a stream skirting a rock.

His section of the crowd squeezed up the final twenty steps and spilled onto Oxford Street's broad sidewalk. He sucked in a deep breath. The street was jammed with vehicles. Low-hanging exhaust fumes stung his nose.

After peeling off the gloves, Firman slipped them in the pocket of his hoodie, and walked three blocks. He stepped into a souvenir shop, slid hangers along their circular rail and selected an extra-large "Mind the Gap" T-shirt. He snapped off the price tag, removed his hoodie, and pulled on the shirt. The clerk watched him on a TV monitor.

Firman handed him a bill. "I'll wear it if you don't mind."

The shopkeeper wore a white turban. He smiled. "You American?"

"Yes."

He nodded his acceptance of Firman's lie and handed over the change.

"Could I have a bag for my old clothes?"

"Ten pence, please."

Firman grinned at the ludicrous request and passed over the coin. He stuffed his shoulder bag and hoodie in the plastic carrier.

"Have a nice day," he said as he left.

In two blocks, he turned down an alley and tossed the bag into a stinking Dumpster.

At 5:30 p.m., he crossed the road to a corner pub packed with white-collar workers. Instead of the welcoming harmonics of an after-office crowd, a church-like quiet prevailed. The congregation stared openmouthed at a wall-mounted flat-screen that displayed a repeating loop of the train as it entered the station and its doors slid back to reveal a carriage full of corpses. They had all traveled on underground rail. There, but for the grace of God . . .

Firman laid a hand on the bar. "Pint of lager, please."

The bartender dragged his eyes from the TV. He poured, and pushed the glass across the counter. "Fuckin' Arabs."

Firman nodded, paid, and settled in at the end of the bar, an incognito star reveling in the impact of his triumphant opening-night performance.

2

The next day . . .

Detective Chief Inspector Steven Quinnborne of Metropolitan Police's Murder Division and Frank Browning—point man for the British Special Branch Terrorism Response Team—stood on either side of a pasty-faced young computer operator in the London Transport Control Center. The technician had access to the largest dynamic network management system in the world, but Quinn couldn't get what he wanted.

Quinn's shoulders stretched his shirt tightly across his back as he hunched forward and peered over the operator's shoulder at the computer screen. Clenching his jaw in frustration, he spat out his words. "Run it again, and keep the camera on the doors." He'd viewed the footage a half-dozen times. Every time the train doors opened, the camera viewpoint shifted to another part of the platform.

"It's not that simple," the operator said. "You asked for the program to lock on the doors from the minute they exit the tunnel. The doors aren't always in shot, so the software loses track."

Quinn sounded out his words as if he were speaking to a child. "I . . . need . . . to . . . see . . . as much footage of the fifth carriage and its central doors as possible. I don't care about your program."

"Okay, why didn't you say? Damned pushy Yank." This was

5

spoken under the technician's breath.

Quinn heard. Anger always made his accent more pronounced, but the kid just wasn't getting it.

The operator tapped at the keyboard, and again the screen showed commuters crowded along the platform, necks craning, focused on the lights of the approaching train as they grew larger in the dark tunnel.

When the train entered the station, the driver's face was a mask of concentration. Quinn knew he'd be watching for jumpers and making sure to hit his marks so the doors would align with the exits.

"Can you slow it down?" Quinn asked.

The operator tapped at a key. "Tell me when."

The train slowed to a crawl. "Like that, good." He leaned in closer, his earlier annoyance replaced by intense concentration. The footage switched, smoothly this time, to the key camera mounted at the center of the platform and looking down from behind the heads of the waiting crowd. The fourth car rolled past, crammed with passengers. The fifth came into the shot. From this angle, the screen showed bodies two and three deep across the floor, some draped over seat backs like discarded coats.

Quinn's gut clenched at the sight. He straightened slightly.

The train stopped. This time, the camera remained on the doors as they slid open and the crowd surged forward.

"Can you rewind to before the doors open? Then go as slowly as possible?"

The operator's fingers flicked across the keyboard, and the doors were closed again. They began to inch open.

"That's as slow as I can go. Any less and we'll be looking at a series of stills."

For the first time since he'd arrived, Quinn looked at the operator. "You can do that?"

"Sure, you want?"

Quinn rested a hand on the operator's shoulder. "Not yet, thanks."

The doors slid open, five inches, six, seven. The passengers waiting on the platform closed in, blocking the camera's view of the interior. Then, as if a bomb had detonated, the front row recoiled, a dramatic response even in slow motion.

Quinn's finger leaped forward and indented the computer's

flexible screen. "There!"

The technician knocked Quinn's hand away.

Quinn ignored the move. "Okay, once more? Begin when the doors start to open and continue until that guy . . ." Without touching the screen this time, Quinn pointed to a bald businessman in a blue suit standing at the platform's edge, ". . . falls back into the woman in the green jacket."

The technician worked his magic. "Ready, should I run?"

"Yes, please. What's your name, by the way?"

They had been introduced forty minutes earlier when he and Frank arrived at the Operations Center, but Quinn hadn't paid attention.

"Austin, most folk call me Aussie."

"Okay, Aussie. Let's go."

The doors opened. The crowd pushed in. They lurched back. The bald man lost his balance and started to fall.

Quinn didn't blink, but it happened so fast he couldn't be sure. He turned to his right. "Frank, are you seeing this?"

Frank nodded. "Someone dived out of the train."

"Aussie, can you enhance it?" Quinn asked.

The screen split in two. On the right, the action replayed again frame by frame, but all they saw was a gray blur. Aussie shook his head. "Too fast. Not enough definition."

On the left, the next camera showed a mass of heads crammed together on the narrow platform and moving as one. Quinn leaned over Aussie's shoulder, straining to catch a glimpse of the lone survivor, but it was impossible in the dense crowd.

"Perhaps we can track his group," Aussie said. "I'll set markers to circle twenty or thirty people." Aussie tapped away as he spoke. "The man in the blue suit's behind him. The blond woman will stand out."

Quinn got the idea. "Use the tall kid with the baseball cap?"

Aussie clicked the target. A red arrow appeared above the kid and, along with another five arrows, moved across the screen, floating above the crowd. The pinpointed group reached the top of the stairs leading out of the platform and started to break apart.

Quinn pointed at the screen, careful not to touch now he considered Aussie a colleague rather than a smart-ass. "What's happening? What's that?"

"Someone's fallen. They're going around," Aussie said. The

arrows flowed past the obstacle and reformed into a group.

"What's ahead?" Quinn asked.

"The ticket barriers; once they pass through they'll have to pick an exit."

The gates had been swung aside so the panicked crowd could get out as fast as possible.

Quinn kept his eyes on the screen. "Frank, if you were the perp, which exit would you choose?"

"The first I could."

Quinn smiled. "Me, too. Aussie, let's work on that assumption."

Aussie split the screen again.

On the left, the group passed through the barriers and scattered. On the right, Aussie displayed video from a camera mounted outside, high on a pole and trained on the Oxford Street south exit. Commuters streamed out of the stairwell. Many stopped a few feet after reaching the pavement, blinking in the sunlight, and causing a backup.

"God, people are stupid. Can't they get out of the way?" Frank said.

Two red-arrowed passengers emerged. Behind them, someone wearing a gray sweatshirt, face obscured by a hood, pulled off his gloves and strode along Oxford Street and out of camera shot.

"There! The gray hoodie. Male!" Quinn said, stating the obvious. "Only one reason to wear a hood and gloves in July."

Aussie backed the footage up, tapped at his keyboard, and a blue arrow hovered above the hoodie's head. "We can't see his face, but the software will map his body shape. The longer he's in the shot, the more attributes to scan. Give me enough time and I'll be able to spot him anywhere."

"Clever," Quinn said. "Where's the next camera?"

"A hundred yards along Oxford Street."

Quinn rubbed at his cheek, as though he was trying to erase a mark. "With eleven thousand cameras in London, they should have this area blanketed, not one every hundred bloody yards."

Between cameras, they lost the killer for over a minute. When he reappeared, the hood still shadowed his face. He walked left to right across the screen.

"Big man, fit-lookin' bugger, too," Frank said.

"Two hundred yards to the next camera," Aussie said, anticipating Quinn's question.

The detective glared at the back of the technician's head as if he were to blame for the camera locations. Time clicked away at the bottom of the screen.

"He should be here by now," Quinn said.

They waited two minutes, three, still nothing. A few business types passed, but no hooded terrorist.

Frank straightened and rubbed the small of his back. "Lost him."

"Let's wait," Quinn remained bent forward, staring at the screen, willing the man to show. The timer showed five minutes, fourteen seconds when a tall tourist in a T-shirt strode along the sidewalk.

He had a blue arrow over his head.

"Come on, you prick, smile for the camera," Quinn said.

As if he had heard, the man looked up. Aussie tapped a key. The screen split, and a face appeared on the left. Dark hair and eyes, well groomed, tanned, and clean-shaven.

"Handsome bastard," Frank said.

"Check his physique, the way he holds himself, the way he walks," Quinn said as the killer strode out of the shot. "That's no brainwashed Arab fanatic. He's a pro."

Their quarry didn't show at the next camera. After ten minutes staring at the screen, Quinn straightened, and rolled and cricked his back.

"Good job, Aussie. Can you extract the piece we viewed and send it to my desk along with the cleanest mug shot you can manage?" Quinn handed him a business card.

"Send it here as well." Frank produced his card.

"Be glad to."

"Thanks," Quinn said. "If you see anything else, call my cell." Out of the corner of his eye, he saw Frank glaring at him and about to speak. Quinn's phone rang and postponed the confrontation.

"It's Mike Mitchell, Quinn. Can you come to the staging area and look at something?"

"What?"

"It's . . . you need to see this for yourself."

"Give me thirty minutes." Quinn closed his phone and turned to Frank. "That was Mike Mitchell."

"The City Coroner, has he got something for me?"

"Dunno, let's go find out."

Frank pulled into traffic. His face was hard and set. "Quinn, this is my jurisdiction."

"We both want to catch the bastard, Frank."

"I know you were first responder, Quinn, but terrorism is my patch. Back off, or I'll make you."

Frank Browning had been Quinn's partner in the Met's Murder Division before his recent move to Special Branch. He knew Frank's limitations, and watching him pissing on a pole to mark his territory was all the proof Quinn needed—Frank wasn't up for a job this big. Uncomfortable silence settled over the remainder of their journey.

Processing two hundred and four bodies was far beyond the resources of the City of London Coroner's Office. The Met had commandeered a local school as a temporary mortuary.

Once they'd passed through the rigorous security procedures at the entrance to the school's gymnasium, Quinn spotted Mike Mitchell observing a pathologist who was bent over a gurney, working on a corpse. Mike had been City of London coroner for twelve years. He and Quinn first met professionally, but their relationship had morphed into friendship, and they got together at least once a month for a beer. Mike joked that he felt obligated to buy for his best customer.

Quinn scanned the room. Sixty or more white-sheeted gurneys were double-parked along the walls. Quinn couldn't tell whether they'd been autopsied or still waited. It brought home the human tragedy of what, until now, he'd been dealing with as hunt-the-hoodie. These people had families and jobs and lives. But now, all they were was dead. Anger surged through him. He forced it down. To catch this murderer he needed focus, not fury.

Quinn tapped the tall, thin doctor on the shoulder. "So what's the big secret, Mike?"

Mike spoke without looking around. "Give me a minute, Quinn." The female pathologist he was observing was bent over a corpse, and speaking in a low, fast voice into a handheld Dictaphone. Once finished, she stepped back, revealing a woman's body. Quinn checked the corpse's face: thirty maybe, no more. No rings, perhaps they'd already been sealed in her personal baggie.

"Damned shame," Quinn said.

"Tell me about it. We've pulled in staff from five counties, and it'll still take us three or four days to process them all. Anyway, thanks for coming, Quinn." Mike nodded to Quinn's partner. "Hi, Frank. I thought you two had a lover's tiff and split up?"

"This is a Special Branch investigation," Frank said and handed Mike his card.

Mike turned to Quinn, who rolled his eyes.

"Oh. Right. Um, come with me." The Coroner led them past the gurneys to a small, windowless office. He closed the door behind them.

"What do you make of that?" Mike pointed to a three-foot-tall, black, headless, armless torso perched at the center of a battered, old metal desk.

"Don't tell me you brought me here to admire a new work of art," Quinn said.

"No, Dummy. What do you think it is?" He waited.

Frank laughed. "Did someone chop off ET's head and legs and leave him here?"

Quinn glared at his ex-partner. This was no time for jokes. "I'm not sure, but the ribs aren't sculpted correctly."

"Close, but no cigar." Mike stepped toward the bust and ran a gloved hand down the front of its neck as if the contact might give him inspiration, provide an explanation of how the object had come to be. "Not sculpted, molded," he said. As though someone poured quick-setting concrete down their throats . . . or, you know, the foam-in-a-can stuff that you squirt into gaps and it expands to fill them? Something entered through the airway, filled the lungs, expanded, and hardened to this black compound. Look here."

He ran his finger along the corrugated neck of the bust. "This is an exact impression of her trachea."

"That's why the ribs are indented. It's molded from the inside," Quinn said.

"Exactly, and that's not all. With this muck in their lungs you'd expect them to die of asphyxiation, right?"

Quinn and Frank nodded.

"Wrong again. See that?" The coroner pointed to a grapefruit-sized indentation midway down the left front of the casting.

"This stuff expanded so fast that her heart was crushed to a stop. I have two hundred and four heart-attack victims in my lab."

The coroner moved back from the bust to allow them an unobstructed view. He held out a box of latex gloves.

"Pick it up. Go ahead."

Quinn started to move but checked himself and let Frank take the lead. Frank pulled on gloves, put his hands either side of the ribcage, and raised the torso a few inches off the desk.

"Solid, but lighter than I expected." He rapped with his knuckles and rubbed the surface. "Feels like those charcoal briquettes you buy for the barbeque."

When Frank finished, Quinn also lifted and felt the material. He checked his hands. They were black. "Soot?"

"Have you seen anything like this before?" Quinn asked the coroner.

"Come on, Quinn . . . no one's seen anything like this before."

3

Nazar Eudon was an oilman. Finding oil, processing oil, and selling oil had made him rich. But nowadays "oil man" wasn't politically correct; so, on the advice of his marketing VP, he had made a token investment in green energy, or the closest to it he could stomach—ethanol production.

The one thing that annoyed Nazar more than being *only* 276th on the *Forbes World's Billionaires* list was wasting his time. Nazar's head of research had invited him to a demonstration at Eudon Ethanol's Ohio facility in Akron. He'd allocated four hours for the visit, and he begrudged every second.

Professor Philip Farjohn's eyes were bright and his face flushed with excitement as he illustrated his points with expansive sweeps of his arms. "We have d . . . d . . . developed a remarkable technology since our l . . . l . . . last meeting, Mr. Eudon."

While the professor talked, Nazar peered through a letter-box-sized window into a thirty-foot-diameter metal fermentation tank. A transparent container the size and shape of a telephone booth occupied the center of the tank, twenty feet below him. A stepladder stood ready beside it.

A clear liquid filled the bottom of the container, which

overflowed with garbage: old tires, newspapers, flattened cardboard, plastic soda bottles, and a pizza box (complete with pizza remnants) were visible. Nazar wondered whether the professor had brought the trash from home. The man was eccentric enough to consider it.

After five minutes of the professor's stammer-filled explanation, Nazar held up his hand to signal a stop. It took a few seconds for the tall, angular man to slow his words and calm his arms. Finally, like a clockwork toy running out of spring tension, he came to rest.

Nazar said, "Professor, I believe it will be more efficient if I tell you what I have understood from your briefing and then allow you to correct any omissions."

"Yes, b . . . b . . . but . . ."

"Professor."

"Sorry, it's ju . . . just . . ."

Nazar's hand edged forward until it touched the professor's large, bony nose. The man jerked back and fell silent.

Nazar pointed to the window. "I'm looking into a fermentation vessel. Normally, it would be loaded with wood chips and flooded with water. Specialized fungi developed at your lab would break down the chips. The resultant mash, when heated, releases the sugars from the feedstock."

"Yes, the p . . . p . . . process takes a huge amount of energy, but—"

Nazar cleared his throat and continued. "Yeasts feed on the sugars and convert them to alcohol, which is distilled to extract ethanol."

"As you say, but now—"

"Your team has developed, or, if I understand correctly, they have used nanotechnology to *build* artificial microbes, atomic-scale machines which you call nanobots. You believe this development constitutes a breakthrough."

"They are 1 . . . 1 . . . less than one nanometer, one billionth of a meter, Mr. Eudon, but amazing, quite amazing." The professor smiled a smug, self-congratulatory grin.

Nazar continued. "You claim these nanobots are intelligent enough to analyze and then break down a wide variety of feedstock. They can disassemble the feedstock at an atomic level and reassemble the atoms into the molecular structure of ethanol, eliminating the lengthy fungal decomposition and expensive heating phases."

The professor nodded along with Nazar's description, and, when his boss finished speaking, he jumped in. "The nanobots bring an additional benefit. When alcohol concentrations rise, the yeast dies, leaving valuable sugars unconverted. With nanobots, we can continue the conversion and harvest the maximum p . . . potential from the f . . . feedstock. Yields are much higher."

"How high?"

"Thirty percent by volume."

Nazar nodded. Finally, he'd heard something interesting. He pointed to the trash in the center of the chamber.

"Professor, it looks as though you cleared out your garage."

The man blushed sufficiently to confirm Nazar's suspicion.

"Initially," the professor said, "we d . . . developed the nanobots to work with wood chips. The breakthrough came when we built the analytical layer into them. Theoretically, they can p . . . process any biomass—anything that grows with s . . . s . . . sunlight."

"What's the liquid?"

"Water. The bots need a supply of hydrogen; they'll extract it from the H2O." He leaned close, his mouth twisted into a conspiratorial grin. "Shall we l . . . let them loose, Mr. Eudon?"

Nazar turned to the viewing window. He'd tolerated enough dramatics.

The professor picked up a wall phone and spoke. A short, bearded man wearing a white lab coat and silver gloves walked through a door in the side of the fermentation tank below and climbed the stepladder until he was level with the top of the junk pile. He unscrewed the cap from a soup-can-sized container and poured a liquid over one of the old tires. Then he pulled off the gloves and dropped them and the empty container into the box.

"Is it safe? I mean, couldn't these nanobots disassemble him?"

"The nanobots operate according to programmed start and stop parameters. These bots will only become active with the application of sunlight, and they're programmed to terminate after eleven minutes."

The lab technician closed the door, sealing the chamber. Nazar heard a whirring sound. He looked up. Sixty feet above, silvered blinds slid back from the domed glass roof of the fermentation vessel. Sunlight flooded in, concentrated by the dome, and shone a spotlight on the garbage pile.

"1:43 p.m." The professor read off a wall clock.

"How much material can they process in eleven minutes?" Nazar asked.

"Well, I've n . . . never used such varied feedstock."

Nazar spun and glared at the professor. "You mean you've never tried this before?"

"Not with this particular m . . . mixture. I thought we should try something special in honor of your visit. This s . . . seemed more . . . um . . . theatrical."

"Hmph." Nazar turned away. He did not enjoy being a guinea pig.

Movement in the chamber caught his attention. Lower-level items moved and caused the trash to bump and settle.

"The tire moved." Nazar said.

"Yes." The professor laughed, an unpleasant, piercing sound, which made Nazar wince. "Yes, it did. L . . . L . . . Look at the pizza."

Nazar watched the pizza slip out of sight as the garbage slid lower, like snow melting in a heated saucepan. The water at the bottom of the vessel had turned bright orange.

"Won't they eat through the box?" Nazar asked.

"Carbon-free glass," the professor replied.

As the last of the junk submerged, Nazar noted the time: 1:48 p.m.—five minutes.

The liquid bubbled and belched and rose higher in the containment vessel. Gradually, the orange coloration faded, and the agitation slowed. Eleven minutes after the process started, the box was half-full of still, clear liquid.

"I see solids at the bottom," Nazar said.

"Carbon-free items: certain types of glass, aluminum cans, and so on."

"I don't understand how a few bots can convert that much material in eleven minutes."

"C . . . convergent assembly. The nanobots we placed on the pile used energy from sunlight to assemble molecular machines. Each machine made more machines, and so on. In the nanoworld, things are p . . . processed at nanospeed. A single assembler performs over one million processes in a second. One makes a million, and each of those makes another million. Within s . . . sixty seconds, the initial stock created a huge army of nanobots."

"But why so much liquid?"

"Obviously the bots don't create m... matter—that's impossible—they are simply rearranging atoms and transforming them into the atomic sequence we program them for. Rather like tearing down a Lego house and rearranging the blocks to make Lego cars."

"What's in the box now?"

The professor squinted at the container. "I'd say about two hundred gallons of l... liquid from which we can distill about sixty gallons of ethanol."

Nazar's eyebrows lifted and his mouth opened, but when no sound came out it triggered another bout of piercing laughter from the professor. This time, Nazar laughed with him. He reached out and shook the professor's hand.

"Professor, this is indeed a breakthrough. What was the catalyst?"

"Not what, Mr. Eudon. Who!"

The professor's flippancy irritated Nazar, but he waited.

"The *who* is Dawud Ferran, or D... David Baker, as he's known in America. Yes, that is who. But why is David Baker here? And the answer to the question is because of you, Mr. Eudon. He's here because of your wise and farsighted investment in the s... skills of your fellow countrymen. His family is from Beirut, Lebanon."

"He came out of my scholarship program?"

"David joined us two years ago after completing his Master's. We had first option on his employment. I interviewed the boy, well, m... man, I suppose, but he is so young. I was very impressed.

"We were using the bots as accelerators, but David examined the problem holistically and went for the ju... jugular." The professor leaned in and spoke in a reverent whisper. "Mr. Eudon, I believe David's nanobots are the most exquisite objects I've ever encountered."

"Professor Farjohn, I'd very much like to meet David."

"Yes, of course." He glanced at the wall clock. "Ah, it's two o'clock. I'm afraid he won't be available for an hour."

"Why can't I meet one of my employees? Is he not working today?"

"David is always here. To be candid, Mr. Eudon, he works constantly—reminds me of myself at his age. Although I confess I am s . . . somewhat in awe of the young man's mind. I wouldn't have been a match for him, even in my prime."

"Why can't I meet him until then?"

"He's at p . . . prayers, Mr. Eudon. Didn't I explain? He prays each afternoon. We've set aside a small room with the orientation of Mecca marked on the w . . . wall for the Muslims on campus. David is always present. He's very devout."

"I understand." Nazar was accustomed to the call to prayers being used in his Middle Eastern operations, often to escape unwelcome work. "I've e-mails to catch up on, please find me a guest office, and arrange for David to meet me once his religious obligations are satisfied."

Nazar spent the next hour running numbers. He didn't understand nanotechnology, but, if the chemical transformation was scalable, David's nanobots could be the holy grail of energy production. Ethanol was an ideal fuel, usable in vehicles, or as a substitute for oil and coal in power plants.

Although producing ethanol from corn was politically expedient in the Corn Belt, it used energy that came from dirty nonrenewable fossil fuels. Nanobots used sunlight and water to transform garbage into ethanol, turning the cost model on its head.

Nazar located Eudon Ethanol Inc. in Akron because the sitting US Senator was an influential member of the Sub-Committee on Energy. After what he'd witnessed today, he would need to move the technology to a more remote location—no publicity, not yet. But first he must secure the brains behind the nanobots.

At three-thirty, Nazar thought he heard a knock at his door. He waited a few seconds and there it was again, a quiet tapping.

"Come in."

When the door opened it seemed to Nazar that a child entered, but something about the posture convinced him it was indeed a man.

"Are you David?"

"I am."

Nazar switched to Arabic.

"*Masa al-khayr.* Please, Dawud, come in and sit. I have been looking forward to meeting you."

The young man walked toward the desk with a self-conscious, shuffling gait; head down, shoulders hunched. Less than five-feet tall, the boy's stooped posture cost him three inches. Unkempt black hair merged into a dark scruffy beard and moustache. He sat opposite Nazar and stared at the floor.

"Professor Farjohn demonstrated your nanobots to me this afternoon."

"I was there."

"Ah, you brought them in?"

"Yes."

"Well, young man, you have done remarkable work. I understand you have only been with us for two years?" The boy, for that's how Nazar saw him, continued to look down. His face remained impassive and sullen. Nazar tried a different approach.

"Where is your family from?"

"Banquet, Ohio."

"I mean originally."

"Beirut, Lebanon."

"Did you know my family is originally from Lebanon?"

"Yes."

"Dawud, I intend to enlarge the scope of the nanobot project. I need to know whether the nanobots will scale up."

"They will."

Nazar smiled. "Good. The professor informs me that you haven't taken a break since you joined us. Is that correct?"

David finally looked up. His eyes were black slits peering from beneath thick dark eyebrows. "I am perfectly satisfied with my work and my working conditions, Mr. Eudon."

"I'm pleased to hear it, but I need to ask more of you. I intend to move the laboratory away from Ohio. I would like to offer you a reward if you are prepared to relocate, perhaps a bonus?"

David's face remained implacable; the monetary incentive made no impression.

"Or an extended vacation, a visit to your homeland to reacquaint with family and friends?"

David cocked his head to the side. "I have a lifelong ambition to complete the Hajj."

"That's most commendable." Nazar stood and offered his hand. David responded.

Nazar gripped the small, soft hand and stared hard into David's eyes. "David, if you stay with the project, I will personally arrange for you to take the Hajj. I can't spare you this year. Do you know the date of next year's pilgrimage?"

"October twelfth."

"Excellent. You will take September and October next year as paid vacation. I will arrange transportation and accommodations in Jeddah."

"Thank you, Mr. Eudon."

As David closed the office door behind him, Nazar smiled to himself. Every Muslim was obligated to complete the annual pilgrimage to Mecca in Saudi Arabia at least once in their lives if they were able. After what Nazar had seen in the lab, David Baker was potentially the most critical resource in his empire. He had found an ironclad way to keep him tied to the project.

A way only a fellow Muslim could understand.

4

A successful prototype project at the Akron facility proved David's nanobots to be robust and scalable. Nazar moved the team to Arizona and began construction of a commercial-scale ethanol production plant. Fourteen months later, toward the middle of September, Nazar made good on his promise. David took eight weeks vacation from the lab and flew home to Banquet, Ohio.

He paid the cab and ran up the path to his parents' doublewide. This was a surprise visit. David knocked and watched through the window as his father pushed himself, weak-armed, out of his TV chair and shuffled across the living room.

When his father opened the door his face split into a wide grin. "Mama. It's Dawud!" He hugged his son and pulled him into the hallway.

David's mother ran to him and held both cheeks in her hands. "Did you eat? Why didn't you call? I could have prepared dinner."

"Let the boy in, Mama." She released her grip on David and closed the front door.

"*Baba*, I have some news."

"How are you, my son?"

"I'm fine. Come. Sit."

He led his parents into the living room. They sat on the sofa, looking up at him like children, and waited for him to speak.

"In three weeks, I'm to take the Hajj."

His father began to cry. David waited. These were tears of joy. Finally, in a pride-filled voice, the old man said, "And the son shall complete the work of the father."

"*Baba*, you gave up your opportunity for the Hajj, so I might achieve mine. Allah recognizes your sacrifice, as do I." David's voice cracked as he felt the power of the words.

"You must wear my Ihram. I brought it from home and held it safe hoping for the day I would hear these words from my firstborn."

"I am honored, Father." David's throat tightened. His eyes too were filled with tears.

"Your mother will wash it tonight. When do you leave?" His father started to stand.

"No. Sit. I don't go until next week." The old man grunted as he sank back into the sofa. "I fly from Akron on October ninth direct to Saudi Arabia. Mr. Eudon has arranged transportation and my hotel in Jeddah. Hajj begins on the twelfth."

"Who will prepare you?"

"I have been studying."

His father wagged a finger. "No. No! You must be prepared. You should meet with Imam Ali."

"*Baba*—"

"I will speak to him."

Ali was Imam to David's father, his mentor from home. To argue would diminish his father's pride. His father had forfeited his homeland and his self-respect to save his family. In bringing them from a Lebanese war zone to the peace and safety of Ohio, he had accepted the charity of Christians, a bitter pill for a proud Muslim to swallow.

The tiny town of Banquet proved ideal for David to clear his mind and prepare for the pilgrimage. He had never seen his *baba* so happy. They prayed together daily.

On his last evening at home, his father gave David the Ihram. Tears glistened in the old man's eyes as he presented the precious garment: two unstitched sheets, laundered and folded, with a pair of simple, open-toed sandals perched on top.

"Dawud, come with me," his father said, and led him to the front door.

Father and son walked in silence until they passed the town-limit sign, "Banquet, Population 723." Only then, surrounded by fields, flat and empty after the corn harvest, did his father speak.

"When I was a young man, a few years younger than you are now, I lived with your grandparents in Sidon, in South Lebanon. One night a terrible noise and shaking woke me. The small dresser where I kept my clothes jumped from the ground, crashed to the floor, and splintered to matchwood." Eyes closed, face screwed into a grimace, his father relived the moment.

"Was it the war, *Baba*?"

His father stopped walking and faced his son, but his gaze was far away. "I pulled on my pants and ran outside. Streaks of light blazed through the sky, so bright it became like day. Planes flew so low I thought they would crash. They roared overhead with the sound of a thousand thunderclaps. Come. Walk."

His father waved him on as though David were the one who had stopped.

"I felt a searing pain in my arm, like being stabbed with a hot poker. My feet left the ground, and I flew through the air and landed, hard. When I next opened my eyes, it was light. I lay on top of a car. I knew I must be on our street. But it was unknown to me."

"Were you concussed?"

A hand wave dismissed David's suggestion. "The houses were all gone. The mosque was a shell of three walls. Tiles from its golden dome were scattered like garbage. Everywhere was fire and smoke. The air stunk of burning rubber. I slid off the car, and my arm dangled by my side; it would not move when I asked." His father flexed his left arm. He had never been able to fully straighten the limb.

"I looked for a marker, something to lead me home through the dust and stone and rubble. Then, near the top of a pile of rocks, like a beacon, my mother's orange and black headscarf flapped in the breeze. She always wore the same colors . . . orange and black." He rubbed his thumb and fingers together, feeling the cloth.

"Many stones lay atop the material. I dragged at them with my one arm and threw them down. When her scarf came free I held it to my face and breathed in her scent. I shouted for them, '*Mama. Baba*'."

His father stopped walking and bent over as though he might throw up. He snatched an inhaler from his pocket and took two rasping puffs.

David had never seen his father so weak, so sad. He didn't know how to react. Tears welled in his eyes.

When the old man recovered, he stared into the distance. "All day I dragged at rocks. No one could help. Out of six hundred Muslims in our village, twenty survived. Weeks later, men came with machines. They dug pits and pushed the rubble in. I never saw their bodies."

"*Baba*, why have you never spoken of this?"

He paused, then sighed. "It is not a memory I wish to recall." After a long silence, he turned back to David, straightened his shoulders, and looked him in the eye. "But, Dawud, you are soon to be a Haji. Understand, when you complete the fifth pillar, when you finish your Hajj, Allah will expect you to shoulder your responsibility. I am from their seed and you from mine. Their deaths are yours to avenge."

His father's face was stone gray, his small fists balled. "My son, here in America we are shielded from the war against Islam. Imam Ali is near the battle. Listen to what he says. Only if each Muslim does his duty can the war be won. Each of us has a part to play. Allah guided me, and I brought you to America. I am old. Now my son must take up the fight. Go to Imam Ali. Trust in his wisdom. He will help you understand how your piece should be placed in Allah's divine puzzle."

Three weeks later, an Asian woman approached David as he left the Akron-Canton Airport express security gate, which was reserved for passengers on private planes. Her almond eyes were warm, and her black hair, pulled tight into a bun, was held with a carved ivory pin.

"David, I'm Keisha, Mr. Nazar's personal assistant." She shook his hand, and he blushed at the softness of her skin. She stood close, and he smelled her perfume as her hand pressed gently on the small of his back to guide him. "Over here."

A sleek jet waited on the concrete. Inside, the pilot stood at the cockpit door. "Welcome aboard, Mr. Baker."

David nodded and took one of six seats. So far, he was the only passenger.

"Would you care for a drink?" Keisha asked.

"Water, thank you."

"Right away. I'll serve a meal once we reach cruising altitude. Just sit back and relax, David. This is a great way to travel." Nazar had promised a guide to accompany him and get him safely to his hotel, but David hadn't expected a woman.

Once they were airborne, Keisha brought food. She leaned toward him to serve, and her white blouse stretched tightly across her breasts. David's pulse raced. Sweat formed under his arms.

Later, as she cleared the dishes, she bent her knees so her face was close and level with his. Her tight black skirt rode up and showed the flesh of her thighs. David filled his mind with prayer to block out the temptation.

"It's a twelve-hour flight. Just press the call button should you require anything, David."

The words triggered more wrong thoughts. Would she really do anything he wished? After she left, he waited a few moments to be sure she wouldn't return. Then, with shaking hands, he laid his prayer mat on the floor in front of the cabin seats, estimated the location of Mecca, and recited morning prayers. He needed to clear his mind. Sexual thoughts were unfitting for a pilgrim of the Hajj.

A few hours into the flight, David needed the bathroom. Not wanting to face the woman again, he opened the door at the rear. His mind reeled from the opulence: walls draped in silks, a huge bed, dozens of liquor bottles hanging from dispensers behind a bar.

Behind him, someone coughed, and he spun around. Keisha stood at the front of his cabin.

"That's Mr. Eudon's private accommodations. Can help you, David?" She smiled, but there was tension in her voice.

"I . . . I need the bathroom."

She walked toward him. He pressed his back flat against the rear seat to give her room. As she turned sideways to pass, her left breast brushed his chest. She positioned herself in the doorway and pointed to the forward cabin. Her naked, tanned arm hung inches from his face. "Your bathroom is through there."

He went quickly, blushing, his head bowed. Behind him, he heard her lock the door to Nazar's room.

They landed in Jeddah at midday on October 10th. Keisha guided him through Passport Control. He could tell by the way the agents stared that they assumed she was his harlot.

Once out of the terminal, Keisha hailed a cab and slid into the back seat next to him. Her skirt rode up her legs; they were smooth and shapely and bare. He sat on his hands, body pressed hard against the car door, and stared out the window. He was a pilgrim. He should not be with her. Thankfully, she stayed silent until they reached the hotel. She paid the cab and left him to follow with his luggage while she handled his check-in.

At the elevator, Keisha said, "You're all set. The bellhop will show you to your room. I hope the Hajj is a rewarding experience for you, David." She held out her hand.

David dared not touch her. "Thank you for your help." His voice came out as a dry-throated croak. He did not make eye contact.

When he reached his room, the message light was flashing. Imam Ali had left his number.

David called back. "I am honored to speak with you, Imam."

"Dawud, your father is so proud. Your Hajj is a wonderful gift for him."

"I am excited and humbled to be visiting Mecca, Imam. I understand you are to instruct me. My mind is open, a blank page ready for your wisdom."

"I have readied fourteen others for their first Hajj. Come in the morning. This mosque will act as your Mikat, your place of preparation. You may stay here tomorrow night before traveling to Mecca."

David slept poorly in the luxurious suite Nazar had arranged for him. He worried about his ability to fulfill the complex pattern of prayer and mental cleansing the Hajj required. How wise his father had been to arrange for Imam Ali to guide him through this unique experience.

After an early breakfast in his room, he packed his things, checked out of the hotel, and took a cab to the mosque. The taxi dropped him at the base of a set of white marble steps. He climbed, removed his shoes, and walked through arched doors into the huge, domed building.

Imam Ali strode toward him across the prayer hall, and the sound of his footsteps echoed with meaning in the open space. Robed in plain black cotton, the Imam stood six feet tall, with a bronzed face and a full, neatly trimmed beard.

He pierced David with an intense stare, and when they shook hands, an electric charge traveled along David's arm. "Welcome,

Dawud, we are ready to begin. Please use my office to change."

At the center of the prayer space, fourteen men, already dressed for Hajj, sat cross-legged in a semicircle. David hurried past them and into the Imam's office.

David's hands trembled as he removed his street clothes. From the suitcase he took out his father's Ihram, wrapped one sheet around his waist like a skirt and the second around his torso, tossing the loose end over his right shoulder.

When he stepped from the Imam's office into the Mosque, the air felt cool against his skin. The men opened a space for him, and he joined them on the floor, feeling self-conscious about his near-nakedness.

"Good, we are all here. Names are unimportant. You are pilgrims now and for the next six days until your pilgrimage is complete and you become hajis. Tomorrow, you will begin to fulfill the fifth pillar of Islam."

The Imam gazed around the group, lingering on each face before continuing.

"I will never forget my first Hajj. The pilgrimage satisfied a deep yearning. Before, I missed something in my life; a piece of my soul remained dark. At Mount Arafat, Allah showed me the way to light that dark place. Each pilgrim experiences the Hajj in his or her own way. But one thing is certain; you are here today because Allah has shaped your lives to make this event happen. Now!"

This last word, spoken with force, echoed around the mosque.

As he studied the Imam's still body and calm face, David's heart pounded, sending blood whooshing through his ears. He had always believed Allah planned a greater purpose for him. The knowledge had drifted like mist at the corner of his eye. At times, during prayers, he turned inward and almost grasped Allah's intention, but always it eluded him. This great man had felt the same. The Hajj had freed him. Allah had shown him his destined path. Perhaps it would also happen for David.

After a few seconds of silence, Imam Ali spoke in a soft voice, "Come. We must practice the key prayers and ensure the ceremony's sequence is understood."

In the evening, they used the mosque's bathrooms to cleanse themselves according to the required rituals. The Imam handed out sleeping mats and showed them to a conference room where they would spend the night. As he was leaving, he turned to David.

"Dawud, can you spare a few moments?"

David followed the Imam to his office.

"Dawud, your father encouraged me to speak to you."

Guilt and fear washed over David. Perhaps he had been remiss in his preparation. Maybe the Imam had listened to his clumsy prayers and decided he was not ready.

"After my first Hajj, I made the decision to become an Imam," Ali said. "The path Allah had chosen for me blazed in my mind bright and clear. Since then, I have occasionally been the unwitting channel for Allah's message to others. An ability I can neither initiate nor control."

Sitting across the desk listening to the Imam, David's body vibrated as though a low-voltage current coursed through his muscles. He clasped his hands together so the Imam would not see them tremble.

"Your father has witnessed this prescience firsthand. In a dream, I saw him leaving Lebanon and taking his family to America. The day after, your father called me for advice. He had received an offer from a Christian group that sponsored families, moving them from war-ravaged territories and giving them haven in Ohio. I told your father of the dream, and he followed the path Allah showed me." When the Imam finished speaking, his eyes were closed, and he became still.

In the silence, David heard the distant sounds of traffic—the world without. He waited, and when Ali opened his eyes again he smiled at David, as if he had just noticed him in the room.

"Now you have come to me and yesterday, on the eve of your Hajj, I dreamed of you. In my dream, you were a warrior for Islam wielding a powerful weapon for Allah. I called your father and asked his advice. As always, he was wise beyond his years."

David thought his heart would burst with pride. This holy man had taken advice from David's *baba*.

"After your Hajj, I wish you to return to the mosque to meet another Imam."

"If my father counsels this, I do it gladly. Who is this man, and why should we meet?"

"This prescience is a vague thing, Dawud, a series of feelings, nuances, and hints shrouded in mist. I believe, at Mecca, you will find the knowledge you seek."

David walked back through the dark prayer-space guided by the light shining under the door of the conference room. He lay on his sleeping mat and pulled up his single cover. Unlike the previous night, the day's worries did not churn in his mind. He did not dwell on the Imam's words, nor think of the harlot on the plane. He had no fears. No qualms. He fell into a deep, dreamless sleep.

Tonight, he was in Allah's hands.

5

Fifteen men wrapped in white sheets and wearing open-toed sandals climbing aboard a bus at five in the morning would look strange in most parts of the world, but not Saudi Arabia. In Jeddah, they didn't warrant a second glance.

Each selected an empty double seat. With so few clothes on, David felt uncomfortable sitting close to another man. He wondered was it the same for the others, or had they turned inward to focus on the experience to come.

The roads were choked with vehicles. The one-hour drive to Mecca became a five-hour crawl. The bus dropped them at a dusty parking lot.

Thousands of pilgrims leaked like white liquid between the buses and flowed toward a distant grouping of tall, elegant spires. The outline of Mecca's buildings was familiar to David; a picture of Masjid Al Haram, the largest mosque in the world, hung on his office wall in Arizona. Covering 360,000 square meters, the equivalent of sixty-six contiguous football fields, this holiest of all mosques housed the Ka'ba. The place that billions of Muslims faced each day as they prayed.

David turned his back on the bus and walked with his fellow pilgrims. Once they cleared the chaos of the parking lot, they joined a human line of cloth and prayer that stretched for two miles to the outer walls of the mosque. David glanced around.

Already there was no trace of the men he'd traveled with. They, and he, were one, blended into the white pilgrim trail.

As he walked, he began to recite the prayers that had filled his mind since he woke. Imam Ali had said: "A haji speaks his prayers to Allah not in a quiet murmur, but as he would to a friend who takes tea with him."

"*Bism Allah, Allahu Akba* (In the name of God, God is Great) . . . *Allahu Akbar, Allahu Akbar* (God is Great, God is Great) . . . *wa lil Lahi Alhamd* (and praise be to God)."

Like spokes of a great wheel, his line and dozens more crept toward the principal mass of pilgrims, tens of thousands, who were performing their Tawaf—walking seven times, counterclockwise around the Ka'ba.

After passing through a gate in the outer wall of the huge open mosque, David shuffled another two-hundred feet, and finally joined the circling crowd.

He moved with the crowd until, as though someone yanked an invisible string attached to the center of his brow, his head turned toward the Ka'ba, three-hundred feet away across a sea of bodies. Forty feet wide, fifty long, and fifty high, the looming black building appeared far larger to him.

A clump of pilgrims gathered at the east corner of the Ka'ba. For a fraction of a second, a space cleared between their heads, and sunlight glinted from the polished setting of the Black Stone.

The Black Stone, a dark, reflective pupil the size of a man's head, set in a four-foot-high vertical silver eye.

The Black Stone, sent from heaven to fall at Adam's feet.

The Black Stone, which reminded every Muslim there was but one God and none before him.

David marked his location relative to the Stone. He pulled his Ihram off his head and slid the right half of the garment down, baring his shoulder. The first of seven circuits of the Ka'ba began from that point. Shuffling through the rotations, David would edge toward the center, never pushing, moving with patience and respect. With Allah's blessing and help, he would kiss the Black Stone before his Tawaf was complete.

After each circuit, when he returned to the position where he had begun his Tawaf, he raised his right hand, pointed to the Stone and chanted his prayer to Allah's greatness.

As he edged nearer to his goal, the rectangular building towered over him. Black curtains draped the walls; embroidered on them in spun gold were the words of the Shahada: *There is no God but God, and Muhammad is the messenger of God.* The purity and truth of the words burned hot in his mind.

When he pointed to the stone for a sixth time and began his final circuit, still sixty feet from the Ka'ba, the crowds were dense, but it seemed to David that a way was made for him. Spaces opened, and as he rounded the south face, his fingers touched the wall of the sacred building.

Ahead, a crush of bodies surrounded the eastern corner. He slowed his pace, taking space as allowed by other pilgrims as they completed their Tawaf and moved to their next rite. His prayers were loud. They filled his mind with the power of their meaning, their strength reinforced by prayer echoes from those around him. Finally, he placed his hand on the warm silver of the Black Stone's setting, the undulating rhythm of prayers vibrated through the metal.

Then the grasping crowds faded, and he glided, untouched, toward the Stone. Leaning forward, he laid his lips where millions of Muslims had before him. Like Muhammad himself, he kissed the Black Stone. Immediately, he was swept away, his place taken by scores of pilgrims, straining and pushing to touch its smooth surface.

It had not been so for David.

Allah had cleared a way for him.

Of this, he was sure.

He drifted in a trance, allowing the crowd to squeeze him outward, toward the less populated areas. After two more circuits, he broke from the throng, found a space, and faced Muqaam Ibrahim—The Place of Abraham—the direction indicated by high green beacons mounted on towers. He opened his prayer mat, prostrated himself before Allah, and thanked him for the precious gift he had bestowed. The prayer chant was on his lips. It was in his mind. It resonated though his body. It consumed him.

His prayers complete, David entered the long air-conditioned tunnel connecting the hills of Safa and Marwah. In a transcendent daze, head high, prayers spilling from his heart, he moved alongside thousands of Muslim brothers and sisters who shared his journey.

At the well of Zamzam, he quenched his thirst with the same water Abraham's wife, Hagar, had used to save the life of her son,

Ismael. He drank five cups, each downed in three gulps. Sated, he filled a water bottle from the coolers provided—a gift for his father.

He walked seven times between the two hills to complete his Sa'i. When he left the tunnel, night had fallen, and he followed a tide of pilgrims to the permanent tent city at Mina. In a crowded marquee, he found a space on the ground, and made his last prayer before lying, exhausted, on the bare earth, to sleep.

David dreamed of the Black Stone. The silver eye appeared before him. He faced the stone with arms outstretched, and a dazzling golden light ushered forth. Its rays bathed his body and warmed him like the sun. The light beam held him fast. It began to lift, and he rose with it until he floated high above the East corner of the Ka'ba. He looked down on the moving mass of white-clad pilgrims circling the holy building. David observed their Tawafs from above, as Allah must see them.

The next morning, he rose early, took food and water, then began his prayers. All day he chanted aloud the hypnotic verses from his Koran. The familiar words carried more meaning spoken in this holy place. That night, he again dreamed of the Black Stone. Its golden light elevated him so that he floated over the pilgrims as they flowed like cream around the Ka'ba.

When he woke on the morning of the third day, it was still dark. After sunrise, he joined a snaking line of pilgrims on the fifteen-mile trek across the plain of Arafat to Wuquf: the hill of forgiveness, the keystone of the Hajj.

By late afternoon, David reached Mount Arafat. For the final few miles of the journey, his eyes had locked on the white marble obelisk that crowned the hill. An inner voice told him to climb and pray at its base.

A crowd, thirty deep, clustered around the stone pillar. He stood as close as possible and read from his Koran. The day waned, and worshippers moved and changed positions. When it was polite to do so, he edged closer until, as the sun's light was setting, he changed places one final time.

David faced the white pillar. The stone marked the place where the Prophet Muhammad had given his last sermon. David lowered his hands and spread them slightly from his sides, palms facing the obelisk, mimicking the stance from his dreams of the Black Stone. He braced his legs and swayed in time to his prayers. Forward and back, his arc of movement increased until his brow touched the smooth, warm marble.

His motion stopped.

The stone held his head as a magnet holds metal.

Passages from the holy book, passages he had never before spoken, ushered from his lips. He opened his eyes, inches from the stone, and a golden light, the light from his dreams, dazzled him to sightlessness.

The stone released him. He straightened and turned. The golden beam warmed his back. When he regained his vision, David saw the land as it had been in the time of Abraham—bare rock, sand, and boulders. The hill of Wufur and the plain beyond were barren and empty of people.

David began to preach. His voice projected in a rhythmic rise and fall as he chanted the words of the Koran: the sacred words given by Allah and transcribed by his prophet Muhammad. He sang as a muezzin, his voice vibrating as the words of Allah poured forth from his heart.

Time passed. The heat from the obelisk diminished, and the force of his prayers lessened until at last they became a whisper. The golden light extinguished, and he fell silent.

Weary, like a water skin drained of its liquid, David slid his back down the stone until he sat. His eyes closed, shutting out the empty desert. A deep, dreamless sleep took him.

David woke with a start. A man in a white Ihram, his face inches away, poked David's arm.

"Al-Mahdi?" he asked.

Confused and displaced by the spiritual enlightenment he had undergone, David blinked to clear his eyes. The hill was again crammed with bodies. A few hundred pilgrims clustered in a semicircle at his feet.

"Al-Mahdi?" He heard it spoken in whispers among the crowd. A hushed reverence filled the air.

The man who had woken him spoke again, in English. "Are you the Mahdi? Are you the Messiah?"

David looked at the gathered people. The murmured sounds of the Koran being read aloud had ceased. A waiting silence hung over the group. All eyes turned to him.

"I am Dawud," he said. Then, *"Bism Allah Allahu Akbar."*

Those sitting close spoke the words back to him.

Again he spoke, but louder. *"Allahu Akbar, Allahu Akbar."*

Voices from below him on the hill echoed his phrases and David completed the prayer, *"wa lil Lahi Alhamd."* The prayer chant spread beyond the group at David's feet. More and more took it up until ten thousand raised voices pledged, as one, their love for Allah.

The faces of the pilgrims were lit with joy from the epiphany they had shared at Mount Arafat.

David, for the first time, saw a clear path ahead. The mist had lifted. Allah had guided Imam Ali, and through that guidance, his father had moved the family to Ohio. That move had enabled David to study, to excel in science, and finally, to create nanobots—a technological breakthrough. He thought of the meeting Imam Ali had arranged with a stranger. Allah had planned this meeting, so David could help this man. *And the son shall complete the work of his father.*

There, on the hill of forgiveness, David pledged obedience to Allah. From this point forward, Allah alone would guide David's path in life. With a huge weight lifted from his shoulders, he began the march back to Mina.

A haji hurried alongside, matching steps with him. "Dawud?"

He recognized one of the pilgrims who had traveled with him from Jeddah. David could not bring himself to speak. He had forgotten how to converse. For three days, he had spoken only to Allah. He nodded to the man.

"Dawud, in America, are you an Imam?"

The question confused him. He shook his head.

"Then how did you learn to recite the Koran as you did on the Mount?"

With difficulty, David formed words and spoke. "I . . . I read from the holy book each day."

"But you spoke from the heart. You preached for an hour. Even Imam Ali cannot move me as you did."

"Allahu Akbar," David said.

"Allahu Akbar," the pilgrim replied.

6

The bus dropped David and the other hajis at the mosque in Jeddah late in the evening of the sixth day. The men hugged as they parted, no longer strangers, now Muslim brothers. When the hajis dispersed to their homes, David remained. The Ihram, so revealing and thin when he boarded the bus before the Hajj, was now a second skin. A warm breeze brushed over his bald pate, shaved clean on the fourth day. He stared at the open doors of Imam Ali's mosque and felt the weight of the moment.

Finally, he climbed the marble steps, removed his sandals, and, with back straight and head high, walked with purpose across the empty prayer space, conscious of the air flowing past his face as he moved.

He knocked on the office door. When he saw Imam Ali, David began to cry. Not with childlike tears of sadness, but from a welling of powerful emotions that spilled down his cheeks. The Imam opened his arms and enfolded him as a father would a long-lost son.

"I see on your face that you have accepted Allah as your one God."

David nodded, his head buried in the Imam's robes.

"I heard of your revelation at Mount Arafat. I called your father and told him how Allah had touched your spirit."

"I saw a golden light."

"You are blessed, Dawud, but with this blessing comes great responsibility."

David pulled back and wiped his face with the loose end of his Ihram. "Allah has shown me my path. I ask your help in attaining it."

Ali placed a hand on David's shoulder. "I promised your father I would aid you as if you were my own son."

David looked Ali full in the face and spoke in the strong, confident voice gained on his Hajj. "I wish to become an Imam."

"Dawud, at Mount Arafat you led the prayers as only an Imam could."

David smiled at the truth in Ali's words. "Imam, before my Hajj, you spoke of a meeting. Allah has commanded me to help this man."

Ali nodded. "He comes tomorrow. But in this thing, I am like Yahya—I opened the way, and I can guide you, but Allah calls to you alone, Dawud. Now come, eat, then you must rest. The Hajj takes a physical toll. Allah needs his servant to be strong."

That night, David slept peacefully on a mat in the conference room.

The next day, he folded the Ihram in his suitcase, showered, and pulled on jeans and a T-shirt. The clothes felt strange, false.

He walked through the prayer hall and knocked on the Imam's door.

"Come!"

Imam Ali sat at a small table beside a large man dressed in black shirt and jeans. The stranger stood and offered his hand. The man's neck was thick, like a bull. A scar, red and angry, distorted the left side of his face. Rough laborer's hands delivered a powerful grip that crushed David's fingers.

"Dawud, this is Imam Ghazi."

Ghazi bowed. "Dawud-bin-Hussein-bin-Ferran, it is an honor. Imam Ali told me of your Hajj, *Allahu Akbar.*" The man's voice was deep and resonant.

"*Allahu Akbar.*" David met the stranger's gaze. "Allah commands that we meet. I am yours to instruct."

Ghazi nodded, and David noted with pride the look of approval on Ali's face.

Ali poured dark, aromatic tea from a silver pot while Ghazi

spoke. "Many years ago, I took my Hajj alongside my good friend, Ali. We were young, twenty-two. We returned changed men and dedicated ourselves to the study of Islam. Those were wonderful days, filled with the joy of doing God's bidding." Ghazi paused to sip his tea, the cup was a toy in his hand.

Ali smiled along with his friend's reminiscence. David felt honored to be accepted in such exalted company.

"In my early thirties, Allah called me to help my Muslim brothers at the place of their greatest need. I parted from Ali and traveled to Jerusalem." Ghazi's face grew solemn.

"Israel is the front line in a war on Islam. I tried to help. I talked to representatives from the UN, and to Western Peace Commissions. I pleaded with rabbis, ministers, and priests. Islam is the one true path for all mankind, yet in Jerusalem, each day, its followers are crushed." Ghazi's raised voice filled the room, strong with passion. Here was a true soldier of Allah.

"The Western powers and the Arab puppets they use to control the Muslim people want one thing; to drive Islam from the face of the Earth. They fear Islam because the words of the Koran expose them as charlatans and thieves." When he picked up his tea again, his hand shook, the spoon rattling in the saucer.

"In Allah's name, I took up arms against the Crusaders, but our weapons are weak, homemade, cheap, and old. We combat the infidel's rockets with sticks and rocks. Earlier this year I was forlorn, ready to give up the fight. I sought council from my wise friend, Ali, and in his words I found clarity."

Ghazi turned to Ali who took over the story. "Ghazi spoke of his frustrations. He cried to think of Allah's servants strapping explosives to their bodies, sacrificing everything yet gaining so little. I said to my friend: 'You cannot beat an enemy that doesn't fear you.' I asked, 'Do they fear the suicide bombers?'"

"No," Ghazi replied.

"Do they fear Hamas's rockets?"

"No again," said Ghazi.

"Did they crumble and accept Islam when the towers fell in New York?"

This time David responded. "No. They fear only weapons of mass destruction."

"Yes . . . yes, Dawud," Ghazi said, "because they know the threat of these weapons cannot be hidden from their people.

Israeli, American, and British citizens do not despise Islam. Their leaders do. Their leaders fear what all leaders fear—losing power. Only when the Islamic warriors' weapons strike fear into the Crusaders will the people of the West understand that they are led by agents of Shaitan who keep them from the one true faith."

Ghazi's eyes were bright fires, and David's mind whirled with the purity of his logic. The Western powers could never allow the spread of Islam. If their citizens accepted Allah and lived according to the teachings of the Koran, there would be no need for godless capitalism and corrupt religions. He had seen the low morals of the West. Not just in Christians and Jews, but in Muslims like Nazar Eudon, with his private plane, liquor cabinet, and executive slut.

"You are right to speak of these things, Imam Ghazi," David said. "I share your devotion, and I understand your need for a weapon powerful enough to correct the balance of power." David smiled; his nanobots could become the weapon they sought. He looked into their eyes, each in turn. "It is for this that Allah has brought me to Jeddah. I can help in your quest."

"*Allahu Akbar*," the Imams said together. "Come, let us give thanks to Him." Ali led them to the prayer space. They set their mats in a line beneath the splendid dome. David knelt between the two holy men and they prayed with one voice. In David's mind, at that moment, they sealed a covenant in front of Allah.

For the rest of the day they discussed David's requirements for a laboratory. Ghazi spoke of his resistance group, which he called, Allah's Revenge. David thought the title fitting and just.

After David left, the Imams sat in Ali's office, taking tea.

"The Saudi connection has funded two attacks," Ali said.

"If Dawud speaks correctly about his weapon, obtaining further funds should not be an impediment."

"Agreed." Ali replaced his cup on the table. "Was he what you expected?"

"Not at all, but the longer I spoke with him the more impressed I became. He has an extraordinary mind. Do you believe he will follow through? Once he returns to America this . . ." Ghazi made a broad sweep with his arm, ". . . may appear too difficult and dangerous."

"Dawud had an epiphany at Mecca," Ali said, "I have guided him in the direction Allah wishes, but to be sure I have asked my brother to speak of our hopes for him as a captain in Allah's Revenge. Dawud feels obligated to his father, as a good son should."

Ghazi raised his eyebrows. "He does not know you are his uncle?"

"My older brother was ever the wisest in our family. He decided long ago, when the Israelis killed our parents, that we would be a more potent force if we developed individual identities."

"In this, it seems he was correct," Ghazi said.

Ali nodded his agreement.

7

Back home in his parents' doublewide, David's father treated him as a returning hero. For a week, they prayed and reflected on his experience in Mecca. The Zamzam water took pride of place on the mantelpiece. His *baba* encouraged David to aid Imam Ghazi in his fight.

In November, he returned to Nazar's Phoenix laboratory and began his preparations.

By January, he was ready.

Last to leave the lab, David crossed to the safe where the "virginbots" were secured: the pure, un-imprinted nanobots from which all other bots were grown. He swiped his access card. Air hissed as it vented into the safe's vacuum. Once the pressures equalized, he opened the thick metal door. The lab's twenty-four-hour video surveillance system recorded his every move.

The virginbots were housed in ten glass vials packed in foam inside a stainless-steel cylinder the size of a soda can. He donned an oven-glove modeled after Mickey Mouse's hand, a running joke among the lab technicians and scientists. He would miss working with his colleagues, but he had a higher purpose to fulfill.

David carried the cylinder across the lab to the programming chamber—a four-foot-square, carbon-free-glass glove box. The apparatus allowed an operator to manipulate items inside without coming into direct contact with them. He placed the virginbots into an induction chamber at the center of the cube.

After closing the glove box door, David slipped his hands into two metal-coated sleeves that extended into the cube. He unscrewed the cap of the containment cylinder and removed one of the glass vials containing virginbots, and placed it to one side.

After withdrawing his hands, he clicked the *Program* icon on the induction chamber's computer. Four heat strips, positioned in the vertical angles of the box, lit, and spread a red glow throughout the cube.

When the temperature gauge reached seventy degrees Fahrenheit, parameters popped up on the computer monitor:

Target –	C_2H_5OH (Ethanol)
Inhibitor –	$C_2H_5OH*30\%$ (Ethanol)
Feedstock –	Bio
Catalyst –	Photon
Activate –	00secs, 00mins, 00hrs, 00days, 00mnth
Terminate –	00secs, 00mins, 00hrs, 00days, 00mnth

This simple interface programmed the virginbots in the induction chamber. Nazar's 'bots produced ethanol, although any carbon-based compound could be specified. Routinely, one tube of cells was programmed and then replicated into the larger quantities required for industrial-scale ethanol production.

The start and stop times were vestiges of the prototyping days when nanobots were given only a few seconds of life to protect against a catastrophic error if a batch of 'bots went rogue.

For Nazar's purposes, thirty percent ethanol was the optimum inhibitor. But any chemical compound could be specified; the nanobots terminated on contact with that compound. In future, David would program a different compound to make the weaponized 'bots safe to handle.

For security, the computer logged every keystroke during programming. However, when David first wrote the imprinting program, he'd incorporated a 'backdoor'. He made his desired changes to Nazar's nanobots. Then he held down the *Ctrl* key and punched in a series of sixteen characters.

The sixteen keystrokes were not logged, and only David knew the sequence.

He clicked, *End Programming*, and the lights went dark. Mickey

Mouse helped him carry the container of imprinted virginbots to the safe-deposit box.

David returned to his desk with the single glass vial he had placed to one side. These cells had *not* been imprinted. They were the only remaining virginbots in the lab and, by implication, in the world.

From his bottom drawer, David retrieved the thermos flask he carried every day with his packed lunch. When he opened the lid, a few wisps of vapor escaped as the dry ice within evaporated. He bedded the test tube snugly in the center of the cold crystals, secured the cap, and placed his precious cargo in his backpack next to his laptop.

David slung the bag over his shoulder and, for the final time, left his Phoenix office.

8

Two weeks before the Oxford Circus tube train attack, Abdul Ahmed weaved past dozens of work cubicles identical to the one he'd just vacated on the third floor of the *Times of London* headquarters. He skipped up the stairs to the fifth floor, nodded to the receptionist, and headed to his senior editor's office.

He glanced at the letter in his hand and tapped on the door.

Rafiq looked up from his monitor. "What's up, Abdul?"

"Sorry to interrupt. Can you take a look at this? I think it might be important." Among his morning mail, Abdul had received a letter, hand-written in Arabic and postmarked from East Jerusalem. He had translated it and now handed a printout and the original to his boss.

Rafiq scanned the document then pointed to the single-word signature, a swirling Arabic rendition of the name Ghazi, which translated as *one-who-struggles*. "Do you know this man?"

"No, but my family may. I could call my uncle and check."

"Let's wait until we've spoken to the chief." Rafiq pressed a speed dial on his desk phone, and the editor-in-chief's secretary picked up. "Amy, is Scott available for ten minutes?"

"I'll see." A few seconds later, she came back on the line. "Come on up, Rafiq."

Abdul had met the editor-in-chief only once when, six months before and fresh out of college, he'd landed his first job as junior Middle-East correspondent for the newspaper.

Two walls of Scott's sixth-floor office were lined with tables covered in papers and Post-it notes. Cleaners were forbidden to enter the room unless Scott was present, in case they disturbed anything. Scott Shearer, a small, wiry man, sat behind an oversized desk, also strewn with papers. White hair, the result, he often claimed, of twenty years spent answering stupid questions, topped a lined face. He looked all of his fifty-five years, plus maybe another ten.

Rafiq handed over the letter and the translation, which his editor began reading as he waved at two chairs on the other side of the desk.

"Whose translation?"

"Mine, sir," Abdul said.

"I've checked, Scott. It's perfect," Rafiq said, and Abdul smiled.

"Can we verify the source?"

"Abdul suspects they got his contact information from his family in Jerusalem. He's volunteered to call his uncle."

Scott lifted his head and stared at Abdul with ferret eyes—gray, and hard. "I'm not sure that's a good idea." The intensity of Scott Shearer's stare was the stuff of Fleet Street legend. Abdul felt its heat. "Have we heard of . . ." Scott released Abdul from his glare and glanced at the translation, ". . . Allah's Revenge before today?"

"Seems to be a new group," Abdul said. "I did a Google search. It's a generic term for any disaster that happens in the West. The financial meltdown was Allah's revenge, AIDS is Allah's revenge, also the 2004 tsunami, 9/11 and so on."

"The letter says they want to meet you, Abdul, to 'instruct' you about their mission and make you . . ." Scott faced Abdul as he emphasized the last few words, ". . . their messenger to the world."

Scott stood, turned his back on them, and paced the length of the full-wall window, which was the only indication they were in the office of the most influential newspaper editor in London. "If Ghazi is a terrorist, you might not want him making house calls on your family. On the other hand . . ." Scott reached the end of the window, stopped, and gazed out at the dreary English rain. ". . . I'm not comfortable involving the police. If it's a hoax, we'll look stupid, and if not, by the time they've finished plodding about it'll be worthless."

"I could take the meeting." The words tumbled from Abdul's mouth and his heart rate tripled. Could this be a breakthrough story so early in his career?

Scott terminated his examination of the window and focused on Abdul. "What do you think, Rafiq?"

"Depends on what we hope to gain." Rafiq also faced his junior correspondent. "Do you want to do this, Abdul?"

"Yes, I think it could be important."

Scott sat opposite them and folded his hands on the desk. Abdul received the stare again. The room went quiet for five beats. Throat tight with nerves, Abdul swallowed, twice.

Scott said, "You do understand the risks? You wouldn't be the first journalist taken hostage."

"I've thought of that, sir. They're an unknown organization. They want publicity. Hamas or Al-Qaida can take hostages and use them as leverage. But if a new group shows bad faith at an initial meeting, no one will ever deal with them."

"You still have family in Jerusalem, right?"

"Yes. My parents and siblings were the only family members to leave."

"Okay, Rafiq, let's set it up." Scott scanned the letter. "They're going to call him at the King David hotel in Jerusalem at 6:00 p.m. next Wednesday. Abdul, why don't you go a few days early? Visit with your family. Adjust to the time zone and the language."

"Thank you sir, I'd like that. It's been many years since I was back."

"No, thank you, young man, and good luck." Scott stood and took a firm grip of Abdul's hand across the desk. "Rafiq will set up a communications regimen. Don't miss a scheduled call or you might find the cavalry smashing into your room and turning you out of bed."

Scott's mouth smiled, but his eyes did not.

9

One week before the tube train massacre, Nazar Eudon stood stage center at a wooden lectern in the Hilton London Metropolis Hotel. Dressed in a seven-thousand-dollar charcoal-gray suit, power tie, and white shirt, he presented a carefully crafted look.

Nazar's face, surgically tightened to wrinkle-free perfection, stared from two huge screens mounted at each side of the stage. Colored contact lenses transformed his brown eyes to a striking green; dark hair, supplemented with implants at the crown, graduated in tone so it blended into his trimmed, silver-gray beard.

Most of the audience at the International Alternative Energy Symposium was pro-renewables. Nazar's selection as keynote speaker had met with resistance from members of the organizing committee. But after his marketing VP e-mailed Nazar's speech to the chairman, Nazar had prevailed.

As he reached the conclusion of his twenty-minute talk, Nazar was about to drop a bomb.

"I am honored that in this room, with my competitors and peers in the energy business, sit Nobel-prize winning scientists, leaders of the world's finest academic institutions, and political representatives from more than thirty nations." As he referred to them, Nazar made eye contact with a few of the five hundred seated luminaries.

"I wish to apologize to you all."

People fidgeted in their seats as he scanned the crowd and allowed his words to hang for a silent three-count.

"I am sixty-four-years old. It has taken me until now to understand that my life's work has contributed more than most to the tragic despoiling of our fragile planet . . . obviously, I am a slow learner." His wry smile triggered a smattering of laughter and eased the tension. "I plan to make amends. Today, I formally and publicly reject the business model that has made me a rich man. Today, from this platform, I am announcing a new direction for Nazar Eudon." Nazar bowed his head to emphasize contrition.

A hushed silence hung over the audience. These were extraordinary words coming from one of the world's most hawkish oilmen.

"From now on, my life, energy, and resources will be dedicated to Eudon Alternative Energy, an organization committed to delivering only clean, renewable energy solutions. Naturally, I can no longer continue to serve the shareholders of Eudon Oil, so today I am resigning as their Chief Executive Officer." Uncertain applause rippled through the meeting hall.

"Ladies and gentlemen, mark this day, a milestone in my life I am honored to have shared with you. I pray that in the eyes of Allah my achievements going forward will be sufficient reparation for the damage I have wreaked on His magnificent earthly creation. I look forward to working with you to make Eudon Alternative Energy's bold vision a reality. Thank you for your time and attention."

Right hand on his heart, Nazar stepped from behind the lectern and bowed. The audience applauded. A few people stood, then more. Shouts and whistles echoed across the auditorium and gradually became a raucous standing ovation. The chairman came from stage left, took Nazar's hand in both of his, and shook with vigor.

With a final wave, Nazar left the stage. Behind him, he heard excited murmuring as the crowd discussed what a huge private initiative to accelerate the development and adoption of alternative energy solutions might mean. But what really had them buzzing was the announcement that the CEO of the fourth-largest oil company in the world planned to turn his back on the goose that laid his golden eggs.

Sandwiched between two burly security guards, he smiled as he strode through the dark backstage. Dropping the announcement on that group of self-serving crooks and charlatans had been a rush. Tonight, his business competitors would raise a glass to the crazy Arab who had committed financial suicide.

They'd be laughing from the other side of their faces when he started producing ethanol at a buck-fifty a barrel.

One of the suits held the elevator door, and Nazar joined six of his staff. They descended to the second floor where he and one bodyguard got out. The rest of the group continued to the ground floor. A second guard held the adjacent elevator for Nazar and they rode it to the roof where they climbed into a waiting helicopter. Less than ten minutes after leaving the stage, he was in the air.

Below him, on the street outside the auditorium, a crush of reporters pressed and jostled his staff as they protected a decoy Nazar Eudon and escorted him, dramatically, toward a waiting black SUV.

At Heathrow airport, a sedan collected him from the helipad and drove him to the steps of his private jet.

Keisha, her black hair pulled back in the tight bun he preferred, awaited him. "Welcome aboard, Mr. Eudon."

"Thank you. I'm relieved to be back and, as always, delighted to see you."

His personal assistant smiled and bowed, her delicate hands clasped in front. "I've laid out a change of clothes. We're scheduled to depart in thirty minutes."

In five paces, he passed through the plane's passenger cabin and opened the door to his private apartment, which occupied half the plane. A black silk jumpsuit lay on top of the colorful, hand-stitched top-cover of his king-sized bed. Letting his clothes drop at his feet, he stripped, then stepped into the bathroom. A switch turned on the shower, the water adjusted to his preferred temperature.

Fabier Martain of Paris had handcrafted the mother-of-pearl-accented porcelain tiles that covered the bathroom walls, ceiling, and floor. The tiles served as a canvas for a hand-painted mural portraying *Hydrophis belcheri*—the most venomous snake in the world. Its vivid gold and dark-green striped scales coiled around the room and culminated on the rear wall of the shower stall where its mouth gaped, ready to strike.

As Nazar traced the snake's fangs with his finger, a cocoon of water jets massaged his body.

He toweled off and, still naked, returned to the living room, slipped on the silk jumpsuit, and pressed the intercom.

"How about one of your special martinis, Keisha?"

Seconds later, the door opened. Nazar lounged on the bed. He admired her as she turned to place a tray of food on the cocktail bar. At first he had lusted after her, and now, ten years later, Keisha had become indispensable to him. She wore a simple black skirt, tiny and tight. Even in three-inch heels she was six inches shorter than he. She bent forward to hand him the drink, delivering the teasing glimpse of breast he so enjoyed. But only titillation; his sexual proclivities did not extend to mature women.

She said, "I have some wonderful sashimi, selected in person from Billingsgate market. Can I tempt you?"

"You constantly tempt me, Keisha, and I'm delighted you do. That sounds wonderful, and then I think I'll catch up on my sleep. What is our flight time?"

"Five hours. We're cleared to Aqaba." She moved the tray of food to his bedside table. Colorful slices of fish, rice, and seaweed garnish were precisely positioned on the stark white plate as though she had painted the meal.

"Please, sit and join me for a few moments."

Her slit skirt rode up her thigh as she perched on the edge of a leather executive chair. With a light touch of her index finger, she woke a computer monitor centered on the table next to her.

"How are the preparations for the press campaign proceeding?" Nazar asked.

"Releases have gone out worldwide. Today's conference attendees received a package as they left. Martin is in Washington this weekend. He's scheduled to do the rounds of the Sunday-morning talk shows. You have an option for *Sixty Minutes;* they've agreed to take it via satellite if you're available."

"What does Martin think?"

"He thinks you should delegate it to him. CBS probably won't take a substitute, but he feels we have a better chance of going viral if we encourage the 'billionaire's epiphany' positioning."

Nazar smiled. Martin Spalling was an expert in manipulation, and his VP knew the savior-and-benefactor-to-the-world image played well to Nazar's ego.

"Tell him to proceed as he thinks best. What about our friends in the Middle East?"

"They appreciated the prior notice. However, it will cause some strain. After all, you are proposing a shift away from their primary product, but there are no contract termination threats. Martin has arranged a press briefing in Eilat on Friday. He hopes you can attend. He has sent an invitation to the *Times of London*. He asks that you pay special attention to their delegate."

"I understand. Eilat will be convenient. Also, message Beijing. Tell them to begin covering my short positions as soon as the markets open."

She typed the message as he spoke.

"Exciting times, Keisha."

"Yes, sir." She stood, bent her knees, and in one graceful movement collected his discarded clothes. "Please, eat, then rest. You have a busy week ahead." Almost imperceptibly, she brushed her hand against his bare arm as she straightened to leave.

With monogrammed ivory chopsticks, Nazar selected a sliver of ginger from the center of its rose-petal arrangement on his plate and slipped it onto his tongue.

His thoughts drifted to Aqaba, a city of whitewashed stone buildings at the southern tip of Jordan. A nugget nestling beneath towering purple mountains. Headquarters for his vast global oil enterprise, its deep-water port was strategically important to Jordan, and to much of the Arab world beyond.

But Nazar wasn't interested in Aqaba because of its strategic location. In a city of one hundred thousand residents, Nazar's dollar-heavy hand reached into every level of government and from there throughout the country of Jordan. A king ruled Jordan, but Nazar was its prince in all but name. He provided security and largesse to the bureaucrats, in particular to those managing the affairs of his beloved Aqaba. In return, he was above the law in this land of the easy bribe.

The reason for his bold announcement in London lay far from the idyllic presentation of a sudden personal epiphany. *Forbes* magazine ranked him 276th in their list of the world's richest people. They based his net worth of $4.6 billion on his seven-percent stake in Eudon Oil. But Nazar had leveraged his stock, risked everything on Dawud Ferran's nanobots. On paper, he was a billionaire. In reality, he was closer to broke.

Since the Professor's demonstration in Ohio, a Chinese investment house had accumulated a large short position in Eudon Oil shares on his behalf. Today's announcement, made after the close of London's stock exchange, would trigger a huge sell-off in Eudon Oil. As chief executive, he was legally bound to declare any trading in company stock, but China was a long way off, and the Chinese were discreet. He expected to clear five hundred million dollars by covering his positions, betting against his company.

Eudon Alternative Energy was a private company. Its progress and potential were not public record. Nazar owned it one hundred percent, and to date he'd invested two billion dollars to move his nanobot team from Ohio and build the refinery complex in the desert.

With the Chinese funds he could complete the plant. Once the ethanol began flowing and the news media realized he had a solution to the energy crisis, then shares of Eudon Alternative Energy would be offered to the public, and he would take his rightful place at the top of the *Forbes* Billionaires list.

Nazar Eudon was destined be the most powerful Arab in history, and the richest man in the world.

10

When Abdul landed at Israel's Ben Gurion International Airport a week after getting the Allah's Revenge letter, nervous energy tingled through him. On his last visit to Israel at age fourteen, a grim-faced Israeli immigration official in a Plexiglas booth had stamped an entry-visa into his passport and glared at Abdul as if he were dirt on his shoe. Now he was returning, a junior correspondent for the *Times of London*, here to become Ghazi's "messenger to the world."

As Abdul strode past the baggage-claim carousels, he took journalistic note of the eclectic crowd. Stressed tourists and costumed nuns mingled with groups of black-suited, dreadlocked Hasidic Jews. Only in Israel.

Abdul walked through the neon-bright, modern airport and out the main exit into the long, broad, concrete arrivals tunnel. Ahead, hundreds of people crowded either side of the entrance, narrowing the corridor as they craned to catch the first glimpse of a son or daughter, aunt or mother. Fifty feet in front, apparently unable to restrain their joy, a half-dozen black-draped women ran forward and clustered around a frail old man, like iron filings latching to a magnet.

Outside, the sticky heat of an Israeli day replaced the air-conditioning of the terminal, and an unstructured crowd invaded Abdul's Western ideal of personal space.

A short, stocky man grabbed his arm. "Taxi. Taxi to Jerusalem. Very cheap." He spoke in Hebrew. When Abdul kept walking, the man switched to Arabic, and then tried English. On all sides, people clamored and shouted. Abdul heard German, French and American accents. Blaring car horns and the roar of jet engines added to the confusion. Abdul yanked his sleeve away from the hawker and muscled through the crowd to the front of the taxi rank.

"King David Hotel, Jerusalem, please."

"Shalom." The driver was an elderly man in his seventies.

The ride along the freeway to Jerusalem was fast and smooth through green, cultivated farmland.

The driver reached back, tapped Abdul on the knee, and spoke. "When I came to Israel with my family in 1947, this was desert; sand and rock and dust. There was nothing. Nothing as far as the eye could see." To illustrate his point, the driver waved a hand out of the car window at a field of cotton. Long black irrigation pipes stretched over olive-green bushes peppered with white buds.

"Nobody wanted the land then. Hah! Now look. Israelis turned the desert green. Israelis built roads, and cities, and the airport. Now the Arabs call it their home. We should leave. Yes, now they want Israel back."

Abdul remained silent. Argument was futile. The driver could accept no other point of view.

"If we give it back, you know what will happen?"

"No," Abdul said, his voice flat with disgust at the driver's racist rant.

"I'll tell you. In twenty years . . . no, in *ten* . . ." Rheumy eyes stared at Abdul in the driver's mirror. "Yes, in ten years this will be desert again! That's the Arab for you." The driver spat out of his window.

As they approached Jerusalem, Abdul strained for a glimpse of the Old City. The transformation from open, arable land to crammed, congested concrete and steel happened suddenly. The cab slowed to a crawl. Traffic was heavy. Vehicles moved in packs, ignoring lane markings. Drivers dived into impossible gaps, gesticulating wildly and leaning on their horns. Teenagers in olive-green Israeli military uniforms with Uzis slung casually across their shoulders dawdled among the crowds.

In contrast, the atrium of the King David Hotel was quiet, calm, and cool. Ceramic floors, high ornate ceilings, and crisply uniformed staff placed him firmly back in the Western world. By 5:00 p.m., he was in his room. He called Rafiq and left a message that he'd arrived.

That evening, his uncles and aunts threw a family party in his honor. More than sixty guests crammed into his uncle's small, whitewashed tenement home and spilled outside into the dusty yard. The kitchen counters were laden with a colorful mezze of olives, warm pita and humus, baba ghanoush, and crisp, fresh salad. Everyone wanted to speak to Abdul, to shake his hand, to impress him with their plans and dreams. His family was big, and loud, and, he thought, wonderful.

Several young women, blatantly brought as potential mates for their English cousin, stood in a group, shyly sneaking glances at him and giggling behind their hands. His father had warned him this might happen. He successfully avoided them until a second uncle on his father's side cornered him.

"Abdul-Haqq, allow me to introduce my daughter, Adiba." The man enunciated his words slowly and carefully. All night, Abdul had struggled with how fast his family spoke their Arabic. Word of his handicap must have spread.

In contrast to her father, a squat dark-skinned man with a stubbly chin, Adiba reminded him of a perfect little doll. She wore form-fitting blue jeans and a simple embroidered cotton top. Her head was covered by a *hijab*—an elegant scarf that framed her face and wrapped around her neck. The fringes of the *hijab* matched her blouse. Head slightly bowed, she turned large brown eyes up to meet Abdul's. The effect befuddled him. She held out her hand. Abdul resisted a strong urge to bend and kiss it, something he had never considered doing in his life. Instead, he gave her a formal handshake and felt color rise in his cheeks.

"I'm pleased to meet you, Adiba."

"Adiba is a writer, like you, Abdul-Haqq." The uncle grinned and showed a row of crooked teeth.

Adiba gave the man a gentle punch on the arm. "Father, please, don't."

"Well, a young woman should learn a trade in these modern times."

Now it was Adiba's turn to blush. This had been a common

theme. His relatives desperately wanted to show they were forward-thinking people.

Adiba shook her head. "As usual, my father is confused." She produced a mock frown and wagged a finger in her father's face as if scolding him. "Abdul-Haqq, I assure you rumors of my writing are greatly exaggerated."

Abdul laughed at the cleverness of the comment.

"Of course, we have met before," she said. "Like that." She pointed to four children playing hide-and-seek under the kitchen table.

"I'm sorry. I remember little of my previous visits here." On this trip, Abdul had expected a feeling of returning home; instead, he felt foreign and out of place.

"That's okay, I don't remember either. My father told me we played together. But that may be another exaggeration."

She gave her father a quizzical look. He shrugged and excused himself, leaving Abdul and Adiba alone. The look on the man's face clearly said, "Mission accomplished."

Abdul was pleased when Adiba made no move to follow him. "Are you a writer?" he asked.

"I study English online. We can't afford for me to attend college. I am grateful, though, that my father is liberated enough to encourage me. Abdul-Haqq, you must be exhausted. Between jet-lag and this crazy crowd bantering you, have you had any time to yourself?"

"Well, everyone here has been wonderful, but I confess I didn't realize how large my Palestinian family was until I saw them together in the same house. I plan to spend time in the Old City tomorrow."

"If you wish," Adiba said, "I could show you around, act as an unofficial guide." Her hand touched his arm, delicately, light as a small bird. "But if you prefer to experience the city alone, I will not be offended."

"Wow, that would be wonderful." Abdul's cheeks burned. His instantaneous reply must have telegraphed how enthusiastic he was to spend more time with her.

"I'll come to your hotel at 9:00 a.m. We can walk to the city," she said.

"You know where I'm staying?"

"Abdul-Haqq, I can assure you everyone in this room knows

you are at the prestigious King David Hotel." She laughed at his lack of guile. "Now I must go back to my father, and you must continue to circulate. Otherwise they," she inclined her head toward the group of women, "will start gossiping." She smiled, this time looking him full in the face.

He shook her hand again. It was delicate, soft, and cool.

Adiba collected him the next morning. They watched in respectful silence as Jews, heads bobbing, prayed at the Wailing Wall. They walked beside awed Christians as they mimicked the route of Christ's last journey—the Via Dolorosa. They exercised their privilege as Muslims to enter the Dome of the Rock and marvel at the mosque's magnificence.

Inexperienced with dating—in college, he'd been too focused on his studies—he found it difficult to take his eyes off his stunning guide. Animated and fascinating, she conveyed not just the history but also the emotions of this remarkable city where the major religions of the world collided.

They browsed through worn, narrow stone pathways in the Arab market where traders had plied their wares for tens of thousands of years. Tourists, Israelis, and Arabs mingled in the Old City, making it difficult to comprehend the strife, death, and sadness wrought because of this place.

She showed him a local café where he insisted on paying for lunch. They ate homemade falafel, fat black olives, and fluffy, light pita, then dawdled over strong, dark espresso. There was more to say than time permitted.

When they parted in front of his hotel, Abdul moved to shake her hand, but she brushed him aside and delivered a warm hug and a light kiss on the cheek. They exchanged e-mail addresses and promised to keep in touch. Abdul watched her walk away until she disappeared in the crowds. His cheek was still tingling when he entered his room.

He spent Wednesday at the hotel, reading, swimming in the pool, thinking of Adiba, and worrying about the upcoming meeting. If Ghazi was what he claimed, this could be Abdul's breakout story, a pivotal event in his nascent career. But now the meeting was imminent, he felt far less confident than in Scott Shearer's office at the *Times of London*.

Although expected, when his room phone rang at 6:00 p.m.

Abdul was startled.

A man's voice, deep and strong, with a harsh rasp, said, "Am I speaking with Abdul-Haqq-bin-Wahid-bin-Tariq-Ahmed?"

"Yes."

"I am Ghazi."

"Where will we meet?" Throat tight with nerves, Abdul swallowed a few times to prevent his voice from cracking.

"In ten minutes, a black Mitsubishi will stop in front of the hotel. The driver will get out and wipe his forehead with a rag. Get in the back seat. He will bring you to me."

Now, as Rafiq had instructed him, Abdul made the first negotiating move.

"I will use a laptop to take notes and a digital recorder to make a transcript of our conversation."

Rafiq had advised, *Don't ask if you can, just tell him you will.*

A momentary pause, then, "This is agreed."

Abdul felt as though he'd won the lottery. The line went dead.

Good-bye to you, too.

In the lobby, he waved off the concierge's attempts to call him a cab and stood outside, watching for the car. A black sedan pulled up. The driver gave the signal. Abdul opened the back door and slid in. The car tore away, tossing him back in his seat.

He said, "Hi."

"You are Abdul-Haqq?"

"Yes."

The driver glanced at Abdul in the mirror. "Speak no more. The journey is short."

Abdul had wondered whether they might blindfold him, but it wasn't necessary; the car's windows were heavily tinted, and already he was lost in the maze of streets. They headed north into the West Bank. But, no matter where they were going, he was in Ghazi's hands until he returned to the hotel. His heart skipped and nerves trickled down his spine as that realization struck home.

For the first time in his life, Abdul was in mortal danger.

After twenty minutes of reckless driving, they pulled into the driveway of a general store. The garage door in front opened and they drove in. The door rolled shut behind the car and left them in darkness.

"Wait." The driver got out and flipped on a light, then opened Abdul's door. "Follow me."

A side door led to a narrow, unlit flight of stone stairs. The air smelled stale and damp. He followed the driver to the top and through a door at the stair head into a windowless room, twelve feet square with bare, whitewashed walls peeling in places. The driver indicated a white plastic lawn chair positioned behind a green-topped card table. The chair faced the door they'd entered by, the only door in the room. A solitary floor lamp pointed at his chair, interrogation-style.

"Ghazi will come soon." The driver left.

A key turned in the lock. The circumstances Abdul found himself in were a huge departure from any he'd encountered before. This trip had seemed logical, even exciting, when he'd volunteered, but right now he yearned for the safety of his work cubicle in London. Fighting a strong urge to talk to himself, he flipped open his laptop and turned on his recorder, keeping his trembling hands busy.

Abdul jumped at the sound of a key in the lock. The door opened again. A tall, thick-chested bull of a man entered, carrying a plastic lawn chair similar to the one Abdul sat in. He placed the chair across the table from Abdul.

"I am Ghazi." His was the voice from the phone. Still standing, he offered his hand.

Abdul stood. Ghazi's hard, callused hand dwarfed Abdul's and delivered a crushing, painful grip. Abdul felt like a small child shaking hands with a grown man. Distracted by the pain, the only feature that Abdul registered was a dark scar that ran from below Ghazi's left eye, down his cheek, and disappeared into the collar of his shirt. Ghazi released him, and they sat.

Abdul started the recorder. "Very well, Ghazi, you asked for this meeting. What do you want to tell me?"

Ghazi thumped his balled fist on the table. "The time of creeping Israeli thievery of Palestinian land is past. The name of our organization is 'Allah's Revenge'. It is also an expression of our intent. Because the Jews only understand terror and bloodshed, we will take our revenge with Jewish blood and the blood of their American and British masters."

The tone of Ghazi's speech was more akin to a radical Imam stirring up a crowd than a man sitting five feet away from his sole audience member.

"Is your organization a part of al-Qaeda?"

"Those who use the name al-Qaeda defile the one God, Allah, by associating His almighty knowledge and power with their cheap tricks and foolishness, their shoe bombs and exploding clothing. Every street gang in Gaza hides behind the pathetic cloak of al-Qaeda."

"You intend to commit terrorist acts in which innocent British, American and Israeli citizens will be harmed. Sounds the same as al-Qaeda. How will we know the difference?"

"Allah has blessed us with a terrible weapon. You will know us by its mark, Abdul-Haqq."

"What kind of weapon?"

Ghazi raised his voice. "You will know us by its mark."

Abdul changed tack. "Why did you contact me?"

"Your family is known to us. They are honorable people. You are in a position to communicate with those who must make the changes we will demand. You will be our messenger."

"What are your demands?"

"The infidels must leave and return to the Palestinians the land that is their birthright. This is also your birthright, Abdul-Haqq-bin-Wahid-bin-Tariq-Ahmed."

Ghazi's chair scraped the ground and he stood. The sudden change startled Abdul. Was this the end of the interview?

"Thank you for coming. I am glad to have met you, and I wish you a safe journey back to England. *Ma'a salama.*"

"Wait." The brevity of the audience shocked Abdul. He sprang to his feet. "When and where will you strike?"

"The infidels will be given one opportunity to retreat. If they refuse, they will know the pain my Palestinian brothers suffer every day. Tell your people to heed our warning or face terrible consequences." Ghazi turned and left the room.

Abdul shut off his recorder. By the time he'd packed away his unused laptop, the driver had appeared at the door. They returned to the hotel at speed and in silence.

When he got back to his hotel room, the message light on the phone was blinking. He'd received two calls: one from Rafiq, checking on him; the second was more interesting.

"Hello, Abdul. This is Adiba. I hope you don't take offense, but my uncle has offered me his car tomorrow. If you like, I can drive you to the airport in the morning." She left her number. The sound of her voice made him smile.

He called Rafiq.

"I'm happy to hear from you, Abdul. Are you okay?"

"Sure, I'm fine, but the meeting was strange, he—"

"Not over the phone. Let's wait till you're back at the office. And Scott wants you to call him right away." Rafiq gave him Scott Shearer's home number.

Abdul hung up from Rafiq and dialed the editor-in-chief. "Mr. Shearer, it's Abdul."

"I'm glad Rafiq reached you in time. Did Ghazi show?"

"Yes, I met him."

"Okay, save it. Nazar Eudon has a press conference tomorrow afternoon in Israel. I want you to represent us."

"Are you sure? I mean, that's a business section piece."

"Well, you're there. You and Eudon have similar backgrounds. His parents were from Palestine. Try to get a more personal angle on his resignation."

"His what?"

"Check the Internet."

"But what if Nazar won't spend time with me?"

"Bring home the press pack, and we'll be no worse off. The meeting's at the Dan Hotel in Eilat. Hire a car. It can't be far."

Abdul didn't tell his dynamic boss he'd never driven a car—he didn't need one in London.

Next he called Adiba.

A gruff male voice answered. "Alo."

"May I speak to Adiba, please? This is Abdul-Haqq."

"Who?"

Abdul was flustered. He'd expected Adiba to answer. He realized, too late, that was unlikely in an Arab household, and it may have been an insult for him to ask for her. He heard voices in the background, and she came on the line.

"Alo, who is this?"

"Hi, Adiba, it's Abdul-Haqq. I hope I haven't caused a problem by calling."

"No, of course not. My father handles a telephone like a sheep with a saucepan."

Abdul grinned. He pictured her wagging a finger at her father as she spoke. He said, "I picked up your message. A ride to the airport would be great, but I just talked to my boss, and I'm not returning till later in the week."

"Oh . . . okay, I understand." She sounded disappointed.

"Unless, that is, you happen to be driving to Eilat."

The line went quiet. *Shit*, Abdul thought. "Sorry, Adiba, that's my strange English sense of humor."

"You are going to Eilat?"

"Yes, I'm due there tomorrow afternoon and—"

"Hold on." Abdul heard a muffled conversation. Adiba had her hand over the mouthpiece.

"Okay, my uncle says I can take you."

"No, I couldn't ask that. I was joking."

"You don't want me to take you?"

"Ah . . . yes, of course I do, but it's too much to ask." Again the line went silent. Abdul realized he was making a horse's ass of himself. He sucked in a breath and tried again. "Adiba, if you are sure, and your uncle says you can use the car, I would love a ride to Eilat. I'm supposed to be there by lunch."

"I'll pick you up outside the hotel at 7:00 a.m. The drive is about four hours."

"Great, I'll book you a room at The Dan Hotel. Bring an overnight bag. Oh, and bring your passport." If they had time, Abdul wanted to cross into Jordan.

11

The next morning, Abdul waited in front of the King David Hotel. After the idiotic way he'd behaved on the phone, he worried she might not show. At 6:55 a.m., a rusty two-door Datsun pulled up, and Adiba leaned over and opened the passenger door.

"Abdul, please put your luggage in back. The trunk lid is broken."

Abdul tossed his bag on the back seat, next to hers. A worn spring poked up through a six-inch rip in the grimy fabric, and candy wrappers littered the rear floor. He climbed in, and Adiba pulled away with a kangaroo jerk. The speedometer didn't work. The car had no air-conditioning, so all windows were open, and a sickening grinding sound accompanied each gear shift.

Adiba drove in silence through the city, hands gripped tightly to the wheel, concentrating on traffic. Once they reached the freeway, she turned to him. "I apologize for the car. My uncle is a pig. If I'd known it was this ugly, I would never have offered to take you." Her cheeks flushed with embarrassment; Abdul thought she looked lovely.

"I'd ride in a donkey cart with you to avoid the vicious old cabbie who brought me from the airport." She laughed. He loved the sound.

Abdul had to shout over the loud thrumming of the wind through the open windows. "Did I embarrass you in front of your family when I called last night?"

"No. Not at all. I am fortunate. My father is the most liberal man I know. He believes many problems of the Arab stem from backward-looking conservative customs. He trusts me, and I would never betray his trust."

"Have you been to Eilat often?" Abdul knew it was a popular vacation spot.

"Once, for my thirteenth birthday with uncle Hassan and two of my cousins. We swam in the ocean. It is a wonderful memory."

"You haven't—" Abdul stopped because Adiba spoke at the same time. "What did you say?"

"No, after you."

They laughed.

"Why did you never go back to Eilat?"

"I have a sister and two brothers, all younger than me. Father works hard, but Arab laborer pay is poor."

"I'm sorry, I didn't mean to criticize." Heat rose in his cheeks. He wished he'd engaged brain before inserting foot in mouth— typical insensitive Westerner.

"Do not be embarrassed. I don't care to lay on a beach in Eilat. I have a wonderful family. My father encourages my writing. My mother makes a beautiful home. We lack for nothing, but our lives must seem very bland to you."

"Not at all. In many ways I envy you. London is so fast-paced that it can be easy to forget what is important in life."

The four-hour drive passed too quickly. The more time Abdul spent with Adiba, the more powerful the attraction. He hoped the feeling was mutual.

While he checked them in at the Dan Hotel, Adiba stood silently by his side, no longer his chatty fellow traveler. The opulence of the hotel appeared to intimidate her.

They ate lunch at the poolside bar. "Are you okay?" Abdul asked once they had ordered.

"Yes." She stared at her plate.

"Sure?"

Adiba pulled in a deep breath and put down her silverware. She faced him for the first time since they'd started eating. "Abdul, for you this grandeur is familiar. I don't belong here. It's nothing you can change."

They ate their meal in uncomfortable silence. Abdul wanted to regain the feeling from the road trip, but he didn't know how. When their plates were cleared and he'd paid the check, he said, "I have to go to the meeting now."

"I understand. I'll wait in my room." She stood and headed for the lobby.

He walked after her, placed a hand on her arm. "Why not take a walk to the beach, see whether you can remember where you swam on your birthday?"

Abdul searched her face, but she looked away. "I prefer not. We could go together, later?"

Abdul released her arm. "Sure," he said, "I'll call you when we're finished."

Abdul found his way to the conference room and joined eight other journalists seated at a large oval table.

Nazar arrived a few minutes later and sat at the head of the table. "Welcome to Eilat. I thank you for taking the time and trouble to meet me. I am yours for an hour, please ask whatever you wish and I will do my best to provide answers." Nazar's striking green eyes sparkled. His voice sounded resonant, powerful, yet Abdul thought his smile conveyed genuine warmth.

Most questions centered on the steep fall in Eudon Oil's stock price, and speculation about his successor as CEO. Nazar repeatedly steered the conversation toward his new venture, Eudon Alternative Energy. When the business discussion tapered off, Abdul asked the one thing that puzzled him the most.

"Mr. Eudon, from a humble beginning you have become one of the richest people in the world. Why risk your wealth and reputation now?"

"Abdul-Haqq, correct?" Abdul was impressed, Nazar had known each of the journalists' names. "A most perceptive question."

Abdul smiled, pleased with himself.

"I have never taken a wife. I birthed no children. Not by chance but by choice. I am a driven individual. I could sit back and relax, but that is not living. To live, one must take risks. To truly live, one must risk everything. I regret that this old fool took so long to understand that the world is on a wrong path, and I bear more responsibility than most. I wish to leave a legacy, not to greed and wealth, but to hope and freedom. And I believe I can."

Nazar's frankness impressed Abdul, and they exchanged an imperceptible nod, one Arab to another.

The meeting ended, and when Abdul's time came to depart, he bowed deeply with hands joined respectfully in front as his mother had taught him. *"Ma'a salama."*

Nazar, smiling, returned the gesture. "Abdul-Haqq, you were the sole representative from the UK here today. It is imperative that my new direction is understood in the country where Eudon Oil's stock is listed. As you will have gathered from today's discussion, my announcement and resignation took a severe toll on the Company's share price. If you have no previous engagement, why not join me at my home in Aqaba for supper tomorrow. I could provide depth for your story. Also, I would enjoy meeting you outside the constraints necessary for this formal press briefing."

Scott Shearer would be delighted by this arrangement, but what about Adiba? ". . . That is most generous, Mr. Eudon. I'd be honored to accept your hospitality."

"You hesitated. Why? Please speak freely. For if you cannot, you are perhaps not the man I hope to meet tomorrow."

"I'm sorry, sir. I expected to be free tomorrow, and I had planned to spend time with a friend, but the arrangement can be changed."

"I suspect she is an attractive friend." Nazar winked. "What is her name?"

"Her name is Adiba, and yes, she is beautiful." Abdul grinned like a schoolboy.

"Well, perhaps you would agree to share her beauty with an old man for a few hours if she is willing to join us. What do you say?"

"I'm sure she'd be excited to meet you."

"Excellent. That's settled. My assistant will make the arrangements. I look forward to seeing you and your Adiba tomorrow."

That evening, Abdul and Adiba sipped mint tea outside a small beachfront café. Their table looked across the Gulf of Aqaba. The light from an occasional hilltop house betrayed the height and scope of the dark mountains that loomed over the city and cradled it against the sea. Nazar's driver was scheduled to collect them at noon the following day, and Abdul still hadn't persuaded her to accompany him. She lacked the confidence to visit the home of such a rich and important Arab.

"I can't, Abdul. I have nothing to wear." Another in a long list of reasons she had paraded before him.

"Adiba, I must go. It's why my boss sent me. But I want to spend time with you. I can only achieve both if you join me." Abdul slid his hand across the small table and laid it on top of hers. She stared at his fingers. Her face screwed tight, as if she were swallowing a lemon. A refusal would break his heart.

"Okay, but you have to help me if I do something stupid and embarrass myself."

A flutter of excitement sped his pulse, and he grinned. "Of course, and you won't. Now. Can we order? I'm starving."

After dinner, they walked for an hour, hand in hand, along the beachfront. He didn't want the evening to end. He escorted Adiba to her room. They faced each other at the open door, and she reached up and kissed his cheek. He held her bare arms and kissed her lightly on the lips. She responded, but then pulled back and wished him goodnight.

At noon the next day, they sat in the lobby until Nazar's sleek black Mercedes pulled up. The driver guided them into the rear seat. "I am Mufeed. Do you have your passports?"

"Yes," Abdul answered for them both.

"The Jordanian border is only a few minutes. The guards know me well, so it will be smooth. Has either of you seen Aqaba before?"

"No," Abdul said. Adiba failed to respond to the driver. She sat erect, hands locked together on her lap, not even leaning back into the seat. Abdul wondered if he'd made a mistake by insisting she come. She seemed so uncomfortable and nervous.

Twenty minutes after they crossed into Jordan, the car slowed as it approached two wrought-iron gates set in a high brick wall and spanning a broad driveway. At the center of each gate, a coat of arms portrayed a green-and-gold-striped snake with its fangs bared, ready to strike. An armed guard in a pale-green uniform, the snake logo stitched to his breast pocket, stepped from his sentry post and checked the vehicle before opening the gates with a remote.

Mufeed drove them up a long, curved driveway, bordered on either side by manicured palms. As they rounded the top of the drive, the house came into view, and Adiba, who had calmed somewhat on the ride, went rigid and grabbed Abdul's hand. Nazar's home was enormous. Abdul counted five stories. Each level featured semicircular balconies facing the harbor below. The white stucco of the walls contrasted with the roof's red quarry tiles. The edge of each roofline finished with a pagoda-style flourish.

The car pulled up in front of a raised marble entrance. Nazar appeared at the oversized doorway and waved to them like a long-lost friend.

"Welcome. I am delighted you came. I meet so few young people in my business." After shaking Abdul's hand, Nazar turned to Adiba. He took her left hand in his right and lifted it to his lips. "And thank you most of all for bringing your charming companion. Adiba, it is a pleasure to meet you."

"Thank you, sir," she said in a small, deferential voice.

"Come. Let us move out of the heat. And, young lady, don't make me feel older than I am. Please, call me Nazar." Adiba delivered a forced smile. Her grip on Abdul's hand was borderline painful.

Nazar proudly showed off his home. He drove them through the grounds in a golf cart, pointing out pieces of sculpture he had acquired. The gardens were built with local stone and exclusively featured native plants, no swimming pool or opulent water display. Nazar explained that it would be disrespectful to the people of Jordan to waste such a valuable commodity on ornamentation. He spoke at length to Abdul about his new business direction.

"After spending time with you, Abdul, I am confident your report will be accurate and fair, which is all I ask. I anticipate making a significant announcement about my alternative energy plans in the next few weeks. I will send you an invitation to the press briefing. It will take place in Phoenix, Arizona, and it will be a UK exclusive for the *Times*." The news thrilled Abdul.

For supper, they selected food from a buffet laid out in a room Nazar told them was modeled on the cocktail lounge at the Hotel Alfonso XIII in Seville, Spain. Red silks draped the ceiling, giving the impression of being inside an elaborate marquee. Pale cream furnishings with clean, simple lines and red accents sat low to the ground. Nazar explained that he had once attended a meeting there. The room had seemed flawless to him, so he commissioned his designer to replicate it.

"An old man's folly, I'm afraid."

"No, it's perfect," Adiba said in a rare spontaneous outburst.

"How is your family, Adiba?" Nazar asked.

Nazar had seemed to understand her discomfort with the opulent surroundings. He had addressed himself to Abdul for most of the day. Only now, when she had freely spoken to him, did he respond with the most polite question one Arab could ask another.

"They are well, thank you for your interest, Nazar." The quaint formality of her reply made Abdul's heart race. She was perfect.

"I have a picture. Would you like to see them?"

Nazar smiled. "I would be honored."

Adiba lifted her purse and produced a worn photograph; she moved to sit next to Nazar and pointed out her family.

"This was taken recently, but I'm sorry the quality is not—"

"Please, name them for me." Nazar studied the small, creased picture.

"Father and mother, of course; these two are my brothers, Dani and Fadil, and this is my younger sister, Lana."

"One day, she will be a beauty like you. How old is Lana?"

Adiba blushed. "Lana just turned sixteen."

"She looks much younger. You know, I was also raised in East Jerusalem. I walked two miles to school each day. What school does Lana attend?"

Listening to their conversation, Abdul felt excluded. Adiba smiled at the photo and became animated, excited by the interest Nazar showed in her younger sister. Abdul sensed the deep love connecting her with the photo of her family, the representation of the five most precious things in her life. Ridiculous, he knew, but he felt jealous.

"Lana," Nazar said. It brought Abdul back from his daydreaming. "A beautiful name and a beautiful family. Thank you for sharing them."

Nazar stood and took a few paces away from his guests. "Now, we must be serious for a few moments. I confess to having had a wonderful, self-indulgent day showing off to you young people, and time has gotten away from us. It is almost 10:00 p.m. I suggest you stay the night and return in the morning to Eilat." Adiba began to protest, but Nazar put up his hand.

"My dear, you, more than Abdul, should know that traveling by road after dark is an unnecessary risk to take. The border crossing is a far more suspicious affair at night."

He softened his tone. "I know you didn't come prepared to stay, but I assure you that I have a guest suite especially tailored to the needs of a woman. I am certain you will find everything you require for a comfortable night."

To Abdul's surprise, Adiba didn't resist the idea; perhaps she did appreciate the dangers of night driving. For himself, he never wanted to leave this wonderful place and their fascinating host.

Nazar guided them to their suites on the second floor and bid them goodnight.

Thirty minutes later, Nazar sat alone at the desk in his bedroom. A black silk robe draped loosely around his naked body. He stared at two fifty-inch, wall-mounted monitors. Each screen split into eight windows, one for each of the cameras in the rooms. A small touch-screen control-panel sat in front of him. In the top left window of one screen, Abdul sat naked and cross-legged on his bed, meditating.

Impressive, he tends to both body and mind.

On the second screen, Adiba explored her room, opening every closet and drawer to investigate the contents. She selected nightclothes from the dresser and carried them to the bathroom. Nazar touched the controls, and her bathroom filled the screen. She sat on the commode. The solid sound of her urine stream played from his speakers.

He enlarged Abdul's screen, placing the couple side-by-side. Still and calm, Abdul's lean body sported a modest six-pack. His olive skin looked smooth, but his musculature was that of a grown man, not a boy. This disappointed Nazar; at the hotel, Abdul had appeared less mature. Still, the boy was easily manipulated. Martin was correct. A positive image in the London press when he made his announcement about the ethanol refinery would be invaluable. Abdul would repay this investment of time and become a good asset for the future.

Nazar turned his attention to the girl. Adiba stripped off her day clothes and folded them carefully across the back of the bathroom chair. As she soaped up in the shower, he zoomed the lens, filling the screen with her face. Water droplets hung on her eyelashes. Without makeup, she seemed almost childlike. Her body, shaped with the curves most men desire, held no attraction for him. But her smooth, innocent face produced a ripple of arousal.

Adiba had spurned the more racy outfits on offer in the guest wardrobe and dressed in a modest full-length cotton nightgown that hung formlessly from her shoulders. Nazar approved. When she lay down to sleep, she left the light on low. He filled the screen with her face. Without the distraction of her woman's body, it was possible for him to imagine her as she once had been—how her younger sister Lana would be now—innocent, frail, and unspoiled. He narrowed his eyes and pictured Lana's childlike face in place of Adiba's. He imagined Lana's thin body beneath the cotton nightgown. Her breasts would be puffy and indistinct, just beginning to form, her pubic hairs soft, sparse wisps. His hand moved inside his dressing gown, and he stole her innocence for his pleasure.

The next morning, Mufeed served fresh fruits and hot croissants on the terrace. He handed Abdul a note and a business card: "Dear friends, I apologize for leaving in haste. Please linger over breakfast. This number will connect you with my secretary, Keisha. If I can ever be of assistance, you can contact me through her."

After the chauffeur returned them to Eilat, they checked out of The Dan, and Adiba drove them to Ben Gurion Airport in the rickety old Datsun.

Adiba insisted on parking and walking into the terminal with him. He could hardly believe the chaos that greeted them when they entered the departure area. Line after line, thousands of people snaked around the concourse. He looked to her for an explanation. Surely a bomb must have gone off before they arrived.

"It is normal," she said.

His mouth dropped open, and she laughed.

"You have much to learn about the Middle East."

She stayed with him for two hours while he pushed his carry-on along the ground toward the security checkpoints. When only a dozen people remained in front of them, she touched his arm.

"I should leave. It will confuse them if they observe me waiting with you and not traveling." On tiptoe, she kissed him full on the mouth, then dropped back to the balls of her feet and brushed a lipstick smear from his bottom lip with her thumb. Her eyes were dark pools. Abdul was sure his cheeks were scarlet. She laughed and moved to turn away, but he caught her shoulders, bent, and kissed her with force before wrapping her in his arms. Her breasts pressed against his chest. She folded into him, held him tightly, and whispered in his ear. "Please e-mail when you are safely home?"

"I will," he said.

She bounced away into the crowd, but turned to blow him a kiss before she finally disappeared.

12

Three days after the attack on the tube train, Detective Chief Inspector Quinnborne perched on the edge of a cluttered table in Scott Shearer's office at the *Times of London*. Scott paced in front of his big window and Abdul and Rafiq sat at Scott's desk. They listened to Abdul's recording of his meeting with Ghazi.

"Can you describe him?" Quinn asked.

"The light was in my eyes, so I only got a glimpse. He had a scar on his face." Abdul indicated with his finger where the cut ran. "He was a couple of inches taller than me, I'm five-eleven. And strong; he crushed my hand when we shook."

"Was anything else said other than what we've heard?"

"No, I set up the equipment before he entered the room. That's the whole recording. The meeting was briefer than I expected."

Quinn glanced at Scott, who spoke to his staff. "Good work, Abdul. You also, Rafiq, I know you were guiding him all the way. Now, if you two will excuse us, I need a few minutes alone with the Chief Inspector." Rafiq headed for the door. Abdul retrieved his digital recorder from the table.

"I'd like a copy," Quinn said, handing Abdul a business card.

Abdul looked at his boss, who nodded. "No problem," Abdul said.

Quinn had known Scott Shearer for over thirty years. He trusted the newspaper man and considered him a friend. Quinn hopped off the desk and thumped a fist into his palm. "You should have called me. You shouldn't have let that kid go by himself."

"I get dozens of these things each year. If I called you every time, I'd never get you out of my office. I couldn't be sure it was a live one 'till we'd checked. Anyway, the *kid* did well, and I phoned you the minute I heard about the Oxford Circus attack. So what are we looking at?"

Quinn walked to the window. "You've put me in a tough spot. This is sensitive information."

"It's the same people who did the train, then?"

"I didn't say that."

"You didn't have to."

Quinn glared at Scott. "You can't use this. If you shine a light on these bastards, they'll be bigger than Elvis overnight."

"What makes you so sure it's Allah's Revenge?"

Quinn's jaws moved back and forth, grinding teeth. If he lied, Scott would know, and he needed access to Abdul. "Off the record?"

Scott nodded.

"They left a note on the train." Quinn grabbed his coat from the rack near the door. "Look, give me the afternoon. I'll get back with you when I can, by tonight at the latest."

An hour after his meeting with Scott, Quinn played Abdul's recording in his boss's office at New Scotland Yard.

"Did you play this for Frank?" Superintendent James Porter spat out the words.

"Not yet."

"Oxford Circus is his case, Quinn."

"Frank worked for me for ten years. Sir, in my opinion, he isn't capable."

"I'm going to pretend I didn't hear that." The superintendent glared at Quinn. "Take it to Frank. If he asks for your help, then I'll assign you to the case. But you'll report to him. Understood?"

Quinn snatched up the recorder, turned on his heel and slammed the door on his way out. He stormed down three flights of stairs to Frank's office and burst in. Frank jumped and slid his feet off the desk. His eyes looked heavy.

"Did I wake you?" Quinn's voice was thick with sarcasm.

"Piss off. Don't you know to knock before you barge into

someone's office?"

Quinn slapped the recorder on the desk and filled Frank in on Abdul's trip. They played the interview twice.

Quinn sat in a chair and Frank stood over him, shaking a fat finger in his face. "Listen Quinn, I don't give a flyin' fuck about your cozy relationship with Scott Shearer. He can't print this."

Frank was enjoying the moment a little too much, but Quinn wanted to stay on the case, so he gritted his teeth and sucked it up. "The name's going to come out. These things always do. Allah's Revenge, whoever or whatever it is, has chosen young Abdul Ahmed. Close the door on Shearer, and we'll lose access to Abdul. Better the devil you know."

"Yeah, what about this Abdul character; he's an Arab, right?"

Quinn glared at his ex-partner. "Scott trusts him."

"And you say his family threw him a party in Jerusalem a couple of nights before he made the recording."

"So what?"

"Maybe Ghazi was there. Maybe he brought a keg. I think we should bring Abdul in."

"Shearer *will* go public if you push his boy around."

Frank's cell phone buzzed. He picked up and listened for a few seconds. "Shit!" The color drained from his face. "E-mail it to me." He moved back to his desk and tapped the keyboard to wake his computer. Quinn followed.

Frank opened an e-mail and clicked a link. A grainy video popped up. It showed the inside of a railway car. The passengers were acting crazy, pulling at their mouths and grabbing their throats as if someone had sucked out all the air. The screen was momentarily filled with a close-up of a young woman's face, red, distorted, terrified. Quinn thought she might be the same girl he'd seen when they visited Mike Mitchell. The camera view shifted higher; along the length of the car, passengers jerked and writhed. There was no sound other than the rattle of the train.

"No screaming?" Frank said.

Quinn didn't answer. Hardly surprising—considering what was growing inside their lungs. Then, like a macabre game of stop-the-music, the passengers collapsed: on the floor, across seat backs, on top of one another. The video ended on a still picture; identical to the scene Quinn had witnessed when he'd first entered the train carriage three days earlier. The footage ran for less than two minutes.

"Who sourced the tape?" Quinn asked.

"It's on the Al Jazeera website under the heading "Allah's Revenge," Frank replied. "They showed it on TV an hour ago. It's gone viral."

13

At the *Times of London* headquarters, less than ninety minutes after the Al Jazeera tape went live, Scott Shearer flipped his cell phone shut to end a call and stabbed the intercom button on his desk. "Amy, get Abdul on the line, stat. Then get in here."

Twenty seconds later, his phone rang.

"You wanted me, Mr. Shearer?" Abdul said.

"Listen carefully. Copy your Allah's Revenge files to a thumb drive. As fast as you can. Then call me back." Scott hung up. Abdul would be wondering what was going on, but that copy might save him a lot of trouble.

Scott paced in front of his office window. Six floors below, police cars skidded to a stop fifty yards either side of the building's entrance, blocking the street from both directions. A black van rounded them on the sidewalk and pulled up in front of the building.

"Amy!" When he turned she was already in his office.

"Go to the third floor. Take the stairs. Collect a thumb drive from Abdul and put it somewhere safe."

She was running before he finished talking.

His desk phone rang.

"Ok, I've done the copy, Mr. Shearer. Is something wrong?"

"Amy is on her way to you. She's coming down the stairs. Meet her. Give her the thumb drive, then come back to the phone and

I'll explain." He heard the phone being laid on the desk.

Hurry Amy. Hurry.

Thirty seconds later, a breathless Abdul came back on the line. "Okay, she has the files. What's going on, Mr. Shearer?"

Before he could answer, Scott heard shouting through Abdul's phone.

"Abdul Ahmed! Where's Abdul Ahmed?"

"I'm Abdul. What—"

By the time Scott reached the third floor, Abdul was bent over his desk, his cheek pressed hard against the surface, head facing the window. Two large policemen in dark-blue flak-jackets held him while a third secured his hands with an orange plastic tie.

"Is this your desk?"

"Yes. Let me up. What's this about? Stop pressing my head. You're hurting me." Abdul pushed up and managed to turn to face the office before the policeman slammed him back down.

Scott shouted, "What the hell do you think you're doing? This is private property."

One of the paper's photojournalists took rapid-fire pictures.

Scott recognized Quinn's old partner, Frank Browning, holding his hand up to shield his face from the camera. He served Scott with a search warrant. Scott didn't look at it. The photographer kept snapping; he was joined by a second, with a video recorder.

"Is this your computer?" Frank asked. Abdul looked to his boss. Scott nodded.

"Yes, that's my computer. Now let me up!" Frank signaled, and one of the two officers removed his hand from Abdul's head. The other pulled Abdul upright, maintaining a fierce grip on his shirt back. Abdul's face was blotched red from pressing into the desk. He faced Frank Browning.

"Abdul Ahmed, under the powers vested in me under the Prevention of Terrorism Act, I am placing you under arrest. Under the terms of the warrant I served on Mr. Scott Shearer, the contents of your desk and your computer will be confiscated and may be used as evidence."

Scott shouted, "Abdul! Abdul!" Abdul looked over at his boss, eyes confused, head trembling. Scott spoke slowly, sounding out his words. "I've called Legal. They're on their way. We're videotaping the arrest. I want you to understand that this newspaper will back you every inch of the way."

"But I haven't done anything wrong," Abdul said.

"I know. What I'm telling you is everyone . . ." Scott swept his arm around the open-plan office. Abdul's colleagues stood in the aisles outside their work pods. They stood on chairs or desks and craned over the partitions. ". . . is with you. You are not alone in this, and I'll do my damndest to get you freed quickly. But for now, these . . . *gentlemen* . . ." His emphasis left no one in doubt that he considered the policemen nothing of the sort. "These gentlemen, unfortunately, are within their rights to arrest you. Abdul, you have nothing to hide and nothing to fear."

"Enough of this; come on!" Frank said.

While Scott had been talking, the contents of Abdul's desk and drawers were crammed into a black trash bag. His computer tower had been unplugged and covered with a similar bag. Both bags were emblazoned with the word *Evidence*. The policeman holding Abdul's shirt pushed him toward the hallway.

Abdul's face was drained of color. His eyes blank, stunned.

Scott positioned himself in front of Abdul and walked ahead of him, giving him something to follow, something to focus on. His colleagues lined the short corridor between Abdul's desk and the office door. They executed a cynical, slow handclap for the police and shouted encouragements to Abdul.

"Go get 'em, Abdul."

"Chin up, mate."

Scott reached the hallway. Two uniformed police officers guarded the elevator and the stairwell.

"Stairs!" Frank barked.

The guard opened the door, and Scott led the way. The photographers followed, still shooting. Scott talked to Abdul all the way downstairs and through the lobby. He was still talking as Abdul was pressed into a police car. He talked of support, of friends and family, of trust and belief in the system. He talked in an even, calm voice. The voice of experience, the voice that said everything would be okay.

Scott stood on the sidewalk, his eyes fixed on Abdul's strained face staring back at him through the police car's rear window until the car turned the corner.

Abdul sat alone behind the bulletproof screen in the rear of the squad car. The two policemen who had held him down on his desk were in front. The one riding shotgun turned. His face was red, angry, and ugly.

"Why'd you do it, raghead?"

Abdul's heart pounded in his chest. Blood roared in his ears as he finally realized what he was being arrested for.

"What the fuck did those people ever do to you?" The policeman had his fist raised, knuckles tight and white, pressed against the glass partition. "I'll tell you something, raghead. By the time we're through with you, you'll wish you'd strapped a fuckin' bomb to your chest and pressed the button . . . fuckin' coward."

"He doesn't give a shit about them, Matt," said the driver. "He's waitin' to get his reward in heaven."

Abdul met the driver's mean eyes in the rearview mirror. "Hey, Abdul, how many virgins do you get for gassin' two hundred innocent people?"

Abdul suddenly needed the bathroom.

Back in his office, Scott flipped open his cell phone and clicked callback.

"Goddamn it, Quinn. You didn't give me much time." Scott gripped his phone tight to his ear and paced back and forward in front of the window.

"I gave you what I could . . . How sure are you of Abdul?" Quinn asked.

It took all of Scott's resolve to contain his anger, but Quinn was the messenger, and without his warning he'd never have secured the files. "I'd bet my life on him. He's a fine young man. You met him." Scott pictured Abdul's face as he'd last seen him, terrified, staring out from the rear window of the cop car. "What happens now?"

"It's a gray area. Under the Prevention of Terrorism Act, they can hold him almost indefinitely."

"I'm going to run the Allah's Revenge story tomorrow," Scott said.

Quinn stayed silent.

"I can't help him any other way except by getting Allah's Revenge into the public domain."

"It's a clusterfuck no matter what you do," Quinn said.

"What if Ghazi tries to get hold of him again?" Scott asked.

"Special Branch will intercept his e-mail and his cell phone.

Scott, if Ghazi contacts you, promise me you'll call."

Scott watched from his window as the last of the police vehicles pulled away and turned the corner.

"I'll call *you*. But not that prick, Browning . . . and Quinn, thanks for helping Abdul."

"I hope I don't regret it." He hung up.

Scott pressed his intercom. "Amy, see if you can get Abdul's father or mother on the phone, will you?"

"Sure."

A few minutes later, his desk phone rang.

"Hello?" A man's voice.

"Mr. Ahmed?"

"Yes."

"This is, Scott Shearer, Abdul's boss at the paper."

"Hello, Mr. Shearer. Abdul has told me so much about you. What may I do for you?"

"Mr. Ahmed, I wanted you to hear this from me first. Five minutes ago, Abdul was arrested by the Special Branch Terrorist Response Team." Scott didn't wait for a response. What was the man going to say? "I called to assure you that your son is a remarkable young man and highly thought of at *The Times*. He has done nothing unlawful. This is a huge misunderstanding. I've scrambled our legal team, and they are working on getting Abdul freed."

Abdul's father still hadn't spoken. Scott understood. He'd be shocked too if his child was snatched at work by a bunch of heavies.

"I'd like to give more details, but not on the phone. Will you be at home this evening?"

"Yes, of course, but what can we do? Where is he?"

"I'm going to give you the number of the paper's attorney, Marcus Pearson. For Abdul's sake, I advise you to speak to him before you talk to anyone else. Will you do that for me, Mr. Ahmed?"

Scott spent the rest of the day with Rafiq, preparing the lead for the morning edition. They polished Abdul's Allah's Revenge article from the thumb drive Amy had hidden, and Scott wrote an impassioned editorial vilifying the new British Police State. He argued that Abdul was more helpful to the nation as a free journalist, doing his job, than as an imprisoned innocent. He speculated that Abdul's arrest was racial profiling. He took preprint copies with him and drove to the Ahmed's home.

The narrow suburban road where Abdul lived with his family was crammed with police cars, TV news vans, dozens of reporters, photographers, and a sizable group of nosy neighbors. The TV cameramen were using the Ahmeds' house as a backdrop for their talking-head shots. He pinned a press badge on his lapel and wandered through the crowd. A few reporters recognized him, most didn't—TV news was a breed apart. He eavesdropped on a heavily-made-up blonde correspondent as she taped her segment.

"According to an anonymous source familiar with the case, this afternoon police apprehended the twenty-six-year-old son of Palestinian immigrants: Abdul-Haqq-bin-Wahid-bin-Tariq-bin-Khalid-Ahmed." She struggled theatrically as she read Abdul's complicated family name from a slip of paper in her hand. "Mr. Ahmed has been detained in connection with Monday's terrorist attack when more than two hundred people lost their lives after a deadly gas was released on a London Transport tube train. Mr. Ahmed's parents are both medical doctors working at Guy's Hospital, London. They moved to England from the Palestinian territories thirty years ago. We've reached out to the family, but the Ahmeds refuse to comment on their son's detention, although we believe they are at home."

The camera zoomed for a few seconds to the front window of the brick-built semi-detached home behind her before panning back to the reporter, who now stood next to a sixty-something man in an ill-fitting blue suit.

"This is Mr. Jackson, a neighbor of the Ahmeds'. Mr. Jackson, how well do you know the family?"

"They've lived here longer than us, and we've been here twelve years." His voice was shaky. "We never suspected anything like this. They kept to themselves, but they were always polite. Abdul seemed such a nice boy, smart as a whip. When he was younger he used to mow our lawn . . . makes you wonder what gets into them."

"Mr. Jackson, when was the last time you saw, Abdul?"

"This morning. I wave to him most mornings. He walks by our house on his way to the train station."

"What about Monday, the day of the tube train attack?"

"You know, I was just saying to the wife, I don't remember seeing him Monday. I might have done, but I don't remember him going by."

"Thank you, Mr. Jackson."

The camera started a slow pan of the street as the reporter closed out the segment in voice-over.

"Yesterday, this was a quiet suburban neighborhood. Today, police suspect it may have been home to a man linked with the largest mass murder in Britain's history. This is Maria Enderhoster, live in Twickenham, West London, for News at Six."

Scott walked past three other news crews shooting similar pieces. He pulled off his press badge before speaking to the policeman guarding the front gate of the Ahmeds' home.

"Scott Shearer. They're expecting me."

"Wait here please, sir." The policeman strode down the path. Cameras flashed and video lenses followed his every step. He knocked on the front door, which opened a crack. After a brief exchange, he signaled Scott, whose walk was also recorded. As the door opened to allow Scott to enter, the photographers all fired at once, and for a few seconds the front of the home was lit as bright as day.

"Ugly crowd," Scott said as he shook hands with Abdul's father in the hall.

"They're your people, Mr. Shearer. You should know."

Scott didn't feel as though they were. Abdul's father took him through the hallway to a small living room, made smaller by too much furniture. The sideboard, mantle, fireplace, and an oak display cabinet were crammed with brass figurines. The room was wallpapered in ornate gold-leaf flowers. Five porcelain ducks flew diagonally across the wall toward a single sash window.

Abdul's mother and sister perched stiffly on a floral-patterned couch. His younger brother sat cross-legged on the floor in front of the television, tuned to the local news station with the sound muted.

"I'm Scott Shearer, Abdul's boss at the paper. Abdul is a good person and a great reporter. He's done nothing wrong." He spoke to them all. The eyes that looked back at him were full of mistrust and disbelief.

"So why did they arrest him? Because he's a Muslim?" Abdul's mother said.

"Well . . . look, I've brought copies of tomorrow's edition of *The Times*. I think it would be more expedient if you read Abdul's article and my editorial to get us on the same page." He handed them each a copy. He kept one for himself and read with them.

He left their home two hours later, exhausted but gratified. He'd provided a spark of hope to a good family. The press corps outside had thinned. A few hopeful reporters asked him what he had been doing in the house. He froze them with his most poisonous glare.

"You can read about it in *The Times* tomorrow."

14

When Quinn got word Abdul was to be released, he called Scott. "I read yesterday's *Times*. You didn't pull any punches."

"What did you expect? Anyway, what about Abdul?"

"He'll be freed this afternoon. Can you pick him up?"

"Thank God." Quinn heard the relief in Scott's voice. "Is he all right?"

Quinn didn't like the implication. "Why wouldn't he be? Despite yesterday's editorial tirade, I assure you London police are not *Stasi-like brutes*."

"We'll see, won't we? Where should I come?"

At 3:00 p.m., Scott waited in his car at the front entrance of a modern red brick building less than a mile from New Scotland Yard. Scott had never noticed the building. He had no idea the Metropolitan Police Service used it. He suspected not many people did.

At ten after, Quinn, bulky and disheveled, dressed in a camel raincoat, walked out of the front door, squinting against the bright sunlight. He held Abdul by the elbow and steered him into the back seat of Scott's BMW. Quinn climbed in the passenger seat.

"Goddamn, Quinnborne!" Scott said, when he saw a yellowing bruise on Abdul's right cheek.

"He slipped going up the stairs," Quinn said.

"*Sure.*"

"Actually, I did, Mr. Shearer," Abdul said. Scott looked into the boy's eyes. He was telling the truth.

"Ha!"

"What's so funny?" Quinn asked.

"No one's going to believe it. Welcome back, Abdul. You okay?"

"I am now. Can we drive away from here, please, sir?"

Scott moved into traffic. "Do you want me to take you home?"

"No. We need to go to your office," Quinn said.

Scott looked in the driver's mirror. Quinn looked right back, his face set and serious.

"He's right," Abdul said. "Ghazi sent me an e-mail. I told the police I wouldn't reply unless they released me. They don't have the secret password he gave me, so they had no choice."

Scott smiled. *Not so naïve after all.* He reached into the back seat and passed his cell phone to Abdul. "Call your parents. They're worried."

Ten minutes later, they parked in *The Times'* underground lot and took the elevator to the sixth-floor.

Amy sat in Scott's outer office. When they walked in, she beamed at Abdul.

"Amy, can you rustle up some tea, please?" Scott asked.

"Pleasure. Welcome home, Abdul." Amy patted his arm as she passed.

Scott led them into his room and closed the door. "Now what?" he asked.

Quinn nodded to Abdul. "Abdul's agreed to let me act as an intermediary with Special Branch."

Scott could well imagine that, after two days of questioning, Abdul wouldn't want any more to do with Special Branch; another intelligent move from the young man. "I'll bet Frank Browning's pissed off about that."

Quinn said, "I'm working for Frank."

Scott stared at Quinn, but the policeman's face was a mask. He decided against commenting. Abdul sat in Scott's chair, logged onto his e-mail, and opened the message Ghazi had sent while he was in custody. Scott and Quinn stood behind him and read the screen.

"We demand release of the following prisoners. They must be

transported to The Dome of the Rock and released into the holy shrine. If you do not comply, we will use the Weapon of Allah to strike off the heads of the infidel regimes."

Below the message was a list of thirty names.

Quinn said, "The Israelis confirm those named are known terrorists. We've passed on the release request, but they won't say whether they are in custody."

"And?" Scott asked.

Quinn upturned his hands and shrugged. "They don't negotiate with terrorists."

"So what do the brainiacs at Special Branch plan to do?"

Quinn turned to his friend. "They want Abdul to arrange another meeting with Ghazi."

"What! No way. You told me I should never have sent him to Israel!" Scott said. He matched Quinn's stance and they faced off—two boxers waiting for the bell. "Last time we didn't know who we were dealing with. Now we do. I can't let Abdul do this. You'll have to send a cop."

Quinn's tone became officious. "Special Branch thinks they'll sever the link if we try to push a substitute."

"And you agree with them?"

He nodded. "If Abdul will go, I'm detailed to accompany him. We'll have Israeli ground support. Abdul won't be involved."

"No, he's just the bait!" Scott said.

Abdul stood, placed a hand on each of their chests and pushed them apart. "I told them I would," Abdul said.

Scott squeezed Abdul's shoulder. "This isn't your job. You're a reporter. These guys are crazies. Just last week they murdered two hundred people with their 'Weapon of Allah'."

"That's why I have to go, before they kill some more."

Quinn took a step back, opening a space, reducing the tension. He softened his voice. "They may not agree to meet. Why not make the offer, see their response, then decide?"

"No harm in trying," Abdul said. He turned to the keyboard and clicked *Reply*.

Scott pressed his lips together to stifle another protest. Quinn handed Abdul a folded sheet of paper from his inside pocket. "Special Branch recommends this wording."

"Your proposed release mechanism is not acceptable. I wish to meet in person to present an alternative." Abdul typed the message and hit send.

"What about the password?" Quinn said.

Abdul turned to him and smiled.

"I see." Quinn didn't smile back.

"Can your people trace the e-mail?" Scott asked.

"They'll try, but they weren't able to locate the sender. I don't understand this Internet stuff, but apparently Ghazi does."

Amy brought tea. Scott handed Abdul a copy of yesterday's *Times*. The Allah's Revenge story was on the front page. Abdul grinned and began to read. Quinn nodded toward the door.

"Walk with me, Scott."

"Just hang on here, Abdul," Scott said. The young man was reading his first lead story; he nodded absently but didn't lift his eyes from the newspaper as the two men left.

"Let's take the stairs," Quinn said.

They descended seven flights in silence. When they reached the parking garage and found no one there, Quinn faced his friend.

"Scott, I understand you want to protect Abdul, but give me some credit. No one's going to get near him while I'm there. It wasn't the password that got him released. Frank overstepped when he brought him in."

"No shit. Legal went ballistic."

"Doesn't matter, he's a marked man from here on in. Frank got his wrist slapped is all. Everyone's paranoid about Muslim terrorists, and Frank's convinced Abdul is his man. Every time Abdul farts, one of Frank's people will be there to smell it. I can help him, Scott."

"I'm not worried about you. Those Special Branch thugs will throw him under a bus if it helps them get Ghazi. And the Israelis . . . come on, Quinn. This stinks. No one knows who Allah's Revenge is, where they are, or what they're capable of. And let's face facts, their first calling card indicates how they feel about murdering innocent people."

Quinn held up both hands. "Okay . . . okay, but, like it or not, he's involved. Don't you think he's safer with me than on his own, having e-mail conversations with a mass murderer?"

Scott sighed and changed the subject. "And the train? Any leads?"

"Off the record?" Quinn asked.

"Sure. Shoot."

"The perp was male. We picked him up on CCTV footage. We sent a mug shot to Interpol; perhaps we'll get lucky and ID him. That's all I've got."

"And the gas?"

Quinn broke eye contact. "The lab boys don't know."

Scott's head snapped up at the hesitation. "How do you expect me to trust you to protect Abdul when you're lying right to my face?"

Quinn's forehead crumpled like a paper bag. Scott recognized the look. The policeman was making a painful decision. Scott waited.

"You can't use this. It'll mean a total shit storm."

Scott kept a look of tired patience on his face as if to say, *what do you take me for, a complete idiot?*

"We don't have any idea what the gas was, but I saw the bodies at the morgue. Scott, this was like nothing I've seen before. Their lungs were packed solid with charcoal. If this gets out, we'll have a panic on our hands. No one will ever ride the tube again."

"Charcoal?"

"Like the stuff you use on the barbeque. All we know is they breathed something in that expanded inside them and solidified. It happened so fast their hearts stopped. Two hundred simultaneous heart attacks, and the process took seconds."

"You will know our work by its mark," Scott said.

"Come again?"

"Ghazi said we'd know it was Allah's Revenge who attacked because they had a terrible weapon." Scott's cell phone rang.

"Hold on, Abdul, we'll be right up." He hung up the phone. "Come on, Quinn. Ghazi's replied." He pressed the elevator call button.

"That was fast," Quinn said.

Scott slapped the policeman on the back. "That's the Internet for you. You should try it sometime."

Quinn grunted.

Back in Scott's office, they read from the computer screen.

"Abdul-Haqq, we trust only you. Be in your room at the King David Hotel, Jerusalem, Saturday at 6:00 p.m. We will contact you. Ghazi."

Abdul wasn't celebrating. There was a big difference between planning and reality. He'd just learned that life lesson.

15

Friday afternoon, six days after Ghazi's e-mail, Abdul turned in his coach-class seat. He and Quinn were flying El-Al. They were halfway to Israel, having been together since arriving at Heathrow at 8:00 a.m., and two men could discuss sports only so long. "So, how does an American join the British police force?" he asked.

"I'm as British as the next man." Quinn exaggerated his American accent as he sounded out the words.

Abdul smiled. "With that accent?"

"Dad moved to Washington with the diplomatic service when I was five. I came home for university."

Abdul turned in his seat. "You were raised in America."

"Let's say I've got an appreciation of both sides of the Pond."

"I've heard the other cops call you 'the Yank'."

Quinn grinned. "There's no cure for stupid."

They laughed. This was common ground—they were both hybrids.

Quinn's long legs jammed hard against the seatback in front— neither the Metropolitan Police nor the *Times* would spring for business class. The flight attendant had cleared away the plastic debris from lunch. Quinn had sweet-talked her into giving him two main courses—the chicken and the beef.

"You married?" Abdul asked.

"Divorced." Quinn took a pull from his third whisky and water because, as he had informed Abdul, he was off duty until they landed.

"I'm sorry."

"Don't be. It's difficult being married to a cop. She was a terrific woman. The marriage lasted eight wonderful years before we split."

The puffy bags under Quinn's eyes seemed to sag lower as he spoke of his ex-wife.

"Would you marry again?"

"Nope. I'm done. It's easier this way. And you?"

Abdul laughed. "No chance. I've only been out of college six months."

"What about Adiba?"

Abdul snapped his head around and glared at Quinn.

"The e-mails were on your computer," Quinn said. "Special Branch located her and put a photo in your dossier. Sorry, Abdul, but I'd rather be up front with you; she's a stunner, by the way."

Abdul felt invaded, as though someone had broken into his bedroom and gone through his drawers.

Quinn changed the subject. "How come you took so long to finish college? They keep you back?"

Abdul gave a wry smile. Humor moved them to a better place, reduced the strain. "A journalism degree takes an extra year."

"Fair enough . . . so, how do you like working for Scott Shearer?"

"Well, I'd only met him once before this Ghazi thing came up. Lowly junior correspondents rarely get his personal attention unless they've screwed up, but I have a lot of respect for him. He visited my family while Special Branch held me. It helped them." Abdul sipped his soda. "You're friends, right?"

"Known him thirty years. He's an honest man. In my profession, I don't meet many."

Each time Abdul pried into the policeman's life, Quinn threw him a crumb and then deflected. He asked, "Any kids?"

"No, we never did."

"Was that why you split?"

Quinn shifted to face Abdul full on. His forehead wrinkled as he processed a reply. The policeman had piercing, pale-blue eyes; a few broken blood vessels floated around the whites, possibly from the Scotch. His face looked "lived in," with scruffy blond eyebrows and a bulbous nose, offset like a boxer's. Abdul assumed it had been broken, possibly more than once.

"When you see the things I do, every day, it's hard to imagine a child living a happy, safe life. Doreen didn't understand. No one does unless they're on the force."

Abdul felt sorry for the big man. "My parents gave up their homeland for us kids. I mean, they were doctors in a place that needed their skills. They moved to England so we could have the opportunities they wished for themselves. They don't talk about it, but I know they miss the family."

"I guess that's what caring people do," Quinn said. "They make sacrifices for the people they love."

They sat quietly awhile. Quinn sipped at his Scotch. Abdul stared at the TV. Quinn broke the silence. "So tell me about Jerusalem."

"Are you religious?"

"Naw. Dad's people were Irish-Catholic." He lifted his whisky glass as if that were sufficient explanation. "We went to church for weddings, baptisms, and funerals."

Abdul smiled. "Jerusalem's a unique place that each visitor views differently. The Bible stories Christians learned by rote as children come to life on the streets of the Old City when they walk and stand where Jesus once walked and stood. The same is true, but different, for Jews, and for Muslims." Abdul faced Quinn, warming to his subject.

"The Dome of the Rock, for example. Sitting high above the city, its golden domed roof dominates the skyline. It's the oldest Islamic building in the world. Muslims believe Muhammad ascended to heaven from the rock over which it's built, and only Muslims may enter the Dome. Many Jews think King Solomon's temple lies beneath, and the rock inside the Dome is where Abraham offered to sacrifice his son. They would like to raze the mosque and excavate the site to reveal the original temple. To Christians, the Dome sits on top of Herod's Temple where, in the Bible story, Jesus cast out the moneychangers. Ironically, atheists point to this dichotomy as proof that religion is a purely human artifice, and God exists only in fables. Everyone sees a different Jerusalem."

"All because of religion," Quinn said.

The pilot announced their final descent to Ben Gurion Airport. Quinn leaned in to Abdul and spoke in a low voice—suddenly all

business. "Okay, Abdul. This is no tourist trip, so let's get some
ground rules agreed. I'm your bodyguard. To keep you safe, I need
your cooperation. When we land, we're going to separate. Ghazi's
people may be watching the airport, and if they are, we'd like them
to think you're here alone. So don't acknowledge me once we walk
off the plane. The Israelis are supposed to be observing us. I hope
they're good enough so no one notices them. Okay so far?"

"Clear."

"Once you're through customs, grab a cab, same as last time.
Go to the hotel. Check in, and wait. I'm in the next room. I'll
knock on the common door, you open the lock, and we can meet.
All right?"

"Yes."

"We'll stay in our rooms until Ghazi calls. Once he makes
contact, the Israelis will take over."

"What will I say to Ghazi?"

"You're never going to meet Ghazi again. You'll listen to his
instructions, agree to do what he says, then put down the phone. A
decoy will take your place. You'll remain with me until we get the
all clear from the Israelis. Depending what happens then, maybe
you'll have time to call on your girlfriend, and perhaps I can visit
this dome thing you told me about. But until I give the okay, don't
contact anyone, including Adiba."

Abdul nodded. "But how will the Israelis handle Ghazi?"

"Not our problem. Our job is to lay low until the crazies are
locked up."

In the airport, Abdul had to stop himself from trying to spot
Israeli agents watching him. After an uneventful cab ride and hotel
check-in, he reached his room thirty minutes before Quinn
knocked.

"Everything okay?" Quinn asked.

"Fine. What took you so long?"

Quinn opened his jacket and revealed a holstered gun. "Took
some persuading to allow me to carry on their turf."

"Huh, so now we wait?"

"Yep. Leave the door unlocked. If you need anything, holler."
Quinn returned to his room. Abdul heard the TV being surfed.
They ordered dinner separately, but once the trays were delivered,
they met up in Quinn's room to eat. Quinn drank only water.

Tired from the trip, Abdul opted for an early night, and Quinn didn't argue.

Abdul showered and put on pajamas, a habit from cold, old England. He pulled back the top cover. A white envelope, with his full Arab name handwritten on the front, lay at the center of his pillow. He opened it and pulled out a note and a photograph. He looked at the picture, and his heart started thumping.

Adiba, her eyes wide and terrified, was strapped with black duct tape to a straight-backed chair. More tape covered her mouth, and a man in Arab robes stood behind her. His face wasn't pictured, but he held a large serrated knife across her throat.

The note said, "At 7:00 p.m. tomorrow, visit the bathroom next to the hotel swimming pool. You will be given further instructions. Tell no one, and you have my word she will be safe. Fail to obey and Adiba will die. Ghazi."

Abdul ran to the bathroom, knelt at the toilet, and threw up.

Quinn's voice came. "You okay, Abdul?"

He must have heard the retching. It sounded as if he was shouting from the bedroom. Abdul had left the note on the bed.

Shit.

With a hand towel to his mouth, he hurried back to the bed. Quinn wasn't there, but he must have been standing right at the adjoining door. Abdul shoved the note under his pillow.

"Fine, thanks, Quinn."

"Okay, I'm here if you need anything."

He climbed under the covers, feeling afraid and out of his depth. Adiba must be terrified. Would they keep her in the chair until tomorrow? His head spun. Should he show Quinn the note? What if Ghazi mentioned her on the call? No. The note meant Ghazi believed they weren't going to meet at 6:00 p.m. He suspected a trap, so the Israeli decoy was in danger? Abdul wanted to tell Quinn, to share the problem. But Ghazi would kill Adiba. Quinn might not believe that, and the Israelis wouldn't give a damn about some Arab girl getting her throat slit.

No, he had to do what Ghazi said. He didn't like the man, but he had to trust his word for Adiba's sake.

A loud banging on the connecting door woke him. He opened his eyes, and it was light outside. He must have finally drifted off.

"Wake up, sleepyhead. It's nine o'clock, breakfast time."

"Be right in."

He threw on his clothes from the previous night and splashed his face before going into Quinn's room.

Quinn had food laid out on the desk. "I ordered enough for three," Quinn said, grinning at Abdul. "Damn, boy, for someone who slept ten hours you look like shit."

Abdul produced a wan smile. "I had an upset stomach. I didn't get much sleep."

"Thought I heard you revisiting your dinner last night."

Abdul ate and spoke little. He hoped the policeman would assume he was ill, or nervous about the phone call with Ghazi. Quinn made up for him on the eating front.

"I think I'll try a nap, nothing else to do, and I'm still tired," Abdul said.

"Go ahead. I'll order lunch about noon." Quinn sounded as if he could hardly wait.

Back in his room, Abdul laid a hand towel over the pillow. He pulled the note out, covered by the towel, and headed to the bathroom, something he'd planned while lying awake the previous night. He sat on the toilet and reread the words. Tears welled in his eyes as he stared at Adiba. Her sweet face masked with tape, and that look of terror in her eyes. This was his fault. They'd taken her because of him.

For the rest of the day, he kept his time spent with Quinn to a minimum. He made it clear he was suffering from horrible diarrhea.

Six o'clock came slowly. Quinn joined him in his room ten minutes before the call. "Try to remember what you said last time. Keep it similar. The most important thing is to believe you are going to meet him, even though you're not."

At 6:00 p.m., the room phone rang.

"This is Ghazi." Abdul recognized the gruff, thick-accented voice.

"Hello, Ghazi, this is Abdul-Haqq."

"Abdul-Haqq, please bring your offer to me. A car will stop outside the hotel in fifteen minutes. The signal will be the same."

Ghazi hung up.

Quinn's cell phone rang. He listened to the caller for a few seconds before speaking. "I understand. Thanks." Quinn ended the call.

Abdul still held the phone to his ear. Quinn waved his hand to tell him to hang up and signaled for Abdul to follow.

They stood back from the window in Quinn's room, looking down on the front of the hotel. The road, as usual, was crammed with vehicles. A young man dressed in a white short-sleeved shirt and jeans, with a laptop case slung over his shoulder, came out from the hotel and stood on the sidewalk.

"He looks a lot like me," Abdul said.

Quinn nodded. The fifteen minutes before a black car pulled up seemed like an hour. The driver climbed out, stretched, and wiped his forehead with a handkerchief.

"Same car, but different guy," Abdul said.

Decoy-Abdul climbed into the back, and they drove off.

"Nice job, Abdul. Let's hope these Mossad guys are as good as they say."

Abdul was sweating. Nervous butterflies scrambled around in his stomach. The decoy was in danger, but so was Adiba. He hated lying to Quinn, and avoided looking at the policeman. "I'm going to take a shower. Then I'm heading to the bar for a cold drink and some fresh air."

"Great idea, mind if I join you?"

"Nope. I'll even buy the first round." Abdul attempted a smile. He went back in his room and bolted the adjoining door. He waited. Quinn didn't say anything. Either he hadn't noticed the lock turn, or he didn't care now the Israelis had taken over.

Abdul showered and changed into a fresh shirt and jeans. He put his passport in his jacket pocket, wallet and phone in his pants. He took the writing pad from the desk into the bathroom. He drummed the pen on the countertop. How could he make Quinn understand? Then he remembered their conversation on the flight over and wrote: *Sorry Quinn, but making sacrifices for the ones they love is what caring people do. I'll be fine. Abdul.* He jammed it, with the original note from Ghazi and the picture of Adiba, behind a clip halfway up the mirror.

He left his room and knocked on Quinn's door. The policeman opened it so quickly he must have been waiting with his hand on the knob. They took the elevator to the lobby.

"Let's use the poolside bar," Abdul said.

They entered the outdoor pool area, Quinn scanned the perimeter. He seemed satisfied. The pool could only be accessed through the hotel. They sat on barstools and ordered. Abdul's hand trembled as he picked up the glass and took a long pull of ice-cold Coke.

"Looks like you needed that," Quinn said, smiling. "Police work's not as easy as it seems, is it?"

"Pretty nerve-wracking," Abdul agreed.

Abdul kept checking the clock behind the bar. At 6:55 p.m., Quinn ordered another round.

"I need the toilet again," Abdul screwed up his face to show the disgusting nature of his mission.

"Good luck with that. I'll wait right here."

When Abdul walked into the bathroom, a man dressed in traditional white robes, his head covered with a white *shumag*, stood at the sink washing his hands. He turned to Abdul and nodded toward a toilet stall. Abdul went in and closed the door. A set of robes hung on the door-hook. He pulled them over his jacket, placed the *shumag* on his head and secured it with a braided rope. He flushed before leaving.

"Come," the Arab said.

They left by a second door, which opened to the lobby. The man took Abdul's elbow and guided him down a hallway to a side exit. A black sedan stood at the curb. The rear door swung open. Abdul climbed in, and the man followed. They pulled away before the door had closed.

Quinn had almost finished his second whisky. He checked his watch.

Ten minutes, poor kid.

By 7:15 p.m., he'd waited long enough.

He went to the bathroom and shouted at the only occupied stall. "Abdul, is that you?"

"Not here," an American voice called back.

"Shit!" Quinn ran through the second door. The lobby was deserted. He scanned the restaurant and seating areas, then grabbed the courtesy phone and called Abdul's room. He visited the poolside bar once more before taking the elevator up to their floor.

He ran through his room and tried the adjoining door—locked. He shoulder-charged. Pain shot through his arm and radiated up his neck. The door was solid.

He pulled his Glock from the holster inside his jacket, stepped back six feet, and put three rounds through the wood surrounding the lock. This time when he kicked the door, the wood splintered, and the door gave.

"Abdul!" He ran through the empty bedroom into the bathroom. He snatched the note off the mirror and read.

The original note in Arabic meant nothing to him, but the photo told the story. He kicked the cupboard and screamed at the bathroom wall. "Goddamn it, Abdul! Why didn't you tell me?"

Quinn ran back into the room. He tore open all the drawers, ripped off the sheets, checked under the bed and the mattress, looking for something, anything, to give him an idea where the little shit had gone.

Out of ideas, he drifted over to the window and gazed at the street below. Vehicles jammed the road. An impatient driver mounted the sidewalk and passed two cars before blasting his horn and slamming back down the curb into a ten-foot gap. Quinn stared at the Hebrew lettering on the street sign opposite.

How would he ever find Abdul in this crazy place?

Someone hammered on the door. "Security. Open up!"

Quinn pocketed the notes and photo before three men barged into the room, guns drawn. Two were uniformed hotel security, the third wore gray flannels and an open-necked white shirt, a Mossad agent, Quinn assumed. Gun snugged in its shoulder holster, and hands raised to show no evil intent, Quinn nodded to the agent. "Abdul's gone."

The guy kept his gun on Quinn, keyed a radio with his free hand, and barked a few words in Hebrew. The radio squawked back.

The agent relayed the question. "Who fired the gun?"

"I did, to get into the room." Quinn eased his hand down, backed toward the connecting door and pointed at the splintered wood. The agent nodded and spoke again into the handset, listened to his instructions, then said, "You wait here for the captain."

16

The sedan tore away from the side door of the hotel and slammed Abdul back in his seat.

The Arab said, "Give me your phone and passport." He switched off Abdul's iPhone and slipped it and the passport inside his robe. When they reached the first intersection, a black SUV blocked traffic from the right, and the driver waved them through. As they turned left, an identical vehicle pulled out in front, forming a convoy. Abdul's heart raced. The man who'd led him from the hotel bathroom hadn't spoken except to demand the phone. His face was a blank, forward-facing mask, and he reeked of stale sweat.

"Where are we going?" Abdul got no reply.

After tracking the lead SUV for twenty minutes, at a service entrance in the rear of a medical facilty the driver pulled into a driveway marked *Ambulance Only*. The tail car pulled up close behind.

"Wait." The smelly man left the vehicle and pulled out a bunch of keys. He unlocked a door labeled *Employees Only* and signaled Abdul to follow.

As he climbed from the car, Abdul's first instinct was to run. He'd come voluntarily. There was no logic to running, but still he wanted to. He went through the door, and the man locked it. Tires squealed outside as the SUVs pulled away.

They were in the receiving area for emergencies. The partition behind which a receptionist had once sat was shattered. Shards of glass lay heaped to one side of the hallway. Abdul wondered whether the place had been bombed. Seeking instructions, his gaze moved back to his escort, and his heart skipped because the man now held a pistol. A cruel prod in the back with the gun barrel sent Abdul walking along the corridor.

With more lights blown than lit and no windows, it proved difficult to see. Abdul stumbled over loose plaster and broken ceiling tiles until the man stopped him in front of a door marked *Office*.

While he waited, his captor shouted something Abdul didn't catch, and an overweight man in baggy sweatpants and a grubby shirt opened the door. He also held a gun. The man from the hotel took up a guard position in the hallway, and Abdul stepped into the room.

The office was large and mostly empty, one wall lined with gray filing cabinets, the others bare except for a crooked calendar hanging by a piece of string from a nail. The room had no windows. Two neon tubes buzzed and flickered in the only working light fixture, and below them Ghazi sat behind an old metal desk. Strangely, Abdul felt relieved to see him.

"Abdul-Haqq, again you have proved yourself an honorable man. Thank you for coming."

"Where's Adiba?"

"Soon I will take you to her. Did you tell anyone of our meeting?"

"You said not to, so I didn't." Abdul thought of the note he'd left for Quinn. "What happened to the decoy the Israelis sent in my place?" Abdul asked.

"This is not your concern. Abdul-Haqq, I apologize, but I must ask you to stay with us for a few days. Provided you follow instructions neither you nor the girl will be harmed. Do we understand each other?"

"Once I've seen Adiba unharmed, I'll trust your word." Abdul tried to sound braver than he felt.

Ghazi turned to the man in sweats who stood to the side with his pistol trained on Abdul's chest. "Show Abdul-Haqq to his room."

With a twitch of his gun, the man indicated a door on the far side of the office, which opened onto a flight of stairs. Abdul climbed to the top and stopped at a small landing with two doors. The man pointed to the right, and Abdul stepped into a room with bare plaster walls and no windows. Paint hung in flakes from water-stained areas on the ceiling. A canvas cot stretched out against one wall, one bulb provided meager light. An open door in the far wall led to a bathroom with commode and washbasin. Two white plastic lawn chairs and a card table, similar to the ones from his first meeting with Ghazi, sat at the center of the room.

The door clicked shut. A key turned in the lock.

Abdul took off the robes from the hotel and dumped them on the bathroom floor. The room was hot and airless so he splashed his face and neck with cold water. Why hadn't he brought a laptop or something to write on so he could record what was happening? He smiled to himself at the stupidity of the thought. He didn't *know* what was happening.

When he stretched out on the cot, canvas seams dug into his back. A low rumble of voices came from the office below.

Maybe he should have been stronger, insisted on seeing Adiba.

Ha. Exactly what leverage did he think he had?

If Quinn had gotten the note translated, what would the policeman do? He wouldn't go to the Israelis; he didn't trust them, but he'd have to report in to Special Branch. London would probably recall him in disgrace.

Abdul swallowed a few times. His throat tightened. Tears were close as the consequences of his actions struck home. If Quinn returned to London, no one in Israel could help him. He circled on those thoughts for a long time.

Abdul heard someone on the stairs. He sat up on the cot. The door opened. Ghazi entered, without a weapon. Abdul's gaze locked on Gahzi's scar. Such a vicious gash: the stitch marks formed a ladder climbing from the man's neck to the corner of his eye. Ghazi's chest was huge, and his hands even larger than Abdul remembered. This man could snap him like a twig. He didn't need a weapon.

"Abdul-Haqq, are you comfortable?"

"I have everything I need except—"

"Come. I'll take you to her."

Ghazi unlocked the door across the landing, knocked, and stepped back to allow Abdul through. The room was identical to his, but this one contained Adiba.

She sprang from the cot and slammed into him so hard he staggered back a step.

"Are you okay?" he asked.

She had him in a death grip, her head buried in his chest, sobbing, unable to answer.

Abdul knew then.

He'd made the right decision.

"Later, I'll bring food," Ghazi said. He left and locked the door behind him.

They held each other until her tears subsided and her grip slackened. When, finally, she pulled back and looked him full in the face, her cheeks were wet and her eyes rimmed with red. "How did you find me?"

Abdul remembered the picture of Adiba strapped to the chair with a knife at her throat. "They threatened to hurt you if I didn't come."

A shudder passed through her. "I was so frightened . . . but how will we get away from these people?"

"Have they harmed you?"

"No. But when they tied me up I thought they would slit my throat." Her fingers trembled as she wiped at her face. He wrapped her in his arms again, moved her to the cot, and sat beside her, stroking her hair. For a long time, they stayed like that, without speaking.

Adiba broke the silence. "Now we're both captives."

"I don't think they mean to harm us. Ghazi—"

"The big one with the scar?"

"Yes. He's their leader. He wants me to publicize Allah's Revenge."

"The group who murdered those people in London?" She pulled back from Abdul and stared at him, a shocked look on her face.

"I came to Israel to meet Ghazi."

"What does he want?"

"Well, he wants the Israelis to leave Palestine. But, meanwhile, he's trying to get some buddies released from Israeli prison." Abdul talked her through the decoy and the note on his pillow.

She kissed him on the cheek. "It was very brave of you to come." He put his arms around her, and Adiba's body sagged against him.

With no windows, he couldn't estimate how much time had passed. He'd left the hotel at seven. He guessed it must be nearly midnight. Adiba lay on the cot and closed her eyes, clearly exhausted. Seated beside her, Abdul studied her face: makeup-free, smooth olive skin, high cheeks, and long dark lashes. Her breathing turned soft and shallow and she drifted to sleep.

When the room door opened, Abdul gave a start. The sudden movement woke Adiba and a scream stifled in her throat. Ghazi brought a tray with bread, cheese, and bottled water, which he placed on the floor.

"Eat. Then Abdul will return to his room." Adiba started to protest, but Abdul held up his hand, and she fell silent. Ghazi left them alone with the food.

"Adiba, these people are Islamic fanatics."

"I understand." She took his fingers in hers and gazed into his face. "It's just . . . I feel safer with you here."

"My room is across the landing. It looks the same as this one. I'll be thinking of you."

She smiled, knelt by his feet, and began to prepare a plate for him.

17

A pissed-off Mossad captain briefed Quinn on the loss of their decoy and left him in his hotel room with instructions to get the hell out of his territory, yesterday if possible.

Quinn hadn't seen this coming, hadn't considered that he needed to be "on" once the Israelis took over. He was furious at himself, such a rookie mistake, never drop your guard. He dreaded relating the story of his incompetence to Frank Browning, but he had no choice, so Quinn called Frank's home number. It was midnight, UK time.

Frank said, "Let me get this straight. The Israelis lost their operative?"

"They were following by helicopter. The car rounded a corner; somehow the bad guys slipped the decoy out of the back seat. They followed the vehicle for fifteen minutes and when it was finally dumped: no decoy."

"And you lost Abdul."

Quinn's guts churned. "He gave me the slip."

"Humph."

Quinn couldn't blame Frank for the sarcasm. "Frank, I need someone who speaks the language. The longer we wait, the less chance we have of finding him."

"Perhaps I can get help from the British Embassy. Stay put until I call you back. I don't want to lose *you* next." Quinn slammed the phone down and started pacing. *British Embassy, what a joke; I haven't lost my fuckin' passport!*

At 9:00 p.m., two hours after Abdul's disappearance, Quinn made the second call he'd been dreading.

Scott Shearer picked up.

"It's Quinn." The line went quiet. "Scott, I need your help. Abdul's gone AWOL."

Scott chewed him out, and Quinn took it. In a strange way, it felt better having someone else shout at him rather than beating himself up. Finally, Scott calmed enough to let Quinn explain what had happened.

"If I tell the Israelis about Adiba, they'll lock me up, or worse, for getting their decoy taken."

"So what are you going to do?" Scott said

"Translate the note. Find Adiba, and I'll find Abdul. In his dossier I've got her full Arab name, her street address and all the e-mails she sent. Perhaps her family can tell me how long she's been missing or where they saw her last."

"Write out her contact information. I'll call you back with a fax number. And we'll need the note, too."

"I don't like faxing this stuff, Scott."

Scott shouted so loud that Quinn had to hold the phone away from his ear. "And exactly how can you make this worse? Take off your stupid policeman's helmet, Quinn. You're in Israel, looking for an Arab girl you've never met. You don't know the language. You don't know where she lives. You don't know jack-shit. Damn it, Quinn! Send the information. I'll call right back."

Quinn was still copying Adiba's address when Scott called him with Rafiq's fax number. "Go to the hotel's business office, send the fax, then get back to your room. I'll call you and conference Rafiq in."

Ten minutes later, Rafiq translated the note for them over the phone.

"Doesn't tell us more than the photo," Quinn said.

"Tells me that Abdul is a brave young man," Scott said with venom in his voice.

"Brave or foolish, either way, how do we get him home?" Rafiq said.

"What about the street address?" Quinn asked.

"I've pulled up a map. I can fax it to the hotel."

"If you'd carry a laptop we could e-mail this stuff to you, damned Neanderthal!" Scott said.

Quinn slapped the dresser hard enough to make his hand sting. He shouted into the phone. "Okay . . . okay. Enough! Look, Scott. I get that you're pissed off. But this isn't helping."

Rafiq spoke in a calm voice, "What are you going to do when you arrive at Adiba's home?"

Quinn stared out of the window at the street below, still crammed with cars. "I'll have to hope someone speaks English. I have a picture of her from Abdul's dossier I can use. Scott, did Abdul fly straight home after meeting Ghazi?"

"No, I sent him to a press conference in Eilat."

"That's something. What then?" Quinn asked. The line went quiet. "Come on, Scott. This is like pulling teeth."

"He had a private meeting with Nazar Eudon. He's—"

"I know who he is. Was he in Eilat?" Quinn paced the room, stretching the phone cord to its limit.

"Yes, but Abdul went to his home in Aqaba, Jordan."

"*Great.* That makes it easier." Quinn's voice dripped with sarcasm.

"What about Adiba?"

"He didn't mention her."

"According to their emails, she was with him in Eilat," Quinn said. "Okay, get me a contact number for Eudon while I visit Adiba's folks."

Quinn slipped a spare magazine for his Glock into his side pocket, put on his leather jacket, and headed for the lobby.

From the business center, he picked up Rafiq's fax and showed the address to the doorman. He slipped the man a bill. "I need a driver who speaks English and Arabic."

The doorman walked along the line of taxis outside the hotel until he found the one he wanted. He signaled, and Quinn got in.

When they pulled into traffic, Quinn said,

"You speak English?"

"A little."

"What's your name?"

"Caleb."

"Pleased to meet you Caleb, I'm Quinn. I might need you to translate." Quinn passed a fifty to the driver, who tucked it into his shirt pocket and grinned. Quinn, speaking slowly, explained he was looking for a girl. He couldn't tell how much the driver understood—probably thought he was after a hooker.

Twenty minutes later, they pulled up in front of a row of single-story white block buildings. The driver pointed to a paint-chipped door beside a small window with sun-bleached, wooden shutters secured behind iron bars. A lit bulb hung from bare wires next to the doorframe. The street was empty and quiet except for an overloud TV playing in one of the houses.

"This one," Caleb said.

Quinn got out. "Wait here."

With the photo of Adiba held high, like an ID, he knocked, then took a step back so his face and Adiba's picture were in the light. The window shutters cracked open an inch and then slammed shut. As he went to knock again, a short, barrel-chested man with a three-day beard, wearing a white undershirt and baggy cotton pants opened the door. He looked from Quinn to the picture.

"My name is Steven Quinnborne. I'm with the British police. I need to speak with Adiba-bint-Tariq-bin-Khalid-Al-Qasim."

The man yelled at him in Arabic. Quinn raised his other hand to indicate he wanted him to stop, but the man was screaming, red-faced, and waving fists as if to throw a punch.

Quinn signaled to the cabbie. "Hey. Caleb, a little help!"

The driver leaned across and shouted something from the open passenger window. Whatever he said caused the man to turn and bark an instruction to those inside, and the front door slammed shut. The man pushed past Quinn and started talking to the driver. Quinn tapped him on the shoulder.

"What's he saying?" Quinn asked the driver.

"His two daughters have been taken. He wants me to tell him whether you are a kidnapper. He says his family has no money, but they want their girls back. Why did you take them, Mr. Quinn?"

Quinn pulled out a handkerchief and wiped away the sweat beading on his face. "I'm no kidnapper. I'm looking for this girl." Quinn pointed to the picture. The driver translated and again Adiba's father began shouting at Quinn and shaking his fist.

"Ask him when he last saw his girls."

The driver spoke.

This time, when the father answered, anger had faded from his voice.

"The youngest disappeared week; she never came home from school. The one pictured, Adiba, two days ago."

"What's his youngest daughter's name?"

When the man heard the question from the cabbie, he turned back to Quinn. Tears streamed down his face. He dropped to his knees and grabbed Quinn's trouser legs. Quinn didn't need a translator to understand the man was begging for his children's lives.

"Caleb, please tell him I am not a kidnapper. I'm a policeman, and I'm looking for his daughter. I want to help."

As the driver spoke, Adiba's father knelt in front of Quinn, staring up, imploring. Finally, he released Quinn's legs, stood, and wiped his face with his sleeve.

Quinn pulled a pen from his pocket.

"Ask him to write down his youngest daughter's name, and get me a phone number I can call if I find either of them."

The man leaned on the taxi roof and wrote on the back of Adiba's picture. Quinn handed it to the driver.

"Read it?"

"Lana-bint-Tariq-bin-Khalid-Al-Qasim, sixteen years old."

Hearing her name spoken aloud, the man began crying again. Quinn heard the pain echoed in a woman's voice from the inside of the home.

"I'll look for them. I'll bring them back," Quinn said. He slapped the man on the shoulder and climbed into the cab. "Let's get out of here."

When he reached his hotel room, he called Scott and told him what had happened.

"Does Abdul know the sister, Lana?" Scott asked.

"She's not mentioned in his e-mails, but she disappeared over a week ago. Maybe Ghazi wanted an insurance policy. Maybe he used her to get Adiba. Maybe the father was confused about dates. Who knows?"

"What now?" Scott said.

"I'm going to Eilat and try to meet Eudon. You said he'd taken a shine to Abdul. Perhaps he can help."

Scott gave Quinn the contact number for Nazar Eudon's office in Aqaba. "Keep me in the loop."

"I will," he said, and hung up.

18

Kimberly Stevens took the elevator up fifty floors to the North Tower Grill in downtown Seoul, and, as promised, Firman was waiting for her. He kissed her cheek, took her arm, and guided her to a seat at the bar.

"Manhattan on the rocks, right?" The drink was waiting. "So good to see you again, Kim." They chatted for twenty minutes until their table was ready. Firman spoke with a slight French accent and looked directly in her eyes. He wore a plain white shirt with two open buttons, gray jacket and slacks. The musculature of his chest and shoulders showed through the fabric.

Maybe this time, she thought. She'd been thinking that for over a year.

Kim had first met Firman at the Toronto G20 summit. He'd taken her to dinner, and they'd arranged to meet the following evening. Firman handled security for one of the dignitaries at the summit. His work schedule intervened, and he'd had to cancel. Ten days ago, he'd called and asked to meet again during this year's conference.

Annually, the leaders of the twenty most powerful countries in the world met at the G20 Summit to agree on global policy. As executive assistant to the Canadian Prime Minister, she'd had a busy day of preparation; even so, Firman had never been far from her mind.

They ate dinner seated side by side in one of the restaurant's famous crescent loveseats. Five hundred feet below, cars looked like Matchbox toys. The city lights sparkled in the distance. The rotating restaurant completed a circuit once every forty-eight minutes. As they began their third rotation, they sipped fifty-dollar cognac from large, thin-walled globes that Firman called snifters.

The black dress she wore, purchased especially for this evening, was the most expensive garment she'd ever bought. It lifted her breasts into a revealing cleavage and followed the curve of her hips.

Firman paid the check.

She'd been sending out signals all night, and he'd been reciprocating. Would it end here? She hoped not.

"Kim, I'm staying at the Ritz-Carlton. They have an excellent cocktail lounge. Can I interest you in a nightcap . . . or must you work tonight?"

"Yes, I'd love to extend the evening. I'm having a wonderful time."

Firman guided her to the elevator. His palm burned through her dress where it rested on her back. In the cab he held her hand. They walked, still hand in hand, into the lobby of his hotel.

"Tell me if I am being too forward, but my room has a better view of the city than the cocktail bar. We could take the nightcap up there."

"Yes, I'd like that." Kim wanted to give a high-five.

The living room in his suite dwarfed her downtown Toronto apartment. Bodyguards must be well paid, she thought.

He fixed Manhattans. They stood close, sipping their drinks and staring through the panoramic windows at the city.

Firman put his drink down. "I have something for you," he said and went to the bedroom. A few seconds later he emerged with a small box, gift-wrapped in silver-accented paper with a red bow. "Please, open it."

Kim grinned like a schoolgirl receiving an unexpected Valentine present. She tore off the wrapping and stared, shocked, at a bottle of Clive Christian No. 1 perfume.

"Firman, I can't accept this. It's too much."

"I insist." He closed his hands around hers with the bottle between them. "Whenever I smell this perfume, I think of you. Do you like it?"

"Yes, of course, but—"

His voice became husky, low. "Wear some for me."

She held the perfume in one hand, ran the other hand behind the lapel of his jacket, and pulled him toward her. The kiss released the sexual tension of the last four hours; no, the last twelve months—sparks flickered against the inside of her eyelids, and she thought her legs would buckle.

"Give me a moment." Kim headed to the bathroom, where she stripped off and crammed her bra and panties into her purse. After a pee, she used the bidet, then sprayed herself with the nine-hundred-dollar perfume and slipped, naked, into her dress.

When she returned to the room, Firman turned and smiled. "Now you smell as beautiful as you look, Ms. Kimberly Stevens."

They made love until three in the morning. Never had she experienced a body so hard and toned. Firman was a considerate lover, and insatiable. She didn't ever want to leave his bed, but the Prime Minister was scheduled to depart the hotel at eight, and he needed her.

"Firman, I must go."

He wrapped his arms around her and held her close. It took an extraordinary act of will to pull away. As she dressed, he watched with a coy smile on his face, and in that moment, under his gaze, she felt like the most desirable woman in the world.

"Kim, there's one more thing I need."

"Firman . . . there's no time. I have to leave."

He smiled. "Will you wear the perfume to the conference today? Although I won't be able to speak to you, I will smell your presence as I stalk the corridors looking for bad guys."

She shook her head. Kim would never dream of wearing such expensive perfume to work.

"Please, Kim, do this for me, just today."

His voice and his eyes were pleading. He was serious about this. She smiled. "Okay. If you insist."

"Promise?"

"Cross my heart." She bent and kissed him one last time where he lay in bed. "Now I must go or I'll be late." Playfully, he held onto her arms.

"Firman. Stop it."

"Promise me again."

"I promise."

He let her go, and she floated along the hotel hallway, beaming from ear to ear. The early-morning traffic was light. She felt racy calling her hotel's front desk at 3:40 a.m. and booking a six-thirty wake-up call. Snuggled under her sheets, Kim drifted to sleep surrounded by the smell of him and her perfume.

When she woke, she showered, toweled dry, and walked naked across the room to her purse. She took out Firman's gift and with two quick strokes sprayed an 'X' of perfume starting at each shoulder, crossing her breasts and finishing at her hips. The aroma was exquisite. She posed in front of the mirror.

"I crossed my heart for you, Firman." A pleasant shiver passed through her as she remembered last night's sexual marathon—wow! Kim slipped into a blue pencil skirt and white blouse. The perfume would always remind her of him. "What a man," she said as she left the room to begin a busy day of organizing at the G20 summit.

At the conference, she strode in front of the Canadian Prime Minister, cleared him through security, and gathered the necessary handouts. Inside the meeting room, she arranged the PM's papers at a magnificent oval table whose stunning centerpiece featured a hand-carved conference logo: twenty rays of light—simulating the Eastern sun rising—emanating from a *chung-sa-cho-rong*, a traditional Korean lantern. Twenty plush, padded chairs circled the table, awaiting the representatives of the elite group of nations.

Staffers buzzed around their dignitaries making sure everything was set for the meeting. Kim watched as a robed assistant to the Saudi Arabian king demonstrated the use of a respiratory inhaler to his royal highness. The aide sucked in the spray with an exaggerated motion, then held the device to his king's lips and depressed, encouraging and praising the monarch as a mother would her child. Boy, there were some spoiled puppies in this room.

At the head of the conference table, a small stage was set with a lonely white lectern at its center, flanked on either side by ten flags, one for each of the member countries.

At a quarter till nine, satisfied the PM had everything he needed, Kim headed for the bathroom. In the hallway, she nodded politely to Maureen Wilson, the American Vice President's executive assistant; the President wasn't scheduled to arrive until tomorrow.

As Kim passed, the aroma of Christian No. 1 perfume drifted into Maureen's nostrils. A few thousand perfume molecules settled on Maureen's tiny nose hairs as they filtered out dust and bacteria. But most swept in with her breath and flowed down her throat. The molecules, each less than three millionths of an inch, settled into the spongy pink alveoli in Maureen's lungs. From there, they absorbed into the surging bloodstream pumping past her honeycombed lung walls, fetching and carrying oxygen to her brain and muscles.

In sixty seconds, Kim's perfume molecules had dispersed throughout Maureen Wilson's body—a microscopic and unwitting gift from the Canadian Prime Minister's executive assistant to the executive assistant to the Vice-President of the United States.

At 8:55 a.m., the South Korean VP called the meeting to order. The heads of the world's richest nations—presidents, premiers, prime ministers, one vice president, and one king—took their places.

Kim, along with over one-hundred assistants and administrative staff, filed into the next room where the Koreans had laid on an elaborate buffet.

A gas will diffuse until its concentration is equally distributed throughout the space available. Since her arrival, Kim had been throwing off an invisible stream of perfume. Had someone viewed the rooms and hallways at a molecular level, they would have observed that every cubic inch of air contained molecules of her scent. They had been breathed and shared by dignitaries and lackeys alike.

Molecules had no sense of status.

At precisely 9:00 a.m., the South Korean president took the stage. He stood behind the lectern and acknowledged the warm applause of his guests. At 9:01, he began a short, well-rehearsed speech of welcome.

Courtesy of Dawud Ferran, Allah's Revenge's newest captain, each of Kim's perfume molecules carried with it a tiny passenger—a programmed nanobot.

At 9:02 a.m., the passengers awoke.

After sixty seconds of exponential replication, trillions of nanobots started analyzing their surroundings, seeking biomass: blood, liver, lung, throat, eye, nose, heart, brain—feedstock for the self-replicating monsters-in-miniature. With organic material as fuel, and body heat for energy, the nanobots disassembled the molecules and reassemble them into a black, charcoal-like substance.

At 9:03 a.m., the Korean president broke off in midsentence, covered his mouth with his hand, and cleared his throat.

"Excuse me," he said and reached for the water perched on the lectern. As he grasped the glass, he grimaced at the hard, black grains he'd coughed into his palm. He gulped the liquid, and, with no time for further apology, began coughing in uncontrollable spasms. He spat out the water because he couldn't swallow. He doubled over, gagging chunks of black charcoal from his lungs into his mouth, and puked them onto the stage.

Coughing broke out around the meeting table. A few concerned staffers poked their heads through the door, and seeing their superiors struggling for breath, tried to assist, but they too experienced an uncomfortable tickle in their throats, then a scratching, then a unique and inexplicable sensation: They wanted to vomit. They wanted to breathe. Neither was possible. They were filling up—drowning from the inside.

By 9:05 a.m., the room was in chaos, decorum at the world's most exclusive meeting overridden by the primal need to survive. Staffers charged into presidents as they ran for the door. In the hallway, security guards writhed on the floor.

Two shots rang out.

The noise brought a rush of secondary guards barging through the polished oak doors at the far end of the hallway, which had until then sealed in most of the perfume-contaminated air.

A green-uniformed Korean guard-captain dropped to one knee and felt for a pulse in the soldier lying nearest the outer door. A pistol lay near his hand, and blood from the man's thigh soaked into his trousers. The guard had shot himself trying to pull his pistol. He was dead.

At 9:09 a.m., following their programming, Dawud's nanobots stopped disassembling biomass.

They stopped assembling charcoal.

They stopped.

The captain ran with his men, guns out, toward the conference room. A pyramid of corpses, piled on top of one another like some weird carnival act, blocked the doorway. The captain stared past the dead, into the room. Most of the bodies were near the doorway. Many had bloody track marks on their necks and faces, souvenirs of a desperate attempt to clear an air passage. Black cinder crammed their mouths, stretching their jaws unnaturally wide, like overstuffed pigs laid out for a medieval feast.

The captain's eyes locked on the center of the room. In the middle of the huge oak table, huddled on top of the magnificent carving, stood two men, and they were alive. Clinging together like limpets, they wore light-gray, ankle-length robes, their heads covered with black-and-white checkered *shumags*. Nothing else in the room moved.

Making an unpleasant snap decision, the captain climbed over the pile of death blocking the doorway.

"Are you okay?" he shouted to the men on the table.

"We are okay," said King Hudayfah, the Saudi Arabian ruler. "Thanks be to Allah, we are okay."

The captain barked orders. "Check for more survivors. Try the next room."

All ten of his security detail had followed him over the warm body-pile. Three of them checked the victims strewn around the floor of the conference room. The others ran into the next room. The captain had tears in his eyes as he sought a pulse on the corpse of his country's president, sprawled on the stage next to the fallen lectern.

One of the guards appeared in the doorway leading to the staff room. "Captain, you need to see this."

The captain spoke to the two survivors. "Please remain on the table until we've secured the area." The King nodded.

Leaping over corpses, the captain ran into the next room. There were forty or fifty more victims, mostly on the floor. His eye was drawn to a couple lying on the buffet table, sprawled across the huge array of food that should have been their breakfast.

"Perhaps they thought getting off the floor would save them?" he said.

"No, sir, I mean this!"

The soldier pointed to a woman in a blue pencil skirt standing stiff and erect against the far wall. The torn remnants of a white blouse hung from her neck. Two lines of black charcoal, as wide as tire-treads, protruded eight inches from her body. Starting at her shoulders and finished at the tops of her thighs they formed a crude X. Both eyeballs dangled against her cheeks, forced out by two macabre black turds protruding from her eye sockets. The fungus-like mass formed a horn on each side of her head where it had squeezed out from her ears.

"Damn," said the captain. Then he threw up.

19

By 9:00 a.m. the day after Abdul's disappearance, Quinn was on his way to Eilat in a Fiat 600, the only rental available at such short notice.

Quinn had felt like a circus novelty act climbing into the smallest car he'd ever seen. The steering wheel jammed against his thighs, so he had to keep switching feet on the pedals to stop his legs from going dead. His head touched the roof, and each bump in the road (and there were plenty) compressed his neck into his shoulders.

The car's thermometer, a flat disk stuck to the dash, read thirty-eight degrees—one hundred Fahrenheit. The sweat-inducing humidity reminded him of childhood family vacations in Florida, but without A/C. With the windows open, dust and sand stirred up by vehicles as they passed him on the highway peppered his face and made his eyes water. The trip to Eilat lasted five hours. It seemed like ten.

He checked into the Dan Hotel, dropped his bag inside the room, stripped, and hit the shower; never had he felt this dirty.

Once clean, he snagged a scotch from the minibar and called Frank Browning, who chewed him out for leaving Jerusalem. Frank didn't believe his story about following a lead. Special Branch was flying in an Arabic-speaking replacement who was arriving in Jerusalem that evening and expected to meet Quinn.

"Tell him to call me," Quinn said. "I'll brief him by phone. I can't get back to Jerusalem until tomorrow." Frank grunted in reply.

Not much he can do about it from London, anyway.

When Quinn finished with Frank, he called the number Scott had given him for Eudon Oil. After being passed around a few times, he reached the voicemail for Nazar Eudon's assistant and left a message. "Mr. Eudon, I'm Detective Chief Inspector Steven Quinnborne of London's Metropolitan Police Service. I need to speak with you about an urgent matter involving Abdul Ahmed, who I believe is known to you." Quinn left his room number; Frank wouldn't issue him an international cell phone—another power trip.

In the lobby, he showed Adiba's photo to the concierge. The guy had never seen her. He turned over the picture to where Adiba's father had written the name of his other daughter. That drew a blank as well. When he returned to the room he had a message from Eudon's assistant, Keisha."

Quinn called her back.

"Mr. Eudon's office."

"This is Detective Quinnborne, I called earlier."

"Hello, Detective, I am Keisha. I told Mr. Eudon of your call. He instructed me to help if I can."

"I was hoping to meet him."

"Mr. Eudon's schedule is packed this week. Perhaps if you explain what you want?"

"I believe Mr. Abdul Ahmed and Ms. Adiba Qasim have been abducted. I understand they recently met with Mr. Eudon. He may be able to help."

"Please allow me to relay this information to him. I will call you back."

"Time is of the essence, Ms. Keisha."

Quinn hung up, frustrated. He hated waiting, but what else could he do? In London, he'd be in control. Operating in a foreign country was like wearing an itchy suit; no matter what he did, he was uncomfortable. He sat on the bed and flicked through a week-old copy of the *Jerusalem Post*. At least it was in English. Suspicions and speculation about the London attack were still front page news: Who was Allah's Revenge? How did they fit with al-Qaeda? Threat levels were elevated across the Western world.

The business section led with Nazar Eudon's shift into alternative energy. Apparently, Eudon Oil's shares had dropped more than fifty percent. No wonder Nazar Eudon was busy. The article speculated on a possible takeover. Bonds were coming due, and the company might not get the loans refinanced because of the stock price. Quinn didn't understand the details, but he got the idea: Nazar Eudon and his company were in the shitter.

Then Superintendent Porter, the division chief, called.

"Quinnborne, Frank briefed me about you losing Abdul. I want you back in Jerusalem tonight. Fareed Marker from Special Branch arrives late this evening. Update him, then get out of Israel before you cause an international incident! You're on the 11:00 a.m. flight tomorrow."

"Sir, I can't bail on the kid. It's my fault he got taken."

"Frank told me you weren't listening. Quinn, you're not the right man for the job. Fareed speaks Arabic and Hebrew. He's got connections with the Israelis. You're a liability. You're off the case. I want to see you in my office on your return."

"Yes, sir." Quinn hung up. He stared blankly at the cheap prints hanging on the wall, then he kicked the bed.

"Fuck."

The phone rang again—Keisha calling back. "Detective, Mr. Eudon is most upset to hear that Abdul and Adiba may be in danger. He's willing to meet you this afternoon. Do you have a vehicle?"

Quinn had his Fiat. "I rented one in Jerusalem."

"Ah, no, you can't cross the border in a rental. I will send a car for you. Can you be ready in an hour? You'll need your passport to cross into Jordan."

"No problem." Quinn didn't understand how meeting Eudon could help either, but at least he was doing something.

He called Scott. "Scott. I need your help."

"Shoot."

"I've got a meeting with Nazar Eudon in fifty minutes."

"Okay."

The line went quiet, just a low static hiss. Quinn searched for a way to avoid telling Scott everything. There wasn't one. "I've been recalled. They're flying in a replacement from Special Branch."

"Oh?"

"Scott, damn it, I'm not going to leave Abdul here. I'm going rogue. I need a cell phone. I might need money."

Scott responded immediately. "Take the meeting with Eudon. I'll arrange the phone. I can't believe they sent you without one. Morons . . . and Quinn?"

"What?"

"You're a good cop."

Quinn's throat tightened. "Thanks, Scott."

"Bring the kid home, safe."

"I will."

He waited thirty minutes in the lobby before a sleek black Mercedes pulled up. The driver held the rear door open for him.

"Mind if I ride up front?"

"As you wish, sir."

They pulled away and headed for Jordan.

"I'm Quinn, by the way." He offered his hand to the driver, who shook it warily.

"Mufeed," he volunteered.

"So we're crossing the border?"

"Mr. Eudon lives in Aqaba, in Jordan."

"You from there?"

"I was born and raised in the capital city, Amman."

"How long have you worked for Eudon?"

"Twelve years."

"What's he like?"

Mufeed focused on the road for a few seconds before replying. "He's a very powerful man."

Quinn noted the pause. "D'you enjoy working for him?"

"Yes, he pays me well." Mufeed slowed as they approached two lines of cars waiting to pass into Jordan. "Here's the border. You'll need your passport." They stopped once on the Israeli side, drove a hundred yards across no-man's land and had their documents checked again by the Jordanians. Both the Israeli and the Jordanian crossing-guards were friendly with the driver. They cleared the border in five minutes.

"You cross the border often?"

"Enough."

Quinn tried again to shift Mufeed out of monosyllabic land. "So, let me ask you, Mufeed. You're an Arab. Do you hate the Israelis?"

"No. I don't hate anyone. But it's complicated."

"Sure seems complicated to me," Quinn said. "I see Arabs and Israelis walking around together like nothing's wrong with the world, just doesn't fit with what we read in the newspapers back home."

Mufeed changed the subject and gave Quinn an Aqaba travelog, pointing out interesting features of the city as they drove through.

Quinn didn't give a damn about Aqaba. He wanted to know about Nazar Eudon. Reading between the lines, he understood that Mufeed's boss was a frightening son-of-a-bitch. Judging by their reception at the border, he guessed the border guards got 'back-handers' from Eudon's chauffeur. Mufeed probably had a piece of that action as well.

Quinn doubted he could get more information, and he didn't want to piss off his ride more than he had, so he stopped talking.

They pulled up at a pair of high wrought-iron gates. A guard came out of a sentry box. He checked Quinn's passport, and he made Mufeed show a pass.

Thorough, Eudon liked his privacy.

As the car stopped in front of the house, a small Asian woman waited at the bottom of the entrance steps.

"Detective Quinnborne?" she said.

"Please, call me Quinn."

"And you must call me Keisha."

"Okay."

They were both smiling.

"Please, follow me. Your meeting will be brief, I'm afraid. Mr. Eudon leaves for the US in an hour." She walked ahead of him up the steps in a skirt short enough to show the beginnings of her butt cheeks. Through a tiled hallway, they entered a side room with book-lined walls. A small conference table stood at one end, and a fancy-looking desk at the other. "If you'll wait in the library, Mr. Eudon will join you."

Quinn browsed the books, most in English, but also French and Spanish titles, and many languages he had no idea about. Did Eudon read them or were they for show?

The door opened and a short, dapper man came in. In pressed blue slacks, a pale yellow shirt, and a gray cravat, he reminded Quinn of a mannequin.

"Mr. Eudon. Thank you for meeting on such short notice, oh, and for sending the car—nice ride."

Eudon shook hands firmly but ignored Quinn's attempt at camaraderie. "Detective Chief Inspector Quinnborne?"

"The same."

"Of the Metropolitan Police Service in London, I understand."

"Right again." Quinn continued to try for lighthearted, even though Nazar's smile looked closer to a smirk.

"I'm curious. What brings a British policeman to Israel?"

"I came here with Abdul. We were scheduled to meet someone in Jerusalem yesterday."

"Associated with the terrible events in London, I presume." Still with the smirk.

Heat rose in Quinn's face. It had been a long day; there was only so much of this supercilious prick he could take. "I'm not at liberty to discuss the nature of the meeting."

"I understand, Detective. Please forgive my curiosity." Nazar switched to a serious face. "Keisha tells me Abdul and Adiba were abducted. Is that correct?"

"That's what we believe."

"Was that before or after your meeting, Detective?" The beginning of another smirk showed on Nazar's face.

Quinn stared hard at the little man. Nazar Eudon was easy to dislike. He shelved the 'good cop' act. "I understand you met Abdul and Adiba recently?"

"Yes. Abdul attended my company's press briefing in Eilat. He struck me as an interesting young man. We come from similar backgrounds. I asked him to join me for supper. He had made arrangements to spend time with his girlfriend, so I invited her along. They indulged an old man for most of the day, and I persuaded them to stay the night. Unfortunately, I left early the next morning and didn't see either of them again. I do hope nothing unpleasant has happened to them. They are a charming couple."

Quinn pulled out the picture of Adiba. "Is this her?"

Nazar tilted his head. The action reminded Quinn of a chicken looking at scratch. "Yes, although the picture doesn't do her justice. Abdul has quite a catch there, I think."

"What about this girl?" Quinn turned over the picture and pointed to the name.

"I don't understand, Detective. What about her?" Nazar got a sudden itch at the side of his nose.

Quinn caught the body language. Nazar understood something. "This is Adiba's younger sister, Lana. She's missing too."

Nazar's lips formed a tight line. "Adiba came because she was with Abdul. I do not know her family."

"Did you and Abdul talk about Allah's Revenge?"

The sudden change of topic didn't faze Nazar. "We never mentioned them. In fact, the first I knew of them was a few days later, after that dreadful Al Jazeera video . . . all those poor people."

"Do you know what kind of gas they used?" Quinn asked.

Nazar blinked once. Then his face turned to stone.

"I invited you here, Detective, because I am fond of Abdul and Adiba. I did not believe I could help, but I was willing to try. However, I do not like to be insulted at any time, and particularly not in my own home. Keisha!" His assistant came in immediately. She must have been standing at the door. "The Chief Inspector is leaving. Good day, Detective." Nazar turned on his heel and marched from the room.

"This way, Detective. Mufeed is waiting."

Quinn followed her micro-skirted butt, listening to the clip-clip of her stilettos.

"Please give Mr. Eudon my apologies, Keisha. I'm culturally clumsy. I meant no harm by what I said. If you hear from Abdul or Adiba, please contact me at the Dan Hotel in Eilat."

When he got back to the hotel, Quinn called Scott. "Nazar knows something. What I can't figure is why he reacted to the younger sister's name."

"Do you think he's the money behind Ghazi?"

"Could be. Maybe he's got both girls and Abdul locked up in his mansion. Maybe anything. I don't know, can't get my arms around it."

"Ghazi sent another e-mail," Scott said.

"Why e-mail Abdul if he's holding him?"

"He addressed it to Special Branch; he knows they're monitoring the account."

"That'll make it look even more like Abdul's in bed with Ghazi. What does he want?"

"Same list of prisoners."

"That's dumb. Why should the Israelis give in this time?"

The line went quiet. When he spoke, Scott's voice had lifted a half octave. "Haven't you seen the news?"

"I'm in Israel and I don't speak Hebrew, remember?"

"Holy Shit! You haven't heard about the G20?" Scott filled Quinn in on the massacre.

"How come the Saudis survived?"

"Official line is they don't know. Praise Allah."

"Yeah, right. What are the Israelis going to do?" Quinn asked.

"Who knows, but the Americans will be pressuring them to act. Their VP was killed . . . What about you?" Scott asked.

Quinn let out a long sigh. "Dunno. I thought of going back to Nazar's pad, uninvited—he's left town, traveling to the US, according to his hot assistant."

"Hot?"

"Whatever. I'm not sure what I'd gain, and I'm wary of spending an extended period in a Jordanian prison."

"Look, Quinn, a cell phone is on its way, should be there in the morning, and some US dollars. Why not wait till the Israelis and Americans make a decision on the prisoner release?"

"Without a plan, doing nothing may be all I've got. I'll call you tomorrow on my new phone. And Scott . . . thanks again."

"Sure, get some rest."

Quinn turned on the TV and found CNN. It didn't take long to catch up: The British Prime Minister, the US Vice President, the French and Canadian Prime Ministers, the list was unbelievable. Leaders of nineteen of the twenty most powerful countries in the world were dead. Suspicion about the Saudis was rife. Baffled biotech experts speculated about the gas. The opening ceremony was scheduled to be televised. Fortunately, the organizers had it on a five-minute delay. The pictures hadn't been released, yet. But it was only a matter of time before everyone understood what these crazies could do to a human body.

20

Nazar felt well rested after the long flight from Aqaba. With a final touch of ownership, Keisha straightened his tie, and he stepped from the plane at Sky Harbor Airport, Phoenix, Arizona into one hundred and twenty Fahrenheit. In the parched desert heat Nazar's eyes were drying out as he descended the plane's steps and crossed under its belly to a waiting Jeep. His driver skirted a line of commercial airplanes, following a painted road to a shiny silver helicopter, which waited, blades drooping like a wilted flower.

Nazar climbed in and nodded to the pilot.

"Welcome aboard, Mr. Eudon. I'm Samuel."

The large, black pilot shook his passenger's hand. "Better put on your cans." He offered a set of oversized headphones then busied himself with takeoff duties.

The rotors began their reluctant rotation. The machine rose laboriously for the first few feet, then, once they had sufficient vertical lift, the pilot tilted the stick forward, and they accelerated toward the towering South Mountains, framed by a cloudless, blue Arizona sky.

"I flew this way last week, amazing what your people have done." The pilot flashed brilliant white teeth.

"I'm eager to see the progress," Nazar said.

"Two years ago, desert, and now . . . wow!"

The pilot's excitement was infectious. Nazar's heart skipped when they crested the mountains and sunlight glinted off the domed roofs of the three completed buildings, fifty miles east. Each silver dome crowned a massive conversion chamber, five-hundred feet in diameter, sunk two-hundred feet into the ground. Circled by hundred-foot-wide concrete aprons, from the air the conversion chambers resembled enormous brimmed hats.

Sam landed on a vast concrete pad dotted with hundreds of feeding stations, ready to discharge distilled ethanol into tankers.

Greg Matteson, Nazar's construction manager, sped toward them, across ten football fields of virgin concrete in his jeep. He parked, and ducked low under the twisting rotors. The Australian boarded and crushed a welcome to Nazar with a plate-sized, callused hand. "Mr. Eudon, thank you for coming, sir. It's an honor to meet you again." He said, "G'day, Sam," to the pilot.

The helicopter took off. Greg, headphones over his ears, directed the pilot and pointed out progress to his boss. They swooped low over one of the unfinished structures. A gaping crater lined by rows of scaffolding marking the future location of the walls. Dozens of concrete trucks hovered around the edge, feeding carbon-free slag concrete through long snaking tubes. Ant-like figures in green-and-gold overalls guided the slurry into rebar-strengthened chambers.

Nazar's voice boomed in the headsets. "What's on your critical path?"

"We had to divert the service road because of unexpected hard-pad; probably looking at five percent overage, but within our tolerances. Frankly, Mr. Eudon, I'm pleased we brought that road in so close to budget. These Yanks sure know how to build a highway." Nazar admired the two-mile-long concrete strip that connected the plant to the interstate and from there to the US's east-west transportation corridor.

"Are we ready?" Nazar asked.

Greg nodded toward a line of trucks. The air shimmered with heat from their idling engines. "Just wave the flag and we're off to the races." Your guests will watch from there." He pointed to a coned-off area near one of the conversion chambers.

"The distillery's been complete and ready to go for six weeks," Greg said, indicating a grouping of dozens of tall, silvered tubes clustered at the center of the plant. The conversion chambers connected to the central distillery through a series of underground pipes like spokes of a wheel to the hub. Once the nanobots did their work, the ethanol solution would flow to the distillery to be purified into automobile-ready fuel.

After twenty minutes of narrated flyover, the pilot returned to Greg's Jeep. They stayed on the ground long enough for the project manager to jump out, duck, and run back to his vehicle. The chopper flew on toward a scaled-down prototype conversion chamber, two miles west of the main plant.

Outside the prototype building, a few people were taking a smoke break near a green-and-gold-striped marquee. When they landed, Martin Spalling drove up in a golf cart.

"Terrific turnout, boss." Nazar shook hands with his marketing VP. He was a handsome man: coiffed blond hair that didn't move, even under the downdraft of the helicopter, clear blue eyes, and a baby-faced complexion. Projecting a look of casual confidence in neatly pressed slacks and an open-necked shirt, Martin was the same height as his boss—one of Nazar's hiring criteria for any employee likely to stand close during photo opportunities. He handed Nazar an agenda.

"Anything changed?" Nazar asked.

"No, just as we agreed."

Nazar slipped the paper into his inside pocket. He had been anticipating this day for more than two years. He had burned cash until there was hardly any left. Now he would savor one of those special moments of triumph that only come to those who take enormous risk.

Martin ran through the plan as he drove the cart. "We're set up in the marquee. You'll give the welcome. Then I'll give a ten-minute technology overview."

"Not the professor?" Nazar asked.

"I took him through it three times yesterday. He stutters. He flubs his lines. And he gets hung up in the details. I'll make him available for questions, but it's better if I do the pitch. I need it high-level. Most of the journalists are generalists, even the ones who think they aren't."

In the marquee, two hundred guests were seated, theater-style. Nazar took his place in the front row next to the senator from Ohio who had been so helpful in the past; making him today's VIP was something of a payback.

Martin called them to order and introduced Nazar, who received a polite sprinkling of applause from staff and from local politicians who had enjoyed a significant boost to their tax base during the plant's construction. As he scanned the press corps, Nazar thought of Abdul. He had been invited, but that was before the boy had disappeared.

Nazar welcomed everyone before handing off to Martin. His VP gave a slick summary of the technology and fielded a few questions.

Nazar tingled inside, remembering the first time he observed nanobots eating pizza boxes and car tires. These people were going to be blown away.

The guests filed across a dusty strip of concrete into the prototype building. For two years, this building had headquartered the scientists and engineers who had perfected the nanobot technology. Nazar had always intended the building to double as a demonstration facility where he'd host car companies, electric utilities, garbage suppliers, government officials, and, most importantly, the Wall Street investment houses responsible for the Initial Public Offering that would rocket him to his rightful place at the top of the *Forbes World's Billionaires* list.

At the center of the building, a fifty-foot diameter circular conversion chamber was sunk thirty feet into the ground. The spectators shuffled into a viewing gallery separated from the chamber by ten-foot-high windows, cambered in, so the onlookers could stand on the other side of the glass in a comfortable air-conditioned environment and look down on twelve dump-truck loads of rotting garbage. Martin picked up the microphone.

"Ladies and gentlemen, you could be excused for wondering why we've asked you here to stare at a pile of trash." A murmur of chuckles and snide comments rippled around the viewing gallery. "Trust me, if we didn't care about you, we wouldn't have sealed you off from the smell." This raised a laugh.

At Martin's nodded signal, additional trash tumbled from the loading bay above, past the viewing-windows, into the pit below. A few spectators jumped back in surprise.

"You are looking at seventy tons of household waste, generously donated by the people of Dewsbury, our nearest town. Thank you, Mr. Mayor."

A gray-haired man in a blue suit waved, enjoying his moment in the limelight.

Martin continued, "Most of this trash was created by energy from the sun. To illustrate, let me tell you the possible story of that plastic milk carton lying near the top of the pile." All eyes focused on the familiar, yellow container.

"Millions of years ago, a seed fell from a plant onto fertile ground. Watered by rain, the seed germinated, pushed its first leaves through the earth, and photosynthesized the sun's energy to manufacture cellulosic material. The plant grew tall, flowered, made its own seeds, and then died. Along with billions of similar plants and the insects that fed on them, our plant decomposed. Over millions of years, the organic matter became buried deep below the surface of the Earth. Massive pressures transformed the rotted plants into sticky, black oil.

"Humans drilled through the earth's crust, tapped the oil, and brought it to the surface. Chemically modified and molded by a plastics manufacturer, it became the yellow milk container below you. Most of what's in this conversion chamber was created using the sun's energy, and that energy is still trapped inside." Martin paused for a few beats to let the concept sink in.

"But trash can't fill a gas tank. We need the energy in a more convenient form. Technology developed by Eudon Alternative Energy will take this pile of garbage and transform it into ethanol, ready for use in vehicles and power stations. Today you will witness that transformation. Ladies and gentlemen, the demonstration takes twenty minutes. Please hold your questions until the end. Thank you." Martin gave another signal.

A metal cherry picker pivoted from the wall and dropped a white canister the size of an oil drum into the center of the tank. On landing, the canister split apart and spilled white powder onto the top of the trash.

The spectators' focus was drawn upward as screens rolled back and uncovered the building's dome, focusing a shaft of sunlight on the trash below.

By the time the guests looked down again, the white canister had melted and sunk into the pile. Vibrations were felt underfoot as the garbage shifted and bumped. The gallery of watchers was strangely silent, captivated by the sight of seventy tons of garbage moving and settling in a huge cauldron. People pointed out specific pieces of debris, following a tire or a sofa as they were consumed.

Orange liquid seeped into spaces in the lowering pile. After fifteen minutes, except for a few floating Styrofoam boxes, most solids had disappeared. Finally, even the white foam melted.

As the activity subsided and the liquid cleared, Martin spoke. "Ladies and gentlemen, before today, fewer than two hundred people had seen what you just witnessed. The liquid in the tank below you is a thirty-percent solution of ethanol, ready to be fed into a fractionating vessel and distilled into fuel suitable for use in automobiles, or power plants: a clean-burning alternative to oil."

Martin fed them the tag line, the sound bite for the news agencies as they led with the story of the miracle in the desert. "We're making gas from garbage, ladies and gentlemen, gas from garbage."

Martin stopped the questions after twenty minutes. He didn't give a damn whether they understood the process as long as they understood the importance of what they had seen. Over lunch, the crowd was animated. Journalists crammed food into their mouths while working their smart phones. Martin had recorded the demonstration and packaged it on DVDs to slip into the care package each guest would take home.

After lunch, four sleek buses pulled up outside the building. Nazar and the guests piled in. They drove down a dirt road to the Interstate, turned east, and in two miles took the turnoff to the main facility. Martin wanted them to grasp the scale of what Nazar had created. The first step came on the newly-built highway.

Martin's audio broadcasted to all four buses. "We anticipate two thousand truck trips each day on this road once the plant is fully operational." He paused to let the number sink in.

"The garbage trucks ahead are loaded with the detritus of home and industry: rotting food, animal waste, plastic and paper. All built with energy from the sun." He tapped his driver on the shoulder and made a *slowdown* signal with his hand. They reduced speed to twenty miles an hour. When they had passed thirty of the idling trucks, Martin spoke again.

"The trucks in this line constitute less than *one* full payload of feedstock for just *one* of the industrial-scale conversion chambers. Three chambers are complete and ready to begin ethanol production today. Construction will continue for another twelve months. Once finished, there will be six conversion chambers, capable of producing sixty-thousand barrels of ethanol every day. Gas from garbage, ladies and gentlemen. Gas from garbage."

The buses pulled into a coned-off area. The luminaries and press corps followed a path painted on the concrete to where a green-and-gold ribbon was strung between two four-foot poles.

Martin spoke through a bullhorn. "It is deemed unsafe for you to approach the conversion chamber. Beyond the feed station is a two-hundred-foot dead drop to the bottom of the tank. However, the package you will receive before leaving will contain video footage of the interior, identical to the prototype, except one thousand times larger. It is now my pleasure to invite Senator Isley, of Ohio's second district, to carry out the ribbon cutting."

The gray-haired politician wobbled forward. One hundred pounds overweight, even in dry desert heat sweat beaded his brow. Nazar walked alongside, and Martin ushered the press photographers to their places. The senator held the ceremonial ribbon, scissors poised over the tape. Nazar Eudon held the ribbon to the senator's right.

The senator said, "I now pronounce Eudon Alternative Energy's ethanol conversion facility open for business." The tape parted and fluttered to the ground to a weak ripple of applause. Nazar shook hands with the senator, and both men grinned for the cameras.

Martin waved a large green-and-gold flag, and, with a roar of engines, eight trucks rolled from the waiting line. Each backed up to a feed station. The rear of the trucks lifted, and garbage slid out. The trucks pulled away, almost in unison, their bodies tilting back to horizontal as they drove off. The next trucks in line took their place.

After three truckloads, eight huge bulldozers roared into life and used their front blades to push the trash into the feed station, and it crashed into the conversion vessel below. The noise and dust and stench were impressive. The guests were quick to respond when Martin suggested they returned to the air-conditioned buses.

After their guests had departed, Nazar, Martin and the professor sat drinking cold beer in the marquee. Nazar raised his can. "Well done, Martin. And you, Professor, your nanobots performed splendidly." A few remaining Eudon staff bustled about, packing equipment. "Professor, I expected to see David.

Where is he?"

"He has t ... t ... taken a short break to visit his family. But not to worry, the nanobot technology is fully automated. Now if you'll excuse me, I am tired and s ... still have a few things I must attend to." Without waiting for a reply, the professor left his beer and hurried away. Nazar stared after him. His abrupt departure seemed odd, even for him.

Martin tipped his drink toward the departing academic. "I swear, he gets more eccentric every time I meet him."

Nazar nodded.

"I'm tired too," Martin said. "For a people person, you know, sometimes I hate people." They both laughed. Nazar understood. "The woman from the *LA Times*," Martin rolled his eyes. "I still don't think she gets it."

"Do you know anyone else there?" Nazar asked. "It's a key publication."

"Oh, they have good people. She's just not one of them. Don't worry, I'll follow up tomorrow. They'll be focused on us like a laser beam after tonight's TV buzz. Get this! Next Sunday, CBS is planning a one-hour *Sixty Minutes* special entitled *Gas from Garbage.*"

"Excellent," Nazar said. He was exhausted. The senator had been very needy, bitching about the heat at every opportunity. He'd loved the ribbon cutting, though, great ego-salve. "I'm flying back to town, want a lift?"

"Thanks, but I have to finish with my people here. I'll talk with you tomorrow. Have a good night. You deserve it." Martin stood and shook his boss's hand. "Nazar, I take my hat off to you, sir. You've got the biggest *cojones* in the world to pull this off."

Nazar accepted the compliment. He'd gone all in, everyone had called, and he'd shown top hand and taken the pot.

At the airport, before he climbed from the helicopter, the pilot shook his hand. "Sir, if you don't mind me talkin' out of turn, you've done wonders for this area. You've brought a lot of jobs, and man, we needed them."

"Thank you, Sam." Nazar reveled in the power. Once the conversion chambers started delivering ethanol, he planned to become as influential in America as he was in Jordan.

Keisha awaited him at the top of the airplane's steps. "Welcome back, Mr. Eudon. We're cleared for takeoff whenever you are ready. It's a six-hour flight to New York."

"Thank you, Keisha; let's get going, shall we? I'll freshen up once we're at cruising altitude."

"Yes, sir. A cocktail?" Nazar nodded and walked back to his air-conditioned private quarters. Keisha brought his drink. He sipped the martini and stared through the window as the plane rose through clear skies. He was about to become the wealthiest man in history. From rags to riches: the income from the ethanol produced in the three completed conversion tanks would be his first unallocated cash flow for two years.

But the stock offering was where the real money was. Nazar had self-funded the project. He who took the risk, reaped the rewards.

As Phoenix dwindled behind him, he finished his drink and moved to the bathroom. He allowed the shower's water jets to envelop him. With the flat of his hand, he stroked droplets from the head of the tiled snake. He had seen one in the wild once, in Australia—a sea serpent less than two feet long. One drop of its venom was sufficient to kill a thousand people. Certain death in fewer than two minutes, not even time for an antidote. Yet, despite its deadly weapon, the snake rarely used its poison, mostly choosing to hold back the fatal dose. He felt strong affinity with the small reptile and its selective attack regime. The snake could kill at will, but only did so at its whim.

Keisha's singsong voice outside the bathroom door interrupted his thoughts.

"I have laid out some comfortable clothes, Mr. Eudon, perhaps a massage?"

"That sounds wonderful."

He stepped from the shower as she entered, dressed in a colorful kimono. He stood, naked, dripping on the tiled floor, eyes focused over her head, tracing the overlapping scales of the snake mural. After patting his face and neck and toweled his hair, Keisha traversed his shoulders and back, pressing and caressing with the soft towel. He spread his legs, and she patted between his cheeks. Dropping to her knees, she supported him against her shoulder and lifted each foot in turn to dry between his toes. Still kneeling, she turned him and repeated the process in reverse.

"Dry now," she said and took his hand as she would a child's and led him to the bed. He lay face down on the fresh towels she had spread. New Age music played as she kneaded the muscles of his neck and shoulders, drawing out the tension. She tapped his back, and he flipped over, admiring her features as she focused, with Zen-like intensity, on the massage.

Twenty minutes later, relaxed, Nazar said, "Thank you, Keisha. That was wonderful."

She stood, placed her hands together in front of her breasts, and bowed deeply. The neck of her kimono gaped. Her nipples were hard, aroused by the contact. She left him, closing the door with a click.

He propped a pillow behind his head, picked up the remote, pointed, and gave life to the sixty-inch flat-screen on the wall at the foot of his bed. He scanned the five icons at the top of the display's desktop: Omar, Marwan, Edward (ah, yes, Edward, the young American boy who had wandered from his parents while on holiday; he smiled an inner smile of remembrance), Lufti, and Lana.

Of course, he would choose Lana—the latest, the freshest. Even after multiple viewings, the experience held sufficient enchantment for him. Soon, he knew, it would fail to promote the same vigorous arousal and he would need to add another icon.

But, for now, Lana was perfect.

The screen flickered to life, and Nazar saw himself, disguised as a doctor. Let the games begin.

21

After an hour of watching CNN in his Eilat hotel, the information started looping. Quinn washed up and headed for the hotel's lounge. Two whiskies in, he felt less stressed. He was the only patron at the bar.

Quinn interrupted the bartender, polishing glasses at the far end. "You Israelis aren't much for drinking, are you?"

"Not like Europeans. Suits me, though." He waved his hand along the shiny, clean bar.

Quinn smiled. "What d'you make of this G20 stuff?" Quinn nodded toward the muted TV on the back wall, which showed the same footage he'd seen in his room.

The bartender glanced at the screen. "Hard to say; Israel isn't invited to the meeting, so—"

"Think the Saudis did it?"

He shrugged. "Who knew they were that smart?"

Quinn laughed. "I'm Quinn."

"Yacob."

"Pleasure." Quinn pushed his glass across the bar. "How about one more for the European?" Yacob poured the Black Label freehand this time, neglecting the metal measure he'd used on the previous two drinks.

Quinn checked his watch: 7:10 p.m. "Thanks. The hotel's awfully quiet. Is this normal?"

"There's a convention in this week, but they went on the sunset desert tour, won't be back till late." Yacob leaned on the bar, no longer feigning work.

"Desert tour, eh? Worth seeing?" Quinn asked.

"Beautiful, and at the same time strange, better in winter, though—too hot this time of year, even at night. Last week they found a young girl out there almost dead from the heat."

"How'd she get into the desert?"

"No one knows, but she was fortunate. Never would have lasted until morning. She'd have died of thirst."

Quinn made a face. "Who found her?"

"My friend, Tsvi. He's a lead driver. The wind had buried most of her under the sand. He thinks that saved her. Strange thing, she had on school clothes. Badly burned, though, so he took her straight to Yoseftal hospital."

Quinn downed his whisky and pulled a bill out of his pocket. "That's for you, Yacob. Put the drinks on my room."

"Sure . . . thanks."

Quinn ran to the lobby and waved the concierge over. "I need a cab to the hospital."

"Are you sick, sir?"

"I'm fine. I'm going to visit someone."

Fifteen minutes later, Quinn arrived at Yoseftal Hospital. He stood at reception and waited while the woman behind the desk finished a phone call.

"Do you speak English?" he asked.

"Yes, of course."

"Great. The girl they found in the desert last week. Is she still here?"

"Are you a relative?" The receptionist turned her head and nodded. Quinn followed her gaze. She'd signaled a security guard, who walked toward them.

"Not related, but I might know who she is, and if I'm right, her parents are desperate to find her."

"May I help you, sir?" The guard, a few inches shorter than Quinn, had a potbelly and a sidearm. His hand rested on his hip, near the gun.

Quinn pulled out the picture of Adiba. "I met this girl's father two days ago. Both of his daughters have disappeared. She's the older one." He showed the image to the guard and the receptionist.

"I don't have a picture of the younger sister, but she went missing from school last week. Here's her name." He flipped the photo over.

"May I borrow this?" The guard held out his hand for the picture.

Quinn hesitated. It was all he had. "I'll need it back."

"And who are you?" the guard asked.

"A friend of the family."

"And you came to Eilat looking for her?"

"Not exactly, I'm here on business."

"What kind of business?"

Quinn glowered at the man.

The guard threw him a suspicious look, but at least the questioning stopped. "Wait here." He made a call on the wall phone. Quinn heard Lana's name. The guard went quiet and struck a waiting pose, holding the handset and staring at Quinn. A few minutes later he spoke again, then hung up, sauntered back to Quinn, and handed him the picture.

"The girl answered to Lana," he said.

"Can I see her?" Quinn asked.

The receptionist spoke to the guard. Quinn couldn't understand the language, but her tone indicated she was rooting for him, so he smiled at her.

The guard relented. "Follow me." They took the elevator to the third floor.

The guard found the duty nurse. "This way," she said to Quinn. She spoke English with an American accent, causing Quinn to reflect on the positive influence of American TV and movies.

He and the guard followed the nurse along a shiny hospital corridor that smelled of disinfectant—same the world over. She led them into a small ward with four beds, all occupied. They walked to the farthest one. The other patients, two old men and one middle-aged woman, wore headphones, watching CNN on a wall-mounted TV.

The fourth bed had screens pulled around. The nurse slid them back, and Quinn saw the girl, head swaddled in white dressings so only her eyes, nose and mouth were visible. The bedcovers were tented. Quinn had seen the setup before. A metal cage under the sheets kept the material from touching her burned skin.

When the nurse spoke to the girl, Quinn detected a different accent and guessed she must be speaking Arabic—English, Hebrew, and Arabic, impressive—the girl stared at Quinn for a few seconds before shaking her head.

The nurse straightened and her demeanor became less welcoming. "She doesn't know you."

"Please, show her this. Ask whether it's her sister." Quinn handed Adiba's picture to the nurse, who held it in front of the girl's face.

"Adiba . . . Adiba!" The girl became agitated and tried to sit up.

The nurse made calm-down motions with her hands.

"I think she's the missing girl," Quinn said. "Her father's phone number is on the back. Call him. He's frantic to find his daughter. Maybe she'll tell her dad what happened."

Quinn turned and nodded to the guard, who had relaxed his gun hand. The nurse punched the number into the bedside phone. After a long wait, she was connected and started speaking, using both girls' names in the conversation. She listened for a few seconds, then put her hand over the mouthpiece. "Are you Quinnborne?" she asked. Quinn nodded.

The nurse held the phone to the girl's ear.

"*Baba!*" Lana said. Tears trickled from her eyes.

The nurse glanced at the security guard, then at Quinn. "Her father says to thank you." Quinn smiled. "This girl was dumped in the desert like a piece of garbage. We think she may have been abused, but she won't talk to us." Her voice was thick with anger. "We have to sedate her whenever the doctor comes. She goes crazy when she sees him. We thought because he is a man, but she didn't react negatively to you."

Quinn shrugged. He was glad he'd found Lana, but from his perspective, it was the wrong sister. He couldn't imagine child abuse being in Ghazi's playbook: too risky, too messy.

Suddenly, Lana began screaming and thrashing. She dropped the phone, jerked upright, and knocked the drip stand into the nurse's face. The woman jumped back in fright and upset the water carafe, which smashed on the floor. Even wrapped like a mummy, the girl bounced her body, trying to get off the bed. The cords connected to her monitor yanked free, triggering a high-pitched alarm.

The security guard pulled his gun. Quinn wanted to hold the girl down, but didn't dare touch her burned skin. He looked to the nurse for guidance. She was shouting the girl's name, attempting to calm her.

"Lana! Lana!" Her father's frantic voice squawked from the telephone, which lay abandoned on the bed.

Quinn read Lana's eyes. The girl was terrified and staring straight at him.

No.

She was staring past him.

He spun around. The TV showed a CNN press conference. A bank of microphones pointed to a sallow-skinned man with silver hair, sparkling green eyes, and a neatly groomed beard. His smiling face filled the screen. The graphic at the bottom read, "Gas from Garbage."

Quinn recognized Nazar Eudon.

And so, apparently, did Lana.

22

In Jeddah, Imam Ali listened to the mellow drone of afternoon prayers coming from the mosque beyond his office door. With two chair legs on the floor, feet on the desk, and arms behind his head, Ali leaned back and spoke into the phone, "The Saudis failed to send the third installment. The contract is canceled."

Ghazi sat on a grubby hospital cot in the abandoned wing of the West Bank medical facility in Israel, and replied to his friend. "They have no stomach for real warfare. They pretend to be Muslim, to care about our Palestinian brothers, but when a tough choice must be made, they cower before their American paymasters. No matter, I have the situation in hand." Across the room, David Baker listened to Ghazi's side of the conversation. "I sent the prisoner release demand again to the Londoners."

"And?" Ali asked.

"No response yet, but be confident. The events in Seoul will change their thinking." Ghazi faced David and raised his voice. "Thanks to Allah's Revenge's newest captain, Dawud Ferran, for the first time in fifteen hundred years the soldiers of Islam have a weapon to defeat the Crusaders." Ghazi smiled at David. The young man's face glowed with pride.

"And if they don't?" Ali asked.

"We will use the weapon."

"Firman is expensive, we will need money."

"Don't worry, brother. I will execute in parallel. We need money even if they do comply. This is only the beginning."

"*Allahu Akbar*," Ali said.

"*Allahu Akbar*," Ghazi replied.

David repeated the words, like an echo.

Above, in Adiba's room, Adiba and Abdul played their tenth game of chess. Ghazi had brought the board, and Abdul had yet to win. In fact, he had yet to cause her a problem. She moved her queen across the board to a protected square directly in front of his king.

"Checkmate again, Mr. Junior Middle East Correspondent." She grinned with delight. Abdul didn't know which would be more enjoyable; winning, or losing again and seeing her victory smile. He leaned over and kissed her full on the lips.

"What was that?" she said.

"My reward for letting you win again."

With a crinkled brow, she wagged her finger at him in mock annoyance. He laughed. She looked so cute when she pulled that face.

The door opened, cutting short his laughter.

The terrorist who had snatched him from the hotel burst into the room. "Abdul-Haqq, you must come."

Abdul and Adiba disliked the man, whom they assumed was Ghazi's number two. He always smelled of stale sweat, and his narrow eyes and crooked mouth gave the appearance of a permanent sneer. Ironically, they both trusted Ghazi, despite the atrocity they knew he had perpetrated in London. Yet they feared this man.

Abdul stood, squeezed Adiba's hand, and followed the terrorist across the landing and through the open door into his room. Ghazi sat in one of the plastic chairs.

"Sit." Abdul took the chair opposite. The grim look on Ghazi's face reminded Abdul of their first meeting in Jerusalem.

"How well do you know Nazar Eudon?" Ghazi asked.

If Abdul had been asked to guess the hundred most likely reasons for this meeting, Nazar Eudon wouldn't make a reserve list. The question surprised him.

"We met in Eilat at a press briefing to clarify his announcement in London about shifting focus to alternative energy. He felt something of a kinship with me because our family backgrounds are similar. He invited me to supper."

"You went to his home?"

Abdul suspected Ghazi was testing the verity of his story. "Yes, Adiba and I stayed the night."

"Can you contact him?"

"He gave me a business card."

"Give it to me." Ghazi held out his hand. Abdul fished out his wallet and handed the card to his captor.

"You must call this Keisha."

"What's this about?"

Ghazi's face hardened and he stared Abdul down. Abdul's head began to tremble under the man's fierce glare. For the past two days, the smelly man had delivered their food, and Abdul had spent every waking hour with Adiba, talking and playing chess. The fact that they were captives had slipped from top-of-mind. Ghazi's angry face brought their predicament back into focus.

"I can call. What do you want me to say?"

Ghazi slammed a sheet of paper on the table in front of Abdul, handwritten in Arabic. "Can you read it?"

"Yes, but I don't understand what it means."

"Come." Ghazi snatched up the note, stood, and walked toward the door. Abdul followed him down the stairs and into the office.

Two men he hadn't seen before sat at a small table, smoking and playing cards. They looked up when he came in the room. The terrorist they disliked was absent. Abdul worried that he might be upstairs bothering Adiba.

Ghazi pointed to a chair beside his desk. Abdul sat, and Ghazi handed the business card to the younger of the two men, who stopped his game, pulled a cell phone from his inside pocket, and made a call. Ghazi placed the note on the desk in front of Abdul. The man with the phone entered a long series of numbers, perhaps using a calling card to disguise the call origin. Finally, he spoke in Arabic. "Is this Mr. Nazar Eudon's office?" he waited for a reply, and then, "Please hold for Abdul Ahmed." He passed the phone to Abdul.

"Hello?" Abdul said.

"I am Keisha, Nazar Eudon's personal assistant. Mr. Eudon mentioned you, Abdul, but we understood you had been abducted.

How may I be of assistance?"

"Hello, Keisha, I'm—" Before Abdul could complete the thought, Ghazi's calloused hand struck him hard across the face. The suddenness and ferocity of the blow knocked the phone from his hand and left his face throbbing. His heart slammed against his ribs, and he stared wide-eyed at Ghazi's furious face. The terrorist jabbed a finger at the notepaper. Abdul picked up the phone. Hand trembling, he read with a quavering voice and through tearing eyes.

"Ms. Keisha, I have a message to deliver."

"I am recording the call. Please continue."

"Allah's Revenge possesses the only viable virginbots in existence. They are for sale. We require one million dollars in cash. I will call in two hours with details of the exchange conditions."

Ghazi snatched the phone from Abdul, ended the call, and barked across at the two thugs.

"Take him upstairs."

Abdul's face ached. Ghazi had hit him hard, and he hadn't been ready. He felt sick to his stomach. The older of the two card players frog-marched him up the stairs and locked him in his room. He worried about Adiba. He wanted to shout across, to check if she was okay. But fear of angering Ghazi prevented him. He'd experienced the man's temper: quick, ugly, and painful.

In the bathroom, he checked in the mirror. Ghazi's handprint stood out, white and red, on his cheek. He filled the sink with cold water, soaked a hand towel, and pressed it to his face to prevent swelling. Obviously, Ghazi's change of mood was the result of a funding issue. Everything always seemed to end up being about money.

Keisha had received the call from Abdul in Nazar's plane, waiting on the tarmac at New York's JFK airport. They had flown there from Phoenix after the grand opening. When Nazar returned from his meetings in Manhattan, they would fly to Washington, DC where Nazar would meet with the Senate's Sub-Committee on Energy. Abdul's call might change those plans, so she sent a text to Nazar.

On the thirty-fifth floor of the Oppenheim building in the heart of Manhattan's financial district, Nazar strategized with his underwriters about Eudon Alternative Energy's planned public offering of stock. When his phone vibrated, he glanced down and immediately reacted to Keisha's emergency code.

"Gentlemen and lady. Please excuse me, I must make a call."

The attractive executive assistant responsible for managing the meeting, the only woman in the room, showed him to an empty office next door. Keisha dictated the message she'd received from Allah's Revenge. How could anyone outside Phoenix know about virginbots? But the information was too specific to ignore. He told Keisha to stay by the phone, and called Professor Farjohn at the lab in Arizona.

"Professor, do you have any issues with the virginbots?"

"Issues, n . . . n . . . no, I . . . I . . . I . . ."

When he heard the stammering, Nazar knew he had a problem. He cut the man off in mid-stutter. "Let me put it another way professor. What is the problem with the virginbots?"

"W . . . w . . . we're working o . . . o . . ."

Nazar cupped a hand around the mouthpiece of his phone and lowered his voice. The underwriters might be listening in the next room. "In less than one hour I must decide whether to purchase new virginbots from another source. Find me someone who can speak without stammering!"

"I . . . I . . . I . . ."

"Professor, let me speak to David."

"N . . . not . . . here."

"Damnit, man!" he hissed, "what's wrong with the virginbots!"

Nazar dug nails into his palm. He shook with anger. His empire could be crumbling and the person with the key information was incapable of speaking a sentence. The more he pressed the less likely the professor would get a word out. Nazar waited. The professor took a series of deep breaths then blurted his words in fast, short, spurts as he exhaled.

"David never returned from his vacation in February."

Nazar was staggered by this news. Why hadn't he been told? He suppressed the tempest of anger he felt toward this pompous idiot. More panting preceded the professor's next block of speech.

"He's contaminated our virginbots stock, so they will auto-destruct at midnight on July 31st."

Nazar's legs buckled, forcing him to perch on the edge of the desk and wait for the next stream of information.

"He stole one vial of virginbots."

Nazar whispered into the mouthpiece. "So ethanol production will stop on July 31st unless we get new virginbots."

"Y . . . y . . . y . . ."

Nazar hung up and called Keisha.

"Send my car immediately."

He composed himself, made his excuses to the bankers, and left the building. His driver was outside when he exited the lobby, and he called Keisha before they'd pulled into traffic.

"Who made the call?"

"Abdul, the journalist from the *Times*."

"Are you sure it was him?"

"Yes, but he sounded under duress. I could tell he was reading the message. I tried to ask about his safety, but the line went dead."

"Tell the pilot we're returning to Phoenix. Call Senator Isley, make my apologies, we'll call next week to re-schedule. When Abdul phones back, tell him we want to make a deal. Phone me immediately after you've spoken to him." Nazar hung up and called his banker in Tel Aviv.

He would need to find a million dollars in cash overnight? It had to be done; Nazar needed to buy time.

Abdul sat on his bed with a cold cloth pressed against his throbbing cheek. Time dragged. Eventually, the older terrorist fetched him downstairs again and pointed to the desk. Abdul sat and waited. The room was silent except for the click of playing cards. Ghazi paced and checked his watch. Finally, he instructed the younger terrorist to make the call. Ghazi laid the phone on the desk in front of Abdul and turned on the speaker.

"Hello?" Keisha said.

He bent forward and spoke. "This is Abdul."

"Abdul, Mr. Eudon wishes to receive the terms of sale."

Ghazi, grim-faced, handed Abdul a note.

Abdul read, "In two days, on July 23rd, bring the money in US dollars to Tel Aviv. I will call this number with details for the exchange. Any deviation from our instructions and further shipments of virginbots will be compromised."

"I understand," she said, and Ghazi snatched the phone away.

23

The morning after finding Lana, Quinn rose early. At the hotel's front desk, he collected the package from Scott—a cell phone, a universal charger, and two thousand American dollars. Quinn left the hotel and headed toward the beach. Scott had programmed his cell number into the phone. Quinn hit speed-dial.

"Scott, the phone and the cash arrived, thanks again."

"Has anyone caught up with you yet?"

"Anyone who?"

"Last night I had a visit from your superintendent and that prick, Frank Browning. They had two Americans with them—blue suits—and they want to speak to you in the worst possible way."

Quinn rounded the corner of the building. In the hotel parking lot, three black SUVs blocked his tiny Fiat. He reversed course and slipped back behind the building.

"Looks like the blue suits are here," he said. "Give me ten minutes. I need to reach my room before they do. Mom always told me to pack a clean pair of jockeys when I went on the lam!"

The lobby was deserted. Quinn took the elevator, crammed his toilet bag and clothes into his grip, but used the stairs on the way down. At lobby level, he opened the stairwell door a crack and peered out. Two stiff-looking men in dark suits stood with four uniformed Israeli police at the front desk. The receptionist called the bellhop over and handed him a key card. The six cops followed him to the elevators. Quinn knew where they were headed.

He slipped into the lobby and down a hallway where a few ground-floor rooms were reserved for smokers. The exit at the end brought him to the opposite side of the hotel, away from the parking lot. He walked briskly toward the beach, but not fast enough to attract attention. No one followed.

He called Scott back. "I'm not sure why I'm running from these guys; after all, we're supposed to be on the same team."

"They may not agree," Scott said. "Think, Quinn: Abdul is the only person who has met Ghazi. Allah's Revenge used Abdul's e-mail to send their demands. Abdul gave you the slip in Jerusalem, and now you've gone missing instead of reporting in. What conclusion would you come to?"

"Damn it all, Scott, I'd think we were both guilty as sin. I'm worried for Abdul. Eventually they'll believe me, but I'm not so sure about him."

"According to the superintendent," Scott said, "you and I are the only people in the universe not convinced that Abdul is an officer in Allah's Revenge. Frankly, Quinn, they've assumed he *is* Ghazi, and they've been set up."

"Yeah, makes sense. Did they mention Nazar Eudon?"

"No, why?"

"Well, he's involved somehow. Adiba's sister, Lana, flipped out last night at the hospital when she saw him on TV. At least I'm the only one working that angle. Maybe Eudon can lead me to Adiba. And wherever she is, that's where we'll find Abdul."

"Quinn, I won't call unless it's an emergency, but keep me in the loop," Scott said.

"I have to. You're all I've got." Quinn looked at the phone's screen. It showed full battery. He powered off. No telling when he'd be able to recharge his link with Scott Shearer, the only person on Earth he could trust.

Scott stared out of his office window at the building across the street: vacant for years like most of Fleet Street's old buildings, blinds shuttered and offices dark. In many ways, he was an old-fashioned dinosaur, stubbornly clinging to his journalistic heritage. Other newspapers had left central London for gray block buildings in cheaper, light-industrial locations. He closed his eyes, trying to put space between Abdul's problems in Israel and the demands of the present in London. A dozen multicolored Post-its peppered the outside glass panel of his door. He'd told Amy not to disturb him; these were only the urgent messages.

The attack at the G20 had every country on high alert. The US Congress, the British Parliament, the French National Assembly, the German Bundestag. Governments across the globe were convened in emergency session. The moment everyone had feared was here. The terrorists had acquired a weapon of mass destruction, used it, and been wildly successful.

Every Western government had emergency plans ready to respond to a rogue nuclear device. But no one knew how to deal with this lethal technology. Although it beggared belief, the Koreans had spent one billion dollars on security for the G20 event. Allah's Revenge had triggered the weapon inside the most secure room in the world.

Not since World War II had anyone seen this level of fear and uncertainty. Stock markets around the globe had plummeted. Central banks were printing money and pouring it into the banking system to prop up their currencies. As editor of one of the world's most respected newspapers, he should be on top of the news, driving his editorial insight through the reporting, making value judgments about where to deploy his journalists.

Instead, all he could think of was his Junior Middle East correspondent. Where was Abdul? What was he doing? Was he safe?

After last night's tense visit from Quinn's boss, Scott felt certain if the authorities found Abdul, he would be shot on sight—the hawks were in the ascendancy. With a resigned sigh, he opened his door, pulled the notes off the glass, and called out. "I'm available, Amy!"

Behind drawn blinds on the sixth floor of the empty building across the street, two men wearing oversized headphones and off-white overalls crouched over a folding picnic table, staring at an open laptop. A black cable snaked across the room, connecting the computer to the center of a silvered umbrella whose concave face pointed at Scott Shearer's office.

When he heard Scott call out for his secretary, one of the men straightened, removed his headset, and pressed a speed-dial on his phone.

After a few seconds, he spoke. "Quinn made contact. Yes, sir. Agent Martin is sending the phone number as I speak. The call originated in Israel." He listened to a question, then replied: "Yes sir, both used cell phones . . . thank you sir . . . yes, sir, we're on it." He ended the call and waved to his partner, who pulled the headset an inch from his ear.

"Superintendent Porter commends us for a job well done." The seated agent smiled and returned to his surveillance.

24

Quinn pocketed the cell phone and took a cab to the hospital. The last time he'd seen Lana's father, the man had been on his knees begging him to find his daughters.

Well, at least he'd found one of them.

When Quinn reached Lana's ward, the short, stocky man sat with his back to the door, holding his daughter's hand. When Lana's eyes widened, her father turned. Quinn came toward them, and the man sprang to his feet and met him at the foot of the bed. Again tears welled in the father's eyes. Quinn offered his hand, but the man pushed it aside and gripped him in a fierce bear hug. He was chattering away in Arabic, a much happier person than the last time Quinn had seen him.

"My father says he is in your debt." Lana's English was heavily accented but clear—an unexpected benefit.

"How do you feel, Lana?" Quinn asked. Her father held on and began thumping Quinn on the back.

"I am still sore, but now my father is here—" she broke down; it took her a few seconds to regroup. "We are waiting for the doctor to discharge me."

Lana's father finally released Quinn. He nodded along with Lana's words, although the man clearly had no idea what she was saying. The other three patients, glad of the distraction, watched until the woman in the next bed turned to the door. Quinn followed her gaze and the nurse entered, accompanied by a dark-skinned man with a heavy beard, dressed in a white lab coat. A stethoscope dangled from his neck.

Lana stiffened and gripped her father's hand. He stroked her hair. The girl looked terrified. The doctor pulled the chart from the foot of the bed and spoke to Lana's father for a few minutes. The father nodded his understanding, and the doctor left.

The nurse began to pull the privacy curtains. "Mr. Quinnborne, Lana needs to get dressed."

He waited outside in the corridor with her father. The nurse reappeared, pushing Lana in a wheelchair. Quinn guessed the staff had contributed the clothes, because her cut-off jeans and white cotton top were two or three sizes too large. Lana's face, drawn and thin, accentuated big doe-eyes framed with long, black lashes. With her neck, face, and left arm still bandaged she looked frail and defenseless. Why would someone hurt this little girl? The thought made Quinn's blood boil.

He and Lana's father followed the wheelchair. When they were in the elevator, Quinn spoke to the nurse. "I wonder, could you ask her father if I could get a ride to Jerusalem?"

She looked puzzled. Probably trying to understand how a British policeman found himself in Eilat without transport. She spoke to Lana's father, who turned and grabbed Quinn's hand in both of his.

"Yes, yes, okay, yes," he said, clearly at the limit of his English language proficiency.

Quinn and Lana waited in the lobby with the nurse while her father collected the car. Finally, a banged-up, white, two-door Datsun pulled up at the front door. The father leaned across, opened the passenger door, and flipped the seat forward. As Quinn squeezed in back, a sharp spring jutting from a tear in the seat fabric dug into his thigh and ripped his trousers. This heap of junk made a good getaway vehicle, but he dreaded the prospect of a four-hour drive with his knees folded into his belly.

The nurse helped Lana into the passenger seat and stood in front of the hospital, waving, as they pulled away.

Once they were out of Eilat, Quinn stopped checking the road, satisfied the blue suits didn't know where he was. Lana's hand trembled as she brushed a few stray hairs from her face. Quinn could hardly believe she was sixteen; twelve seemed closer to the mark.

"Lana?" She turned in her seat. Hollow cheeks and dark rings under her huge brown eyes betrayed the stress she'd been under. She glanced at his face before her gaze shyly wandered to the side window.

"Do you know a man called Ghazi?" he asked.

She held his gaze for a moment and shook her head. The answer surprised him, but he sensed the girl was telling the truth.

He came at the problem from a different direction. "Lana, where is Adiba?"

"In Jerusalem. At home." She turned to her father and asked him a question. He answered with a few gruff grunts.

"Father says she is at home."

Quinn looked in the driving mirror, and Lana's father gave a shake of his head. Quinn acknowledged with a small nod.

Okay, he doesn't want to upset her any more. Adiba disappeared after Lana, so, if the girl hadn't seen her sister that ruled out his idea that Ghazi had used Lana as bait.

Quinn tried another tack. "When did you meet Nazar Eudon?" he asked.

"I don't know Nazar Eudon."

She didn't look at him, but he was sure she told the truth. Lana didn't know who Nazar was, but she had recognized his face.

"The man you saw on the TV, in the hospital. You became upset when you saw him, remember?"

Her eyes stretched wide and tears welled so quickly that Quinn immediately regretted asking, but he needed to understand if Nazar was involved with Adiba's abduction. Sisters abducted within a week of each other—even in the Middle East, surely that wasn't normal.

Lana spoke rapid-fire to her father. He barked back at her, the car swerved as his concentration wavered from the road. Quinn waited through their heated conversation, trying to gather what he could from tone of voice.

Finally, Lana turned again. "My father says you may not ask these things. It is not civilized for a man to speak of such matters with a girl."

Lana's father caught Quinn's eye in the driving mirror.

"No!" he barked.

"Please tell your father I'm sorry for offending you and him."

She spoke to her father, who continued to glare at Quinn, his face fixed and angry.

Quinn stewed for ten minutes, frustrated, but stymied. He couldn't mention Nazar again, and he couldn't figure out how Lana connected with Abdul and Ghazi. Maybe when they arrived in Jerusalem he'd have another chance. He got out his phone and powered it on, then pulled a piece of hotel notepaper from his wallet and punched in the number.

"Mr. Eudon's office."

"I'd like to speak to Mr. Eudon, please."

"Hello, Mr. Quinnborne, this is Keisha. What may I do for you?"

"Ah, you recognized my voice . . . do you have any news on Abdul or Adiba?"

"No, nothing," Keisha said.

When Quinn spoke his daughter's name, Lana's father started to talk loudly, in Arabic. Quinn put a finger in his ear to block the noise.

"I've moved from the Dan hotel. Please take a note of this number? It's my cell." He began to recite the number, but she cut him off.

"I have the number, detective. Thank you. Is there anything else?"

"No, just . . . call if you have any news about Abdul, and again I apologize for upsetting Mr. Eudon." Quinn hated groveling, but friends were scarce. He turned the phone off to save battery and shifted in the seat. His left leg had already gone to sleep.

25

When she finished speaking to Quinn, Keisha knocked on Nazar's cabin door. They were en route from New York to Phoenix. Nazar intended to meet the professor and learn first-hand about the problem with the virginbots.

"Come." He lounged on his bed, scrolling through the news on a tablet computer. The world was in chaos. Even the launch of his ethanol plant, the solution to the world's energy crisis, had been pushed off the front page by the G20 attack.

"I received a call from Inspector Quinnborne."

Nazar wrinkled his nose.

"He's still looking for Abdul and Adiba."

"Where is he?"

"He didn't say, but he's checked out of the Dan, so he may be leaving Eilat."

"Sit," he said and patted the bed.

She sat close and pressed a bare leg against Nazar's.

"Perhaps this brute can help in our dealings with the terrorists." Nazar absently stroked her naked thigh with the back of his hand. Keisha recognized the distant look in his eyes: he was planning, running scenarios, weighing options. Nazar was a brilliant man. She waited, watching her leader, her muse.

After two hours driving, cramped and hot, Lana delighted

Quinn when she asked for a bathroom break. They pulled into a gas station, and Quinn extracted himself from the car like a cork from a bottle. Stiff-legged with dark saddlebags of sweat soaked through his shirt's underarms, he limped to the restroom and cleaned grime from his face. With no A/C they'd been driving with windows open. He toweled off and switched on his phone. Keisha had left a message: "Mr. Quinnborne, I need to speak with you urgently."

He called back, and she picked up. "Mr. Quinnborne, thank you for returning my call. Please call me on a landline; your number may be compromised."

Quinn jerked the phone from his ear and held it at arm's length like a biting snake. He powered off and considered the trashcan. Never get rid of an asset unless you have to—advice learned from his father, good advice. He slipped the device into his pocket and headed for the blue payphone attached to the side of the gas station. At least they still had payphones in Israel. After three failed tries, he figured out what codes to enter and finally got connected.

Keisha answered. "Abdul contacted us," she said. "The terrorists intend to use him as a courier. They have stolen something of value to Mr. Eudon and wish to sell it back to him. Mr. Eudon wants you to act as our intermediary in the transaction. You would be compensated for your services. Perhaps you can help us and at the same time find Abdul."

"Where and when will the exchange happen?"

"We do not have specifics yet, but you need to be in Tel Aviv by tomorrow, July 23rd."

"I'll be there."

"Excellent. Please call me on a landline when you arrive."

Back on the road, Quinn spoke, through Lana, to her father and explained that he needed to get to Tel Aviv.

She translated her father's reply. "Father has to return the car to his brother-in-law, Hassan, in Jaffa, which is near Tel Aviv. You will be welcome to stay the night in Hassan's home, if you wish."

Quinn smiled. He couldn't imagine turning up on his brother-in-law's doorstep and expecting him to provide a bed for a stranger. "Thank your father for me." This killed two birds because a hotel would want his passport, and the Israeli police would love to be the first to find the missing English detective.

Hold on Abdul, I'm coming.

26

Late afternoon, Mountain Standard Time, Nazar Eudon's helicopter landed outside the prototype building in Arizona. Two days before, this had been the scene of great excitement as Nazar's team had demonstrated their extraordinary energy breakthrough.

This time, Mason Phillips, head of security, drove the golf cart. Mason escorted Nazar along a hallway and into a large open laboratory. The professor stood with three white-coated technicians in the center of the room. They stared at a plastic cube, murmuring in low nervous voices. The cube reminded Nazar of a popcorn machine.

"Mr. Eudon, welcome." The professor used the technique of speaking inside an exhalation of breath. It made the conversation strangely discontinuous, but Nazar preferred it to the damn stammering. The professor offered his hand, and Nazar glared at it as though it were a piece of dog shit. The three colleagues averted their eyes, and the academic turned bright red. He took a deep breath and spoke. "I decided to show you the problem rather than trying to explain."

"An excellent idea," Nazar said, his voice dripping with sarcasm.

The professor nodded to a short, plump woman who stood at the computer keyboard. After a few keystrokes, the computer monitor sprang to life.

Nazar studied the display:

Target –	C2H5OH (Ethanol)
Inhibitor –	C2H5OH*30% (Ethanol)
Feedstock –	Bio
Catalyst –	Photon
Activate –	00secs, 00mins, 00hrs, 00days, 00mnth
Terminate –	59secs, 59mins, 23hrs, 31days, 07mnth

The woman pointed to the screen. "This is the nanobot programming interface. Under normal operating procedures, we place a sample of virginbots into the induction chamber." She indicated a small glass vial at the center of the glove box. "Then we raise the temperature." When she depressed a key on the computer, four red strip lights came on, one inside each corner of the cube. "Once the temperature reaches twenty-one Celsius, we modify these parameters and imprint the constraints on the virginbots in the induction vessel. The imprinted cells are removed and grown to make larger quantities, clones of themselves with the same imprinted parameters, which go to the production facility."

"I understand. So what's the problem?" Nazar, relieved, wondered whether the professor's crisis was nothing of the sort. After all, scientists and businessmen had different ideas of what constituted a problem.

"David imprinted all of our virginbots the day he left. The problem lies here." The woman pointed to the last line on the screen. "This parameter dictates that the virginbots will stop converting feedstock on July 31st."

Nazar smiled. *These idiots!* "Why don't you put in a later date?" he said.

"We can't."

The statement hit him like a punch to the gut.

"I don't understand. If this is normal procedure, why not?"

The woman pressed the 'Tab' key. The cursor jumped to each field in turn, but then skipped past the last one.

"The Terminate field is not accessible," the woman said.

"How did this happen?"

Mason, the security chief, spoke. "The surveillance video from January tenth shows David removing one vial of virginbots from the containment vessel before placing the remaining stock into this device and modifying their programming."

One of the lab technicians spoke up. "The computer saves a log of every keystroke entered by an operator, a failsafe device so we can track an erroneous parameter. The log shows the date you see in the Terminate field being input by David."

Mason pointed at the date. "The video shows that David Baker made more key depressions than we have recorded on the log file."

"He entered additional data we have no record of?" Nazar said.

The professor spoke for the first time since he greeted Nazar. "Exactly."

Nazar studied the man. He had always been thin, but he had lost weight. His face was gaunt and pale, eyes bloodshot with purple rings beneath. Nazar thought he detected makeup.

"How is this possible?" Nazar still did not understand why these eggheads couldn't change the programming.

"David sabotaged the virginbots," Mason said. "He must have built a backdoor into the control program, enabling him to change and lock the final date sequence without the computer logging his keystrokes."

"Can't you patch the program? Change it back again?"

"That is only possible if we have the program's source code," Mason replied. "And we don't."

"You knew this at the opening ceremony. Why the fuck didn't you tell me?"

"We've been t . . . trying to f . . . f . . . fix the problem since we discovered it in January."

"And you didn't think it was important to share that information?"

His question was met with silence.

Finally, Mason spoke. "Put plainly, Mr. Eudon," the security chief said, "we don't know how he made the change and we can't reverse it. Our ability to generate nanobots, and consequently our ability to generate ethanol will cease at midnight on July 31st. We don't know why he picked that date."

Nazar turned away, heart racing, temper teetered on the verge of exploding. He spat out his words, encapsulating the disgust he harbored for these incompetent, overpaid idiots. "Dawud's religious fervor is well known to us, yes?"

"Yes, sir," Mason said.

Nazar spun and faced the group, fists clenched and face flushed with anger. Only Mason maintained eye contact; the others stared at the computer screen as if through pure willpower they could change the termination date. "July 31st is the end of Ramadan," Nazar spat out the words. "August 1st, Eid-al-Fitr, is the day all Muslims feast after a month of fasting. These nanobots won't be breaking their fast." He couldn't afford to unleash his fury on these scientists. Their lax protocols had placed in jeopardy two years of careful planning, his fortune, and his place in history. But if Abdul delivered new virginbots, he would need the professor and his staff.

Nazar stormed out of the lab. He needed fresh air.

27

Firman looked up from the blackjack table while the dealer shuffled the deck. Again he spotted the woman, walking away from him this time: hourglass body, backless, black dress, and a single-string pearl choker. He tracked her with his eyes, a hunter savoring his prey. At the restaurant's hostess station, across the gaming room floor from where he sat, she stopped to check the menu. The maitre d' oozed over her for a few seconds before she slipped out of sight into the restaurant.

"Monsieur?" The dealer waited for his bet. Firman, playing in the private area reserved for high rollers, pushed his pile toward her.

"Color me up please, Marcella."

She changed Firman's chips for thousand-dollar markers and signaled the pit boss. Who, full of self-importance in a stiff dinner jacket, sauntered over to check her count. "Sixteen thousand two hundred," the dealer said.

The pit boss glanced at the pile and nodded. "Thank you, Mr. Lechay. Is there anything else I can help you with?"

"I'd like to eat; could you check for a table?"

"Certainly, sir." The suit waved to a uniformed guard who was positioned at the entrance to the playing area to keep tourists away from the high rollers; Firman's table had a five-hundred-dollar minimum bet, and no maximum. The pit boss spoke in the guard's ear and he set off toward the restaurant. "Jose will seat you, Mr. Lechay. Have a wonderful evening."

Firman always came to Aruba after a job. However successful his assignment, he liked to lay low for a few weeks, check the news, in case the client broke any confidences and implicated him. The gambling was inconsequential; he played enough to be comped a suite.

Aruba had exceptional diving, warm weather, and clean beaches. An autonomous Dutch colony, if problems arose, a significant bribe could make extradition difficult, and the tiny island boasted direct flights to Europe, the US, and South America.

Jose, the maître d', came out of the restaurant and looked over. Firman read the man's nod, left the dealer two black chips, and went in search of the dress.

He spotted her sitting alone at a table for two. Instead of the place prepared for him, Firman pointed to a table that would allow him to observe her. She glanced in his direction—the way the staff fawned over him, he was difficult to miss. Dressed in chinos and a blue linen shirt, tailored to present his body well, Firman expected the woman to notice him. By the time two waiters had fussed him to his table, she was again staring out of the window.

He settled in, asked for a glass of Chablis, and followed her gaze. Below them, lights from the beachside bar made the breakers sparkle along the sand. A band played soft rock on the hotel's boardwalk, and a crowd had gathered ready for the nighttime party. Every night was party night in Aruba.

He ordered foie-gras followed by lobster. The waiter brought a small plate of amuse-bouche with his wine.

The woman seemed intent on the scene outside. She had a classic profile. Yes, classic described her well; she was constructed like a pre-Raphaelite work of art: dark auburn hair pulled back tightly and held by a subtle, silver comb at the bun; tanned, flawless skin and a strong Spanish nose; ample breasts filled out the dress and offered an attractive cleavage, and her ramrod-straight posture accentuated the curve of her waist as it melted into her hip. A tingle of anticipation passed through him—the chase could be as exciting as the conquest.

She turned and caught him staring. He smiled, and she held his eye for a fraction before signaling the waiter. Although she made a point of not looking over again, as she returned to her study of the beach, he noticed a sly smile on her lips.

Firman finished his meal by sipping and swirling a two-hundred-dollar brandy in an oversized snifter. The woman was ready for her check. Three further occurrences of eye contact during dinner led him to believe it might be an interesting night. She called the waiter, gave him her key card, and he waltzed off to close out her tab.

Then, for the first time, she looked directly at Firman. The effect startled him: her finely balanced features were dark, tempting, and sensuous; burned-chocolate eyes seemed filled with mischief, and her mouth hinted at a half-smile. The waiter returned with her key and broke the spell. She signed and stood.

Warmed by the brandy and the inviting last look, Firman drank her in as she walked toward him. A full woman, unlike those rake-thin New York models, her hips swayed as she stepped out: a magnificent specimen, curved and tight at the same time. She smiled openly now, and he was uncertain what she planned to do. As she reached his table, she brushed his arm with her left hand, and with her right, dropped her dinner receipt in his glass. The contact lasted under a second.

Firman could not have been more surprised if she had smacked him across the face and admonished him for staring. The floating receipt, unlike the plastic room key, had her room number printed at the top. After signaling for his bill, he fished out her invitation, and savored the last few drops of brandy.

Give her a few minutes—mustn't seem like a hasty teenager.

On the same floor as his, her room was a one-thousand-dollar-a-night executive suite: impressive. Firman strode past his door and rapped on hers, tingling with anticipation. A meticulous planner, he rarely experienced the unknown, and she intrigued him.

A few seconds passed, and then a brief shadow as she checked the spyhole. Opening the door wide, one hand on the frame and the other on the doorknob, she showed herself to him. The bathrobe she'd changed into yawned open, and her olive skin glowed against the fluffy white material. As her arms stretched around his neck, he received a tantalizing glimpse of dark nipples. She pulled him into the room, and kicked the door shut behind them.

He buried his face in her hair and breathed in her perfume: subtle, musky, but feminine. Inside the robe, his hands traced the curve of her waist and slid around to cup her butt cheeks: smooth, and taut. He felt a scratch on his neck, from her nail perhaps, then another, sharper this time, like an insect bite. His hand went up to swat away the pain.

Then he collapsed in a pile at her feet.

When Firman woke, he felt constrained, as though he had twisted in his sleep and gotten caught up in the sheets. Unable to untangle himself, he opened his eyes. He was in a travel-trailer, or RV. Curtains covered the windows. A canvas straitjacket encased his upper body, its sleeves attached to the bunk bed he lay on. Naked from the waist down, his legs were spread wide and strapped to rails that ran along the sides of the bed. He tested the bonds but couldn't move any limb more than an inch. To his right, a half-full saline bag dripped through an IV into a shunt in his groin. He was alone.

He shouted, so his captors would come. "Hey, let me up!" No point in delaying the inevitable; better to understand with whom he was dealing. A door opened behind him, and a tall, well-built man with a shaved head and a chiseled face—mid forties—moved into his range of vision and stood over him.

"Good morning, Mr. Lechay. I trust you slept well?"

"Sure, I had a wonderful night. Now what?"

The man smiled, a warm smile, the smile of someone in control and in no hurry. The man picked an eight-by-ten photograph off a small table to his right, turned it over and held it so Firman could see a blown-up image of himself, face and torso. Firman recognized the "Mind The Gap" T-shirt he had bought in London after the Oxford Circus transaction. He still had the shirt at home; a souvenir of what, until this moment, he had thought of as a perfectly executed job. The man, smiling, showed a second photo: Firman again, this time entering the lobby of the Ritz-Carlton hotel in Seoul holding Kimberly Stevens' hand; she had on her cute black dress.

"What's your point?" he said.

"May I call you, Firman, Mr. Lechay?"

"Knock yourself out."

The smile didn't change. Firman understood he was in deep

trouble with this man.

"Clearly," the man placed the photos back on the table, "you have been careless. However, I have no personal interest in your business. No vendetta inspires me to bring you to justice or have you punished for your crimes. What I need is information. If you furnish what I desire, I will have no qualms about releasing you. Although, I recommend you refrain from entering the USA, or Canada. Oh, or Britain. A shame to be limited, but that still leaves most of the world for you to enjoy. Wouldn't you agree?"

"What if I don't have this information?"

"But you do." The man nodded toward the IV stand. "You understand the options available to me to help you remember?"

"What do you need?" Firman owed allegiance to no one except himself. If he didn't give the information willingly, they'd use drugs or torture to take it. Although he had little faith in the man's promise to release him, in a zero-sum game, Firman saw no advantage in holding back—he was screwed no matter what he did. If he complied and made life easy for his captor, then some outside factor, something unknown to him, some subtle benefit might accrue if Firman were allowed to live.

"We want to contact your paymaster for these transactions."

"I'll give you everything I know, but first, take this contraption off me, and let me put on pants," Firman said.

"I'm sorry, that's not appropriate at this stage."

The man waited. Firman hadn't expected a positive response, but he had nothing to lose by asking, so why not? "Both transactions were initiated from the same source—Allah's Revenge, although the M.O. differed in each case. I had only one face-to-face meeting, before the first contract, where I received the weapon and instructions from a man named Ghazi." Firman waited to be sure this was what the man expected.

"Thank you, Firman. That information correlates. I need a location."

"Israel. He operated out of a medical facility in the West Bank. I met him and a technician named Dawud. The weapon for the second transaction was shipped to me in Seoul."

"How did you arrive at the location?"

"I drove: 245 Mozel Street. I used the rear goods entrance. Ghazi has an office halfway along the main hallway."

The man moved out of Firman's sight line. The door closed. He heard voices in the next room.

Firman took two deep breaths, tensed his muscles, and jerked his body from side to side, using every fiber of his being to tip over the bed. It didn't move, but the trailer began to rock; the bunk was secured to the floor. Next, he strained his legs, first left, then right, then together. He pushed so hard that he pissed himself. The straps didn't give an inch. The bars held, solid and unyielding. Focusing on his right arm, the stronger one, he pulled, trying to slide his hand up into the sleeve of the straitjacket to gain a purchase. When the cramping pain in his shoulder became unbearable, he was forced to quit. Never before had he been in this situation, been under someone else's control. He had been lax. Caught by the most ancient folly of man: he'd let his cock rule his head.

The door opened. The man came into view, accompanied by the woman from the restaurant, dressed in jeans and a roll-neck sweater. When she smiled at him—her face impassive and unfeeling—fear trickled down his back like ice water. She was a killer. She was like him.

The bald man spoke in his calm, measured voice. "Thank you, Firman. You have been most cooperative. Just one further question: how come the gas didn't affect you?"

"Ghazi supplied me with an inhaler. The weapon was airborne. I used the inhaler to coat my airways, and it made me immune."

The woman spoke, her voice flat and cold. "Fascinating. Mr. Lechay, I have to put you out while we move you. I apologize, but be assured, when the drug wears off you will have your pants on."

She glanced at his groin, and a smile flickered across her lips. A strange thought passed through Firman's mind: his penis would be tiny, flaccid and withdrawn, like a turtle hiding in its shell. Fear does that; the body instinctively protects the reproductive organs. The woman picked a small glass vial from the table. The smile remained on her lips as she used a hypodermic to transfer about twenty CCs of clear liquid into the plug at the top of his IV.

"What is that?" he asked.

"As I said, something to put you out while we move you, Mr. Lechay."

"It's not necessary, I'll—"

Damn, that was fast.

It was Firman's last thought.

28

When they arrived at Lana's home in Jerusalem, Quinn followed her and her father in. Ten people stood clustered in a living room no more than fifteen feet by twelve. Large, colorful cushions were scattered around the floor. A small, stooped woman in a black dress and *hijab* held Lana at arm's length. Tears poured down her face as she studied her bandaged daughter, and Lana shook with sobs. The other women surrounded mother and daughter with their hands held high, wailing and crying, their voices melded together, like a chorus of alley cats.

The men talked loudly and all at once, slapping backs and shaking hands. The emotions were palpable. These were good people, Quinn thought. Not so different from his father's family back in Ireland: hardworking blue-collars without much, but overflowing with love of family.

Once Lana had been touched and held by everyone in the room, her father called for silence and addressed the room. Quinn heard his name mentioned, and all eyes turned to him. He was the giant, Gulliver, in Lilliput. None of women weighed more than a hundred pounds, and Lana, at a couple of inches over five feet, stood tallest of the group. Quinn found himself stooping; although the headroom was probably seven feet, it seemed like he might bump the ceiling if he straightened. A dozen sets of eyes stared at him, heads nodding as they listened to the father's speech.

When the man finished, everyone rushed to Quinn. They surrounded him, and he didn't need to understand the words: they were thanking him, all at once. The intensity of their gratitude moved him. His eyes welled with tears as he shared their relief from the pain and worry they'd suffered over Lana, miraculously returned to them by this stranger from a distant land.

Quinn was anxious to get going, but he stayed for coffee served in tiny espresso cups, strong, gritty, and sweet. He welcomed the jolt. They sat on cushions or on the floor. Lana's mother offered him a large slice of honey-soaked cake. The family waited until he took the first bite. He nodded and smiled.

"Mmm. Delicious."

Lana's mother grinned, then everyone ate a small piece of the cake. He hadn't been eating regularly for the last couple of days, and the sweet cake hit the spot.

Finally, his need for action overrode his obligation to be polite, and he knelt beside Lana. "I'd like you to thank your family for their hospitality. Please tell your father I have to get to Tel Aviv now. Tell him I'm going to look for Adiba."

Lana stared hard at him. "Why is Adiba in Tel Aviv?" She turned to her father and barked something in Arabic. Her mother came across and tried to wrap her arms around her daughter, but Lana pushed her off and jumped to her feet. She screamed at Quinn. "Where is Adiba? What have you done with my sister?"

Before Quinn could respond, Lana's father gripped her by the shoulders and spoke firmly to her. Quinn watched the girl's expression melt from anger to fear. Finally, she wiped at her face and spoke to Quinn. "You must bring her back, Mr. Quinn. Bring back my Adiba."

"I'll try, Lana."

The girl nodded, once. In her mind a deal was made. Then she spoke to her father.

"Mr. Quinn, my father will take you to Tel Aviv now." Quinn stood, and she took his hand and shook formally. "Thank you for saving me."

Lana's father led the way, and Quinn climbed into the Datsun, relieved to be in the front seat this time. Lana's mother came out of the house, ran around the car to the passenger side, and handed Quinn a package wrapped in brown paper. She smiled at him, kissed her finger, and touched it to his forehead. He and Lana's father pulled away. Quinn opened the package and finished the honey cake before they reached Jerusalem's outskirts.

They drove for about an hour until they pulled up in front of a painted clapboard building, larger than Lana's home.

Maybe this was the moneyed side of the family.

Lana's father signaled for Quinn to remain in the car. He went to the door and knocked. The brother-in-law appeared, similar to Lana's father: short and stocky, with a dark beard and mustache. The two men talked for a few minutes. Quinn watched through the windshield until he was waved over.

Lana's uncle greeted him, "Mr. Quinn, on behalf of my family I want to thank you for saving Lana. I am Hassan. Welcome to my home. Please come in."

Relieved that the uncle spoke English, Quinn shook the man's hand and stepped through the front door directly into the living area. A low table sat in the center of the room: hand-carved wood, ornamented with beaten copper, and well used. His ex-wife had a similar piece; to her it was an ornament. A sofa and two beanbag chairs completed the furnishings. When his gaze landed on the white telephone sitting on a small table at the corner of the room, Quinn smiled. Perhaps his luck was changing.

Quinn pointed to the phone. "May I make a call?"

"Yes . . . yes, please." Hassan herded him to the phone and dragged a large cushion across the room. Quinn hadn't sat on a beanbag since he was a boy. He wondered whether he'd be able to get up again. He pulled Keisha's number from his pocket and plunked himself down, back against the wall. Hassan politely moved to the opposite side of the room and began a low-voiced conversation with his brother-in-law. He dialed, and she answered on the first ring.

"This is Keisha."

"It's Quinn. Do you have further information?"

"Are you on a cell phone, Detective?"

"No."

"Excellent. You will need to take notes."

29

The day after his phone call to Keisha, Abdul stood in the downstairs office of the medical center while Ghazi paced in front of him. Thirty minutes earlier, Abdul had left a tearful and frightened Adiba in her room. Finally, Ghazi stopped, leaned in so his face was close enough for Abdul to feel his breath and fixed him with a hard stare. "Complete this task and you have my word that you and the girl will go free."

Abdul didn't want to know about the alternative if he didn't complete the task. A sharp rap on the outer door signaled it was time. He slipped his arms through the straps of a small backpack that contained a bottle of water for him and a vacuum flask he must deliver to Nazar Eudon's representative.

Ghazi returned Abdul's passport and handed him a digital watch. "Remember Adiba," he said. "Allah be with you." He slapped Abdul on the back.

The man he and Adiba knew as Stinky opened the office door, and Abdul followed him to the car. Stinky dropped him in a bustling parking lot near downtown Jerusalem. Walking free among so many people seemed strange to Abdul; he'd grown accustomed to being a captive. Scanning the line of buses, engines idling, waited for passengers, he spotted one with 'Historic Jaffa Tour' marked on its front window.

The dozen passengers already seated on the bus watched him as he climbed the steps and stood next to the driver. His hand trembled as he handed over the ticket Ghazi had given him. The driver stared at him. Perhaps his face had been posted; the man seemed to recognize him. Abdul glanced behind, but the next passenger stood on the bus step, blocking his exit. The driver tore a piece off his ticket and returned the remainder to Abdul with a flyer, in English, detailing the trip.

"Shalom. Welcome aboard. Sit anywhere. We leave in twenty minutes."

Heart pounding, he selected a seat.

Abdul sighed with relief when the bus finally pulled out and no one had doubled-up with him in the seat. A two-hour conversation with an enthusiastic tourist would have been excruciating.

They approached the ancient town of Jaffa from the east. Not until they parked did Abdul notice the clear, blue Mediterranean shimmering five hundred feet below.

He and his fellow tourists gathered like day-old chicks around the tour guide, who held a bright-yellow umbrella above her head for them to follow. Abdul walked the first few hundred feet with the group. After they entered a cobblestoned pedestrian area, the guide began describing one of the many archeological digs going on in the city, and Abdul drifted away.

He pulled out the tourist map he'd received from the driver and located his destination—the Church of Saint George. Abdul checked the cheap watch Ghazi had given him. They'd arrived in Jaffa at 11:00 a.m. By 11:30 he must be kneeling in a pew on the left side of the church, and someone would exchange backpacks. It seemed simple enough.

He strode up the hill toward the main part of the town. Twenty yards ahead, on his right, two Israeli police officers leaned on a railing in front of the sandblasted exterior of an ancient church. They stopped talking and stared at him as he passed. Looking straight ahead, Abdul put one hand in his pocket, acting nonchalant.

Through his peripheral vision, he saw them peel away and follow. Behind, he heard the metal taps on the heels of their boots, as they gained on him.

They split, drew level either side of him, and matched his pace.

"Shalom," the officer on his left said.

"Hello," he answered in English.

"On vacation?" the other officer asked.

"Yes." His answer came out as a dry-throated croak. "Yes," he repeated, clearer this time.

"Where are you staying?" the first man asked.

They suspected something. Could they know who he was?

"The King David, in Jerusalem."

"Ah, beautiful."

He turned to the officer, tried to smile, but it froze on his face and probably looked weird.

"Where are you from?" the officer asked.

"London."

"Ah, fish and chips." The officers laughed. Abdul offered his grimace again.

"Enjoy Jaffa," the officer on his left said, and they veered off toward a side street.

With legs like two slithers of jelly, Abdul took deep breaths to slow his racing heart. After a twenty-count, he found the courage to glance behind. The policemen had gone. He pulled out a handkerchief and wiped his face.

According to the brochure, the church's principal attraction was a large fresco of Saint George slaying the dragon. Saint George's body reputedly lay in a mausoleum below the altar. Abdul reached the church with time to spare. He had no idea whether Ghazi had sent men to watch him, but he thought it likely.

Inside the church, a solitary woman knelt in the front pew on the right, head bowed and hands steepled in front. He heard her murmured prayers in the quiet of the church; could she be the contact? Two tourists stood at the front of the middle aisle, gawking at the huge, golden chandelier that dominated the center of the church. He slipped into a pew halfway along the left-hand side, pulled off the backpack, placed it on the seat, and knelt.

When he closed his eyes, morning prayers, gouged into his subconscious and unused for years, sprang to mind. Softly, under his breath, he spoke to Allah, asking His help. Never having prayed in a Christian church before, he wanted to blend in, so he mimicked the woman's pose, palms together, fingers pointing to the sky.

Ten minutes passed. The woman rose to leave. As she turned, she caught his eye and nodded; one believer to another—if she only knew.

Footsteps sounded behind; someone walking down his aisle. They stopped before passing him. Abdul's heart fluttered. He swallowed.

This was it.

The pew behind him creaked, and the edge of his seat touched his back as the newcomer's weight pressed on the kneeling board behind.

The hairs on his neck stood on end. At the corner of his eye, he saw a bulky backpack placed on his seat. In one smooth movement the same hand, a man's, lifted Abdul's pack. The pew creaked again, and shoes scuffed as the man rose and left. The footsteps receded.

"Do not speak to the courier. Do not look at the courier, or our agreement is void," Ghazi had warned.

The new backpack, unlike his, bulged and looked heavy. He lifted it off the bench—maybe twenty pounds. So that was how a million dollars felt. He checked his watch—11:35, and waited five more minutes before hefting the backpack onto both shoulders and leaving the church.

Now all he had to do was board the bus by two, return to the square in Jerusalem, and wait for Stinky to pick him up. Then he and Adiba would be free. Somehow, it seemed too easy.

He walked back through the renovated older part of Jaffa. The ancient stone buildings, sandblasted clean and gentrified by the Israelis, housed art galleries, bars, restaurants, and souvenir shops. He selected a café some distance from the marked tourist route, away from his fellow bus passengers who would be following their yellow umbrella and listening to the Israeli's revisionist history of this once great Arab city. At a corner table, he ordered a sandwich and coffee.

With the backpack firmly lodged under his seat, a million dollars between his legs, and his passport in his pocket, why not go to the police? Explain what was happening. They could follow him to the medical building. Storm the place. Capture Ghazi and set him and Adiba free.

Who was he fooling? The police would lock him up. Question him for hours. Make calls to check his story. He would miss the bus. Stinky would go back to Ghazi empty handed, and Adiba would die.

Shakily, he sipped his coffee and tried to read a six-month-old

Newsweek from the paper rack. But he couldn't concentrate on the articles. Their content seemed alien and insignificant to him. The focus of his existence had narrowed to two small rooms in a bombed-out medical center in Jerusalem, where the first woman he had ever loved waited for him to set her free. Would Ghazi be true to his word? Abdul had no option but to trust the man. Ghazi had Adiba, and so he held all the cards.

Time dragged. At 1:45 p.m., he was the first back to the bus. The door hissed when the driver opened it, and Abdul took the same seat he had used on the outward journey. Sitting in silence, sweat cooling on his forehead in the air conditioning, he sandwiched the backpack next to the window and waited. To his relief, everyone returned, and the bus departed on time.

When he alighted in Jerusalem, backpack firmly secured on both shoulders, he looked around for Stinky's vehicle. Panic took him: what if something went wrong on Ghazi's end, what if he wasn't picked up? Would that constitute a death sentence for Adiba? Alone, he could never find the medical building.

When he spotted the terrorist's black sedan parked across the square, his heart rate tripled. Actually happy to see the terrorist, he quickened his pace, opened the passenger door, slung the backpack into the empty back seat, and got in.

"You're early," Stinky said.

He pulled away, driving at a more sedate pace than Abdul had seen from him on previous rides. "Put on your seat belt," he barked.

Not for safety's sake, Abdul realized. The man didn't want to draw attention to the vehicle. A million dollars in a backpack would be difficult to explain. The drive to headquarters took thirty minutes.

While the driver opened the rear door and pulled out the backpack, Abdul waited. "Okay, come." He followed the man to the office. Stinky dumped the backpack on the desk in front of Ghazi, who opened the straps and pulled out a brick of hundred-dollar bills. For the first time, Ghazi smiled.

"You have done well, Abdul."

"Now fulfill your obligation," Abdul tried to speak with authority, although he was unsure whether Ghazi would indeed deliver.

"First, I need your passport for one more night. Tomorrow we will facilitate your release. Just one more night, Abdul-Haqq. I promise. We must make arrangements so Allah's Revenge will not be compromised."

Abdul handed over his passport. "Tomorrow, then. May I see Adiba now?"

"Go." Ghazi pointed to the stairwell door. Abdul walked up the stairs and into Adiba's unlocked room without a guard; a small difference, but one that increased his confidence that Ghazi would fulfill his end of the bargain.

30

As Quinn sat in Hassan's car and observed the medical building, he opened the wrapper of a Subway sandwich, bought that morning in Jaffa. He savored a large bite, the first food since breakfast, and it was 4:30 p.m. Hassan's Datsun, a piece of junk, made a perfect stakeout vehicle. His position, two blocks from the building, provided a clear view of the rear entrance Abdul had used when he returned from Jaffa.

When Quinn phoned Keisha from Hassan's home that morning, she had directed him to collect a backpack from a tourist information booth in Jaffa. A note in the side pocket described the exchange procedure and told him in which direction to walk away from the church. Not until he rounded a corner, three blocks from the church, did he understand how the transaction would be completed. Mufeed, Nazar's driver from Eilat, waited on the sidewalk next to Nazar's black Mercedes.

"Hello again, Mr. Quinn. Is that for me?"

Quinn handed the bag to the driver.

"Just a moment." Mufeed opened the trunk, lifted a false floor, placed the backpack inside, and grabbed a small parcel, which he handed to Quinn.

Once Mufeed left, Quinn checked the street—empty. The package was about an inch thick. He tore enough paper to see a bundle of hundred-dollar bills. After slipping the cash in his

175

pocket, Quinn returned to the corner and watched the church entrance. When Abdul came out, he followed.

It had taken all his willpower not to tap Abdul on the shoulder in the church. But he didn't know who might be watching, and Abdul was there under duress; at least so Quinn hoped. No wonder the authorities thought Abdul had joined Allah's Revenge. You'd have to know the boy to believe how naive he was and how much Adiba meant to him.

As darkness fell, Quinn settled down in the driver's seat, and prepared for a long, uncomfortable night.

Quinn wasn't the only one watching Allah's Revenge's headquarters. Two hundred miles above him, high-resolution cameras on a US-military fixed-orbit satellite focused on the medical building and beamed the pictures to Vandenberg Air Force Base. The location had been under surveillance since Firman had revealed the address two days earlier in Aruba.

31

The President of the United States arrived ten minutes late for the meeting. The chairman of the Joint Chiefs of Staff stood. They shook hands and exchanged pleasantries.

"What do you have for me, Frances?" The president gestured, and they sat side by side at a small conference table.

"The location of the terrorist group, Allah's Revenge."

"What about the weapon?"

"We have eyes on their HQ. Their leader, Abdul Ahmed is in the building. We believe the weapon is with him, sir."

"Excellent work. Can we retrieve it?"

The old soldier sighed, and spread his hands on the table. "The location is Jerusalem. Should we contact the Israelis?"

"Who owns the information?"

"We have sole ownership, sir." A hint of pride leaked into his voice.

"Can you execute an extraction?"

"We have the capability, sir." His voice was strong, certain.

"Well, Frances, sometimes it's better to apologize than to ask permission." The president stood and slapped the leader of his armed forces on the shoulder.

"Yes, sir."

The president, smile gone, looked down on the old soldier. "Make it fast. Make it clean. But secure that weapon."

"Understood, Mr. President."

They shook hands and the president left.

The old soldier pressed a speed dial on his Blackberry and gave the order.

32

Scott buzzed Rafiq up to his office, signaled for him to sit, and handed him a press release just received from the Israeli Government's press office.

"Today, The State of Israel will free a number of West Bank citizens who have been helping the Israeli authorities with their inquiries. This action is intended as a goodwill gesture, confirmation of Israel's desire to forge a deep and lasting peace with its Palestinian neighbors."

Rafiq finished reading and stared, open-mouthed at his boss.

"What do you think?" Scott asked.

"The Israelis must be under severe American pressure."

"Quite likely: the Yanks lost their VP in Seoul."

Rafiq scanned the release again. "Did they announce the prisoners' names?"

"No, but you can bet the farm they're on the list Allah's Revenge e-mailed to Abdul." Scott stalked back and forth in front of his window. He had a sickly feeling in the pit of his stomach. "Rafiq, this is one of the most difficult decisions I've ever faced."

Rafiq waited.

"If we don't call them on this, we're not doing our job, but if we create a stink we might be putting Abdul at risk. Well, more at risk than he already is."

Rafiq stood and joined Scott at the window. He laid a hand on his boss's shoulder. "You can't take this personally. If we don't cry foul, we'll be the only news outlet that doesn't. The shit is going to hit the fan no matter what. You won't put Abdul in more danger by following through."

"I hope you're right. This prisoner release represents a seismic shift in the world's power structure. Don't the Americans understand this will make things worse? The terrorists' next demand will be for more than the release of a bunch of thugs from prison. Why'd they give in?"

"Buying time?" Rafiq said.

Scott hadn't considered that angle. Perhaps this wasn't capitulation, but a ploy. "You may be right. In that case, they're hoping to get Ghazi before the next attack."

"Perhaps the Israelis have planted a mole in the prisoner group," Rafiq dropped his hand and stepped back a pace from his boss. "Any news from Quinn?"

Scott shook his head. "Nothing."

33

Keisha waited at the bottom of the airplane's steps for Mufeed to arrive. Even though Jaffa was a five-hour drive, Nazar had insisted she depart from Aqaba. He feared the Israelis would prevent her from taking off from Ben Gurion.

She wore a loose-fitting jumpsuit. With Nazar still in Arizona, there was no need to dress up. Mufeed arrived, slid the car alongside the plane, and lifted the backpack from the trunk. When he handed it to her, he held on for a second too long, so she yanked the bag from him. He flashed tobacco-stained teeth as he released the strap.

She unzipped the backpack and checked inside. The vacuum flask Nazar had told her to expect nestled in the bottom. Without speaking to the driver, she climbed the steps, feeling his eyes on her. The hairs on her arms prickled to attention; Mufeed gave her the creeps.

With one stop for refueling, Keisha flew directly to Arizona. She carried the bag on the helicopter. This being her first visit to the plant, the pilot described the scale of the project and the benefits to the local economy; what an amazing concept, to make gas from garbage. Keisha hadn't considered the technology before. Her focus was tightly centered on Nazar's needs. But she agreed with Samuel. Her muse was indeed a brilliant and powerful man.

When they reached the prototype building, Sam helped her

from the chopper. He averted his eyes from the tiny skirt she had changed into for her meeting with Nazar, and she appreciated his manners.

A woman wearing a white lab coat collected her in a golf cart. Inside the prototype building, they passed through a hallway to a laboratory. Nazar stood at the center of the room with three men.

She handed Nazar the backpack, and he passed it to the tallest of the group, Professor Farjohn, whom she recognized from publicity pictures. The man looked gaunt. His hand trembled as he pulled the thermos from the bag. The flask hissed when opened, and vapor misted out of the top.

One of the men extracted a thin glass tube from the flask and placed it into a receptacle in the center of a clear plastic box sitting on the table. He keyed into a computer. A pump came on, and red light filled the box.

Nobody spoke as they stared at the monitor. Their bodies blocked her view, so she moved around the semicircle of white coats and found a gap to peer through.

"Yes!" the professor exclaimed.

Keisha read the screen:

Target –	C2H5OH (Ethanol)
Inhibitor –	C2H5OH*30% (Ethanol)
Feedstock –	Bio
Catalyst –	Photon
Activate –	00secs, 00mins, 00hrs, 00days, 00mnth
Terminate –	59secs, 59mins, 23hrs, 14days, 08mnth

One of the scientists slapped the professor on the back. They were all grinning.

"The nanobots are extended until midnight, August fourteenth. We bought two weeks," Nazar said. "Well done, Keisha." He stroked her hair and she leaned into him. "You must return to Aqaba immediately. I expect further transactions."

Keisha didn't understand what had happened with the thermos, but she tingled with pride because she had pleased him.

Two weeks bought Nazar breathing space. Given time, he could negotiate a better deal. Worst-case scenario, a half-million dollars a week was manageable.

34

The sound of a vehicle passing at speed woke Quinn. An unmarked white van skidded into the service entrance of the medical building. The rear doors sprang open and six men, all in black, jumped out and flattened against the wall.

They wore night-vision goggles, and carried automatic weapons.

Quinn checked his wristwatch, 4:00 a.m., not a courtesy call; he shook water from his bottle onto a handkerchief and wiped his face.

One of the men went to the same door Abdul had gone through earlier. He seemed to try the handle, then ran back and took his place beside his team. A startling flash of light made Quinn turn away a fraction of a second before the explosion rattled his car window.

The men charged through the blown door. Quinn heard gunfire. Pulling his Glock, he chambered a shell then patted his pocket, checking for the spare magazine. He could only watch and wait; he was no match for what had smashed into the building.

Keep your head down, Abdul.

Commotion downstairs woke Abdul with a start. An explosion shook his bed, and he sprang to his feet. Ghazi's gruff voice barked orders. Abdul grabbed his clothes and rushed across the landing to Adiba's room. Since his return from Jaffa, the doors were no longer locked, although they were still prisoners. Adiba sat up in bed, eyes stretched wide.

"Get dressed," he said as he pulled on his jeans. She jumped out of bed in her bra and panties and snatched up her clothes. Theirs were the only rooms on this floor. Nowhere to hide, and he didn't dare go downstairs, so when they were dressed he sat on her cot and pulled her close. She shook so much her teeth chattered. "They're not here for us. Just sit tight." Abdul said. He hoped he was right.

By 4:03 a.m., a raging gunfight vibrated through the building. Adiba covered her ears. The noise was terrifying. Then, suddenly, it stopped. Abdul checked the time again: 4:05 a.m. Two minutes, it seemed longer.

When Adiba began to speak, Abdul put a hand over her mouth and signaled for silence with his finger to his lips. He crept to the door, and when he pressed his ear against the thin wood, he heard the stern voice of command.

"Dawson. Two wounded for extraction. You three, come with me."

Abdul was shocked. He'd expected Hebrew not American.

Then, in passable Arabic this time, the same man shouted, "Stand and show yourself!"

Some of Ghazi's people must be alive.

The American screamed, "Drop your weapon, now!" A moment's silence preceded another short burst of automatic weapons fire. Then silence again. Blood pounded in Abdul's ears.

A second American shouted, "Captain? Holy shit!"

An unnatural quiet descended for five beats of Abdul's racing heart before being pierced by a series of high-pitched shrieks that sounded hardly human. Adiba scurried across and pressed herself to his body. Her breath came in quick, shallow pants. He put his arm around her without lifting his ear from the door.

Abdul checked the time, 4:10. He whispered, "We should wait. We don't know who's still downstairs." Adiba nodded and squeezed his arm. He kissed her forehead and pulled her close. She tasted of salt. Silence enveloped the building. He checked his watch again. Time was standing still.

"Five minutes, let's give it five minutes," he whispered.

By 4:14, nothing had changed, and he began to breathe easier. Then he heard someone moving downstairs. Abdul's heart sank.

He had dared to hope the Americans had killed the terrorists, and he and Adiba would walk away from this terrible situation and go back to their lives.

Her eyes went wide. She heard it too.

Someone *was* downstairs.

"Abdul! Abdul!"

A man shouting; he thought he recognized the voice, but how?

"Abdul. Adiba!"

This time he was sure. "That's Quinn," he said.

"Quinn. How?" Adiba whispered.

"Dunno, but that's him all right."

Abdul opened the door, poked his head out.

"Quinn, is that you?" he shouted.

"Thank God. I thought you were dead for sure." Quinn charged up the stairs, three at a time.

Abdul and Adiba stepped onto the landing.

"You okay?" Quinn asked, and he spanned his long arms around the two of them and pulled them into a bear hug.

When he released them, the big man said, "Hi, Adiba. I'm Quinn. Come on. We need to move. Someone's bound to show after that racket."

They followed him downstairs. Abdul scanned the office: papers scattered everywhere, walls ripped apart where rapid-fire weapons had strafed them. Abdul couldn't believe guns created such havoc and destruction.

Abdul pointed to the large man spread-eagled over the side of his upturned metal desk, chest torn open and covered in blood; in his hand he held an aerosol can. "That's Ghazi."

Stinky slumped against a filing cabinet with part of his face missing and chunks of his flesh splattered over the filing cabinets behind him. The card players lay across each other on the ground, blood pooled around them. Two men in black combat gear, nigh-vision goggles still strapped to their faces, blocked the door leading to the hallway. Another, dressed the same, sprawled near the aerosol in Ghazi's outstretched hand.

"Come on, let's go." Quinn stepped over the dead soldiers and stood in the hallway, waving impatiently.

Abdul turned to follow, but he heard a noise. "Wait, what was that?"

"Come on, Abdul. No time."

"Listen." Abdul held up his hand for silence. The sound was familiar to him. Maybe that's why he had noticed, because his mind recognized the patterns, unmistakable to any Muslim.

Someone was saying morning prayers.

Abdul moved toward the open door at the rear of the office. He had never been through this way. Stepping around the dead soldiers, he stopped at the threshold of a large laboratory, one hundred feet square with dozens of equipment-covered worktables and computer stations. Five feet inside the room, another man in black combat gear knelt with his back to them. Abdul wasn't sure whether he was alive, but he didn't see any blood. He prodded the soldier's shoulder with his foot and shouted. "Oi!"

The man toppled, slowly, like a vase tumbling from a shelf. His body remained rigid, locked in the kneeling position. When he hit the ground his neck twisted around. Abdul stared but couldn't fathom what he saw. Where the soldier's face should have been was a mass of black foam. Abdul checked a second soldier, a few feet farther into the room and flat on his back. A black block of charcoal, bigger than a basketball, protruded from his flak jacket in place of his head. Two more of the invading soldiers lay dead beyond him with heads and faces distorted and disfigured by the same black compound.

A hand slammed onto Abdul's shoulder, and he jumped a mile.

"Come on. These soldiers will be missed. The Israelis have plenty more where they came from," Quinn said.

"I heard them talking, Quinn. They weren't Israeli. They were American," Abdul said.

"What? Well, whoever. Let's go." Quinn stared past Abdul at the four bodies and the black charcoal and muttered, "I've seen this movie before."

"What about him?" Abdul pointed across the room. Past a line of flip-charts covered in math symbols and diagrams. Past a glove box. Past a row of tables crammed with computer equipment. On the far side of the lab, one hundred feet from the door, a solitary figure knelt on a prayer mat with his back to them, bobbing up and down in supplication and singing in a low, rhythmic voice.

"It's a kid," Quinn said. He shouted. "Hey! Are you okay?" The child ignored him. "Fuck it. Let's get out of here."

"We can't leave him," Abdul said.

Quinn sighed and pushed past Abdul. "Come on then." He

jogged across the lab. Abdul followed.

Adiba appeared in the doorway behind them. "What's happening?"

Abdul shouted over his shoulder. "There's a child over here. We have to help him."

Adiba stayed where she was, staring at the fallen soldiers and their ravaged faces.

Quinn reached him first. He banged the boy on the back and shouted. "Hey! Kid!"

The kid jumped and turned to face them. But this was no child; he had a heavy beard and dark caterpillar eyebrows. Lost in his prayers, he'd apparently been unaware of their presence. Abdul spoke to the man in Arabic.

"The Israeli police will be here soon. We are going to get out before they arrive. You should come."

"*Allahu Akbar.*"

"*Allahu Akbar,*" Abdul replied.

"I am Dawud."

Quinn shouted. "Abdul. Now! Come on!" He shifted from one foot to the other, staring at the door.

David stood and rolled up his prayer mat.

"Tell your buddy to move his ass." Quinn grabbed Abdul by the shirt and dragged him across the room.

Abdul shouted to David. "We must hurry."

David slung a backpack over his shoulder and followed Quinn and Abdul. Adiba joined them at the door, and Quinn led them outside. The white van was parked with its engine running. Quinn checked inside—empty.

The Yanks were going to have some explaining to do.

They hurried to the Datsun.

"Uncle Hassan's car," Adiba said.

Abdul smiled. He had fond memories of the Datsun from their trip to Eilat.

"A piece of shit is what it is," Quinn said. "I hope the engine will pull four people. Come on. Climb in."

Abdul pushed Adiba into the backseat and squeezed in next to her. David rode shotgun. Quinn slammed the gas pedal to the floor and the car squealed in protest.

"I hope one of you knows the way to Hassan's from here." Quinn pulled onto a main road. At the first intersection, Adiba read the signs and directed him. The morning commute had begun, and Quinn merged with the workaday traffic—hiding in plain sight.

"Hey, you! Put your seat belt on." When David didn't respond, Quinn punched David's arm. "Abdul, tell him. I don't want any undue attention from the cops."

Abdul spoke in Arabic to David. When he didn't react, Abdul leaned in and whispered in his ear. "Dawud, put on your seat belt, please." David still didn't move.

"Nice job bringing that along," Quinn said.

"Quiet," Abdul said. He knelt on the floor and squeezed between the front seats, so he could look at David's face.

"Now what?"

"Please, Quinn, be quiet. I'll fix the belt." Abdul reached around and clipped the safety harness in place. He stayed on his knees, staring at David and listening.

"What's wrong with him?" Quinn asked.

"It's extraordinary. He's reciting passages from the Koran, whole passages. I don't think he can hear us. He's in a trance," Abdul said.

"Great, now we've got a Jesus freak on board."

"Wrong prophet, Quinn."

"Huh? Whatever."

Remaining between the front seats, Abdul turned to Quinn and laid a hand on the big man's shoulder. "I'm sorry I ran out on you at the hotel. Thanks for rescuing us."

"Sure, anytime," Quinn said. "I got you. Problem is I don't know what the hell to do next."

"Why don't we just go home?" Abdul said as he flopped back into the seat next to Adiba. She squeezed his arm and beamed at him.

Quinn laughed.

"What's so funny?"

"Shit, boy. They'd shoot you on sight. The world and its sister think you did the G20 attack," Quinn said.

"What?" Abdul asked.

"Oh, brother. I guess that solves the problem of what to talk about for the next hour." Quinn caught Abdul and Adiba up on the terrorist attack in Seoul.

"They think my Abdul did that?" Adiba said.

Abdul squeezed her hand. His heart skipped when she called

him 'my Abdul'. He liked how it sounded.

Quinn said, "You too, missy. According to the authorities, you two are the new Bonnie and Clyde. No one believes Abdul ran off to rescue you."

Adiba frowned. "But—"

"And they have me pegged as an accomplice. Seriously guys, I wouldn't believe us if I didn't know Abdul. At one stage, even I began to doubt."

Abdul checked Quinn's eyes in the rearview mirror. He was serious.

"Scott Shearer's the only friend we've got. But he's in London, and I can't call him on my cell because it's being traced. Anyway, I'm not sure even he can help; we're pretty deep in the shit pile. Excuse my language, Adiba."

Then David spoke. "Nazar Eudon will help you."

Abdul looked in astonishment at David. Firstly, because he had been listening, and Abdul had assumed he was off in another world. But more surprising, he spoke English with an American accent.

Quinn glanced at Abdul in the driver's mirror, eyebrows raised. Abdul shrugged.

"Come again?" Quinn said.

"I have something of great value to Nazar Eudon. He will take any risk to obtain it."

"Now you've deigned to talk to us, what's your part in this, David?" Quinn asked.

"I am following Allah's plan. I may not question the part I play."

"Well, I hope you've got a direct line upstairs, because we sure could use His help to get out of this mess."

"Have faith, Mr. Quinn. These events have divine purpose. Never try and second-guess Allah."

They arrived at Uncle Hassan's on the outskirts of Jaffa at 6:15 a.m. Quinn drove past the house and circled the block.

"You went past," Adiba said.

"Just making sure we're the only ones visiting your uncle. The police may be watching your family in case you show up."

Nothing seemed suspicious, so he pulled up in front. Automatically, he touched his Glock; it was snug in its holder inside his jacket.

"Let me go first," Quinn said.

Abdul watched the big man's back as he knocked. Quinn had risked a lot to find him and Adiba. He wished now he'd taken the policeman into his confidence when he'd received the note at the hotel. Could that really be less than two weeks ago? So much had happened. He squeezed Adiba's hand, and she responded. He gazed into her eyes. They were dark-brown pools. Her cheeks were flushed with excitement.

Yes. It had been worth it.

Quinn signaled them, and disappeared into the house. They followed.

Inside, Hassan grabbed Adiba and rocked and cried with her in his arms. He was chattering at her when something he said made her pull away.

"You found Lana?"

"Yes . . . yes. Mr. Quinn, he found her."

Abdul and Adiba turned to Quinn.

"What? It's not as if I rescued her from slave traders. I found her in a hospital."

"Is she all right?" Adiba asked.

Hassan said, "The young heal fast. She'll be okay in time."

"I must go to her," Adiba said.

Quinn looked at Abdul and gave a shake of the head.

Abdul took her hand. "Adiba, that's going to have to wait. Quinn thinks the police will be watching your home."

"But we haven't done anything bad. I was kidnapped; you came to rescue me. I don't understand. Why can't I go home?"

Hassan touched a hand to her cheek. "The police visited your parents. They say you are a terrorist."

"A terrorist!"

"Of course we didn't believe them, but I think Mr. Quinn is right. If they find you, it will not go well."

Tears rolled down her cheeks. Abdul wrapped his arm around her.

"Hassan, I need to make a phone call," Quinn said.

"Yes, of course." He pointed to the corner of the room. Quinn waved for David to follow.

"Time to find out whether you're right about Nazar Eudon, David."

"I am," he said, and smiled.

Quinn dialed Keisha's number.

"Ah, Mr. Quinn. Thank you for the excellent work in retrieving our property. I trust the payment was satisfactory?"

Quinn touched his jacket pocket. He'd forgotten the packet Mufeed had handed him in Jaffa.

"Does Eudon know a young man named David?"

There was a pause.

"David Baker is an employee of ours. Do you know where he is?"

"Is your last name Baker?" Quinn asked. David nodded. "He's with me, and he says he has something of value to Mr. Eudon. Does that make sense?"

"Perhaps."

"Okay, well it seems we have the basics for a trade. I'm in Jaffa with Abdul, Adiba and David Baker."

"I'm listening," she said.

"We very much want to leave Israel."

"And you say David has something for Mr. Eudon?"

Quinn nodded to David. "She wants to know what you've got."

David slipped his backpack off his shoulder, took out a vacuum flask, and held it for Quinn to see.

"He's got a thermos." Quinn felt stupid saying that.

She responded immediately. "Give me thirty minutes, then call back." And the line went dead.

"I'll be damned," Quinn said. "Come on, David, maybe Hassan can rustle up some food, I'm starving." Quinn put his arm around David's shoulders. The young man only came up to his chest. Quinn had no idea what was going on with the thermos, but with Eudon's money on their side, their odds improved.

Quinn waited an hour before calling Keisha back.

"We must get you to Aqaba," she said. "We can fly from there to Arizona. Will that satisfy you?"

"Yes." Their chances of getting out of this mess alive were better in the US than in Israel.

"Do you have a vehicle?"

"Yes, but it's old and unreliable."

"Time is of the essence, Mr. Quinn. Do you believe the car will travel one hundred miles?"

"Yes, should be fine."

"Very well. Please leave in the morning and drive south to Be'er

Sheva. There's a popular rest stop. You once called me from there."

"Okay, I know it."

"Be there by noon tomorrow. Wait in the café and Mufeed will fetch you."

35

They stayed the night at Hassan's home. The men slept on the floor, Adiba with her aunt. In the morning, the women made breakfast; bread and cheese, and Quinn, for one, was grateful. He'd been on a forced diet these last few days, his stomach always grumbling.

Keisha's phone call had reminded him of the money he got from Mufeed in Jaffa. Quinn turned his back on the room and pulled out the packet—a thick wad of crisp, hundred-dollar bills. He riffled the notes and slipped about fifty in his inside pocket. The rest he left in the package.

Quinn studied the three people for whom he was now responsible. A strange bunch: Adiba sat on the sofa, deep in conversation with her uncle, her brow wrinkled into a frown. He heard Lana's name used, Hassan was probably describing her sister's ordeal. Abdul leaned back on a brown beanbag, eyes closed. He'd lost weight; puppy fat no longer puffed his cheeks. Dark rings below his eyes illustrated the strain of little sleep and much worry. David, in a lotus position, straight-backed, rocking to-and-fro, lips moving as he mumbled his prayers.

"Okay, team." Quinn forced levity into his voice. "We're off on another road trip." The room fell silent. Adiba, Abdul and David stared at him like children forced to visit the dentist. The weight of responsibility pressed down. This was his fault. He should never have let Abdul run. He had to make it right.

"Hassan, I need to borrow your car one more time."

"Of course."

Quinn suspected the man would answer the same if he told him he wanted his house. Family ran deep with these people, and, in Hassan's mind, Quinn had saved both of his nieces.

"It's safer if I don't tell you where we're headed."

Hassan nodded.

The three fugitives stood beside Quinn, awaiting instructions.

"Let me check." Quinn opened the door and peered out. At one end of the street, a group of children played a game with sticks and a ball. "Clear. Move 'em out."

Abdul took Adiba's hand and pulled her along. After returning to her family, she was reluctant to leave. David followed, backpack slung over his shoulder. Quinn wondered whether he had the weapon in the flask. That would have to be faced—he didn't want to be responsible for another mass murder.

At the doorway, as the others climbed into the Datsun, Hassan gave Quinn a plastic carrier bag. "Some of my wife's cake and a flask of coffee for the journey, my friend."

His wife bowed deeply and spoke in broken English. "Much thanks for Lana, Mr. Quinnborne."

Quinn smiled and handed Hassan the packet of money he'd got from Mufeed. These people needed it more than he did. "Give this to your brother-in-law to help with Lana's medical bills."

Hassan took the package without questioning. With tears in his eyes, he nodded toward Adiba. "Look after her."

Quinn smiled. As he opened the driver's door, he pointed to the bundle in Hassan's hand. "If there's any of that left, you might want to consider a better car."

Hassan looked puzzled, and Quinn drove off, smiling to himself as he thought how Hassan would react when he counted out ten thousand dollars in cash.

He drove, stop-start, through busy Tel Aviv. Once they hit the freeway, traffic cleared and they made the speed limit.

Five miles out of the city, two police cars sped by on the opposite side of the four-lane. As they passed, they turned on their sirens. Quinn checked the rear-view mirror. The police vehicles crossed the median and started after them, lights flashing and sirens blaring.

"Shit, here we go, boys and girls," Quinn said.

No use trying to outrun them in the Datsun, so Quinn slowed and eased to the edge of the road. The police reached them in thirty seconds.

Adiba tapped his shoulder. "What will we do, Mr. Quinn?"

"Let me do the talking," he said. As soon as the words left his lips, he realized how ridiculous that was; he didn't even speak Hebrew.

The police tore past and roared down the freeway. Quinn's heart was racing, but at least he knew they weren't looking for the Datsun. A glance in the mirror showed Abdul and Adiba glued together in the back seat—Abdul, face pale and strained, and Adiba, wide-eyed like a trapped animal. David rocked and muttered as usual; Quinn wondered whether he'd even noticed the incident. Maybe there was something to this religion stuff after all.

For the next ten minutes, Quinn struggled with how to broach the subject of the weapon. Finally, he decided head-on was best. "David," Quinn said. "The soldiers who died at the door of your lab, what killed them?"

"Imam Ghazi sprayed them with the nanoweapon."

Quinn remembered seeing an aerosol in the dead terrorist's hand.

"The stuff he sprayed on them, was that used on the London Tube train and in Seoul?" When David didn't answer, Quinn glanced across, but he hadn't started mumbling again. He appeared to be considering the question.

"Mr. Quinn, I do not know Imam Ghazi's plans. My allegiance is to Allah. Allah spoke to me. He told me to help Imam Ghazi."

"So you don't care about all the innocent people Allah's Revenge has killed?"

"In Allah's plan, our time on Earth is but a precursor to our lives after, with Him."

"Whatever. So, is the same stuff in your flask?"

"In the flask, I have virginbots. They may be used to create or to destroy."

Quinn took a deep breath; the kid spoke in riddles. "So how is Nazar Eudon connected to Allah's Revenge?"

"He never could be. Nazar worships money, not Allah. He keeps a harlot. He is not pure of heart."

"So why does he want the flask so badly?"

"Nazar uses the virginbots to create money."

"Abdul, you understanding any of this?" Quinn asked.

"Do the virginbots have something to do with Eudon Alternative Energy?" Abdul asked.

"He programs them to create ethanol," David said.

"So what's in the flask can't kill people, like at the medical center?" Quinn asked.

"The virginbots are inert; programming dictates their actions."

"Holy shit," Abdul said.

"Well, I'm sure glad you understand this, Abdul. How about helping a poor, dumb policeman?"

"The virginbots are building-blocks. Ghazi used them to create a weapon. Eudon programs them to create ethanol."

"So, without what's in the flask, his billion-dollar refinery in the desert is useless?" Quinn asked.

"Useless," David echoed.

"Okay, we have a serious leverage," Quinn said. He rubbed his forehead trying to make his brow relax.

They arrived at the service station, the one Quinn had stopped at on his way to Jaffa three days earlier with Lana and her father.

"Go ahead and eat. I'll fill the tank so Hassan won't be stuck when he collects the car. I'll meet you inside."

David held his seat forward while Abdul and Adiba squeezed out of the back. When David grabbed his backpack, Quinn held the strap. "Why not let me take care of that?"

Without hesitation, David released the bag and followed the others.

Quinn shouted after them. "Hey, Abdul, order me a double cheeseburger, large fries, large coke ... and Texas toast. I'm buying." Who knew when he'd get the next meal?

Quinn gassed up the Datsun then parked in the center of the lot. Somehow, he'd contact Hassan and tell him where to find the vehicle. In the restaurant, he handed David his backpack, and tore into his cheeseburger. They didn't understand Texas toast in Israel, so he closed out with a slab of honey cake; he saved the piece from Hassan's wife—homemade was always better.

"Not as good as your mom's," he said to Adiba with his mouth full of the sticky dessert.

Before they'd finished their coffees, the Mercedes rolled into the parking lot. Mufeed got out and stood beside his vehicle. Quinn paid, and they headed for the car.

"Hi, Mufeed. Got room for four more?"

"Please, get in, hurry." Mufeed's eyes kept darting toward a parked police cruiser.

They drove for two hours, following signs for the Jordanian border. Closer to Eilat, they passed through small towns, then they hit a stretch of road bordered on either side by desert, no houses and few vehicles.

Mufeed pulled over. "I have to smuggle you over the border," he said.

Quinn wondered how.

"I'm sorry. It will be uncomfortable. Come."

Mufeed got out. When they followed, Quinn caught the driver staring at David's backpack. It put him on alert. Mufeed popped the trunk, dragged out two heavy suitcases, and pulled a lever. The back seat slid forward, and a false floor lifted to reveal a large empty cavity.

"You must climb in here."

The space didn't appear big enough.

"Quickly."

"You're biggest, Quinn. Climb in, and we'll position around you," Abdul said.

Quinn squeezed in, his back pressed against the passenger side. The storage area was deeper than he expected. The rear seats of the car had been hollowed out to make more space.

Mufeed's taken people over the border before. The thought gave Quinn some confidence, and at the same time sounded alarm bells.

David climbed in with his backpack and curled his body so Quinn spooned him, then Abdul and Adiba joined them—sardines in a can. Mufeed closed the lid. A light came on, and Quinn heard a hiss of gas.

Oxygen, quite a setup.

The car set off. He felt every bump, and even with the pumped air, the confined space became stuffy.

The car stopped.

Must be the Israeli border. Quinn started counting out time.

None of them spoke, but Quinn could hear the tension in their breathing. The car remained stationary for a count of one-hundred-eighty then stopping again.

Jordanian border.

A metallic click above them, then voices; Quinn knew by their tone that the border guard was asking Mufeed questions.

They must be checking the trunk.

Heart pounding, Quinn tried not to focus on what would happen if they were caught sneaking a weapon of mass destruction into Jordan.

Two more clicks preceded the noise of something being moved on the partition above their heads.

They're opening the suitcases.

Quinn recognized Mufeed's voice, then a loud bang, and a firm thump as the trunk lock engaged. Sweat ran down his chest. Adiba stifled a sob. Abdul shushed her gently.

As they pulled away, he stopped counting—seven minutes to clear the Jordanian border. It had seemed longer.

They drove on. The Mercedes took sharp turns. Quinn visualized the route out of Aqaba as the road climbed the hills to Nazar's home. The car stopped again, and Mufeed opened the partition. Daylight dazzled Quinn's eyes.

"Quickly, get in the car."

Mufeed had pulled over on a quiet stretch of road. Adiba was upset, sobbing and muttering. Abdul wiped her tears with his handkerchief and whispered into her ear. Quinn didn't know what was said, but he understood her fear: she'd just spent thirty frightening minutes trapped in a trunk.

Unlike on his previous visit, the security guard waved them straight through the open gates to Nazar's home: they were expected. When the car pulled up to the house, Keisha waited for them, dressed in a black jumpsuit, sloppy and asexual compared with the last time he'd seen her. He still remembered following those legs up the stairs.

"Welcome. I hope the journey wasn't too terrible for you. You are safe now. Please come in. Let me show you to your rooms; I'm sure you want to freshen up." They followed her into the main hallway. "David, you're in the downstairs guest room. Mufeed will take you."

David, stooped and tiny, backpack hooked over his shoulders, followed the driver. Keisha led the rest of them upstairs. Adiba and

Abdul were shown to separate rooms. She put Quinn in the room next to Abdul's.

After he dropped Hassan's plastic carrier bag on his bed, Quinn went along the hall and knocked on Abdul's door. Abdul didn't answer; instead, he poked his head out from Adiba's room and waved Quinn over. Adiba was slumped in a chair, her body wracked with deep sobs.

"What's wrong?"

Abdul handed him a crumpled photograph. He recognized Adiba, Lana and two young boys, bracketed by Adiba's parents.

"She found it in the trunk of the Mercedes. It's Lana's," Abdul said.

"Son of a bitch."

He recalled Lana's reaction when she saw Nazar on the TV at the hospital—no wonder. He must have snatched her then smuggled her across the border.

"She blames herself," Abdul said.

"Don't be silly, Adiba. This has nothing to do with you."

"When I came here with Abdul, Nazar asked me her name; I showed him the picture; we each have one." Her voice cracked and she began to sob again.

Abdul raked his fingers through his hair and gave Quinn a look that said—she's right. "When we visited, Nazar did show a lot of interest in Lana. He even asked where she went to school."

Quinn stood over Adiba and placed a hand on her shoulder. This made a terrible situation worse. "Adiba," he said.

She looked up at him, eyes brimming with tears. Quinn struggled to keep the fury out of his voice. The thought of Nazar hurting Lana, that frail little girl he'd seen in the hospital, pushed him to the limit. "This isn't your fault. The guy's a fuckin' creep."

But right now, every gun-toting law-enforcer had him, Abdul, and Adiba in their sights. They were marked: the Israelis, the British, and the Americans believed the easiest way to stop Allah's Revenge was to kill the three of them. Nazar Eudon offered a way out of Jordan, their only way. In the US, given some breathing space, he could maybe get their death sentence lifted. Although even with Nazar's help, it was a long shot. Without him . . . "Listen, guys, we need Nazar," Quinn said.

Abdul snapped, "After what he did to Lana!"

"He's a despicable pig, and I want to hurt him just as much as you two, but we're stuck in his house, and we've entered Jordan illegally. The only reason we aren't already dead is because we have David and his magic flask. We need Nazar's plane to get out of here. If we clear our names, then we can focus on getting Nazar Eudon what he deserves. But right now, he's our only option."

His speech was met with silence.

At the end of the hallway, in Nazar's bedroom, Keisha studied the TV monitors and listened to their conversation. Nazar had given her explicit instructions. "Bring David and the flask. Lose the others if you can. If not, bring all four, and I'll deal with Quinnborne, Abdul and Adiba when you arrive."

This development regarding Lana further complicated the situation and made it more important that she leave Quinnborne behind.

When Keisha was Lana's age, Nazar had found her sexually attractive. She had feared him at first, but once she understood how excited she could make him, she looked forward to playing his rough games. That he no longer desired her did hurt, but she had adapted to her role: helping him, supporting him. These fools couldn't possibly understand his needs. They couldn't comprehend his greatness, his power and intelligence. He needed her now. The policeman posed a threat, and she would protect Nazar any way she could.

That evening, Keisha laid out a generous buffet. They ate. Then, fatigued, everyone elected for an early night. She told them they would fly to Arizona the next morning.

Later, she watched on the CCTV in Nazar's room as Abdul, Adiba and Quinn prepared for bed. Once they settled, she called Mufeed. "Get the car. Meet me out front."

Keisha crept past the guest rooms and down the stairs, still in her scruffy black jumpsuit to avoid upsetting David. He had been uncomfortable with her attire on the trip to Jeddah. She tapped on his door and went in without waiting. Kneeling on his prayer mat with his back to her, David rocked and reciting evening prayers. The backpack lay on the bed.

She lifted the flap and peeked inside. The flask was there.

She moved closer to David and spoke softly to him. When he didn't hear her, she shook his shoulder, and he gave a start.

"David, we must take the flask to Mr. Eudon now."

"Allah's will be done." He stood, collected his backpack, and followed her out of the room without asking for the others. She loaded him into the rear of the car and sat up front to save him the embarrassment of sitting next to her in the dark back seat. They drove for twenty minutes in silence. David's lips moved constantly. Airport security waved them through. No one in Aqaba would challenge Nazar's car.

Once David was on the plane, she decided to secure the flask.

"David. May I have the virginbots?"

"I don't have them."

He did. She had checked his bag in the room.

"David, give me the flask."

He reached in his backpack and passed it to her.

"That's better. Why did you say no?"

"You asked for the virginbots. They are not in the flask."

Keisha staggered back as though punched in the chest.

She had failed Nazar.

36

Quinn stood in the doorway of Abdul's room. "Abdul . . . Abdul, wake up."

Abdul turned on the reading light. "What? What's the time?"

"A little after midnight."

He rubbed his eyes. "What the hell?"

"I need your help." Quinn signaled for him to come.

"What's going on?"

"Keisha's taken David."

Abdul sat bolt upright. "How . . . Shit. We're fried."

"No, I don't think so. She'll be back, but I have to make a phone call first."

In his jockeys, Abdul joined Quinn in the hallway. "I thought David and the virginbots were our leverage?"

"I have the flask." Quinn held up the small thermos.

"What about David?"

"He's got Hassan's coffee. I switched flasks at the service station."

"Huh . . . okay, what do you need?"

Quinn pointed to the window at the end of their hallway. "Call me when she returns. I'm going to try the phone in the far bedroom, that's where she came from."

He ran down the hallway. When he entered Nazar's room, his eyes locked on the screens displaying the camera feeds from their bedrooms.

Damn. He hadn't anticipated that. The desk phone had a dial tone. Direct line, nice. He dialed Scott Shearer's home number. Come on, Scott. Be your usual boring self. Be in.

A sleepy voice answered. "Hello?"

"Scott?"

"Quinn! Where the hell are you? Where's Abdul?"

"He's with me, so is Adiba."

"Thank god!"

"Scott, I don't have long. I'm in a jam. Turn on your recorder." Quinn delivered a potted history of the past few days, but didn't tell him where they were or where they were headed. If the authorities had qualms before, once they knew he had the weapon he felt sure they'd shoot first and talk later.

"I need a way to convince the world we're not part of Allah's Revenge. I have the weapon. I'll deliver it in exchange for a safe exit from this screw-up—"

Abdul appeared at the bedroom door. "She's back."

"Scott, I gotta go. Do what you can. I'll call tomorrow with a location for the exchange." He hung up, ran to Abdul, and pushed him along the hallway. "Get back in bed. She mustn't know we've been up." They dashed down the hallway and into their rooms before the front door opened.

Keisha pounded up the stairs and opened Quinn's bedroom door. "Quinnborne, wake up!"

Quinn pulled the covers off his face. "Is it time to go?"

Keisha turned on the light with her left hand. With her right, she leveled a nickel-plated Colt revolver at Quinn's head. "Where is the flask?"

Her hand trembled, but from this range, she wasn't likely to miss. "It's not polite to point a gun at a man in his bed."

Her voice shook. "I will fire if you don't tell me." She seemed angry enough to spit nails.

In a calm, level voice, he said, "Okay, I'm going to show you. Don't do anything hasty."

Quinn slid his hands from under the covers. He held the Glock, its barrel aimed point-blank at the center of the thermos. The flask meant more to her than anything—he hoped.

"What's more important, Keisha? Killing me, or taking the thermos to Nazar?"

He waited for the logic to sink in and tried to slow his pounding heart.

She lowered the gun. "Very well."

"Once we're in America the flask is yours, but until then it's our ticket to ride. So when do we leave?"

"The plane's ready. David's already onboard. I'll wait downstairs for you and your friends."

Abdul was dressed when Quinn knocked on his room door. They went together and woke Adiba. Once she was ready, Quinn sat them both down on the bed. "Our rooms were monitored. Keisha probably listened while we spoke about Lana."

"Good. She is a woman. Now she will hate Nazar too," Adiba said.

"You'd think so," Quinn said, "or maybe it gives her more incentive to protect him. Let's not count on her, okay?" Abdul nodded, but Adiba looked confused.

Keisha drove the Mercedes. Mufeed had remained at the airport with David. She led them up the steps to the plane. Quinn walked behind her, while Abdul clutched the plastic carrier bag with the flask. The plane pulled away as soon as the cabin door shut.

Abdul glared at David. "Why didn't you tell us you were leaving?"

"Allah did not command me to."

"After Quinn saved your neck in Jerusalem, don't you think you owed him at least a warning?"

"Since the Hajj, I have given myself to Allah completely. It was His wish for me to help Imam Ghazi in Jerusalem, and He, not Mr. Quinn, chose to spare me while Ghazi perished. Allah directed me to go with the woman tonight, but His divine intervention caused Quinn to exchange the flasks, which is why you are here now, Abdul."

"You knew about the switch?" Abdul said.

Face calm and sure, David, "The flasks look quite different."

"And you didn't say anything?" Abdul sat next to David. "You think everything in life is predestined. That we're all puppets acting out the master plan of some divine being. What about free will?"

"We have free will. We can choose to live according to Allah's rules, or not. Abdul, before my Hajj, I was unhappy, anxious, and uncertain—like you. But now, while I follow His teachings, I have no worries. Through the words of the Koran, Allah steers my choices. This is the best path, a path of peace, purpose, and fulfillment. For me, it has been a wonderful awakening."

"What are you going to do when we see Nazar?" Abdul asked.

"I will do what Allah guides me to do." A brilliant smile lighted David's face and transformed his countenance. Abdul didn't remember seeing the man smile before.

"But what about the innocent people who died in London, and in Seoul, and the soldiers back at the lab? And what about their families, grieving for their lost loved ones?"

"If they lived their lives according to the teachings of the Koran, then I rejoice for them—they are with Allah in heaven. If they were unbelievers, then their lives were worthless anyway."

Abdul didn't know how to respond. It could be argued that a religious zealot like David couldn't be blamed for the murders; as with a psychopath, he was disconnected from reality. Within his distorted frame of reference, he'd done nothing wrong. Worse still, he believed he was doing good, doing God's will.

Abdul wanted to understand more about the nanobots. The knowledge might prove useful to Quinn when they reached Arizona. "David, how can the virginbots be a weapon for Ghazi and a fuel for Nazar?"

David's face brightened. For twenty minutes, he presented his technology to Abdul; animated and engaged, he seemed like a different person. Although the concepts were outside of Abdul's sphere of knowledge, David explained them at a level he could comprehend. By the time David finished and fell silent, Abdul understood the basic tenets of the nanobots and how programming dictated their actions. He also realized that he was in the presence of a brilliant mind.

"Thank you, David. I appreciate you taking the time to share your work."

David inclined his head a little to the side. "Would you like to pray with me, Abdul?" The question took Abdul by surprise.

David rose and moved to the front of the cabin. He rolled out his mat. Abdul yearned to join him. To relieve the stress and allow his mind to melt into the soft rhythm of prayer. As if on autopilot, Abdul followed and knelt beside David. They prayed for fifteen minutes. When they were finished David beamed at Abdul.

"*Allahu Akbar*," he said.

"*Allahu Akbar*," Abdul replied. He felt calmer than he had for days, and more conflicted than at any time in his life.

37

Nazar's jet arrived at Phoenix airport late in the morning. Quinn peered out the window as they taxied, checking for any kind of welcoming committee. A Jeep pulled alongside. The driver pushed a set of steps to the side of the fuselage, and climbed to the front of the plane. Quinn cracked open the cabin door and watched Keisha. She'd told him an arrangement had been made with the ground crew to get them through without passport checks. Keisha handed over a thick envelope, which disappeared into the driver's inside pocket.

Abdul stood behind Quinn with one arm wrapped around Adiba. His free hand held the plastic carrier with the flask. David sat calmly in his seat.

"Welcome back, Miss Keisha." The man from the Jeep spoke with a soft Southern accent, but when he keyed his two-way radio, the hairs on Quinn's neck bristled. The driver flirted with Keisha, who had changed into a tiny red skirt and a tight, revealing top. She coyly covered her mouth with one hand and laughed at his patter. A few minutes passed before a second Jeep arrived and collected the driver, leaving them with a vehicle.

Quinn opened the cabin door. "Let's go."

Keisha drove them across the concrete apron to the heliport.

Quinn considered his options. He could shoot her, take the Jeep, drive to the terminal, and surrender. But he was public enemy number three. His travelling companions were numbers one and two, and, if Scott had done his job, the authorities would know he had a WMD. He didn't recall much conversation happening when SEAL Team 6 met Osama bin Laden. No, too many unknowns. He needed to speak to Scott first. Learn the lay of the land. For now, they were safer with Eudon's people; *they* didn't see the flask as a weapon.

They abandoned the Jeep and walked, heads bowed, to a waiting helicopter, rotors already spinning. The pilot was a large black man. Quinn gauged his threat potential. He didn't seem hostile.

The cockpit was cramped. Quinn sat next to David. Abdul and Adiba took the seat behind. Keisha rode shotgun. She passed a set of cans to Quinn, and he monitored Keisha and the pilot's small talk.

Quinn needed a plan, but he didn't know where to start. He trusted Scott, but couldn't risk calling him on the cell phone and giving away their location. Once they reached the plant, he might get access to a landline. With so many unknowns, he'd have to wing it. Perhaps David was right. Perhaps Allah *was* managing the show.

As they approached the refinery, Quinn spoke into his mic. "Is that all Nazar's?"

"Amazing, eh?" the pilot said. "I'm Sam, by the way. I often fly out here, shocks the heck out of me every trip."

They landed on a concrete pad near a domed building.

Two golf buggies came toward them, each driven by a man in a green-and-gold uniform—security, Quinn assumed. He took the bag containing the flask from Abdul, and they rode the carts to the building. Quinn let Keisha climb out of the cart first and whispered to David.

"Stay close to me. Think of it as Allah's will."

David smiled. "You are a good man, Mr. Quinn, but you are an unbeliever. You can never know the will of Allah."

"But whatever I do is Allah's will anyway, right?" David frustrated him, but he had no way to influence him. Heck, he hardly knew the man. He followed Keisha and kept a tight grip on David's arm. When they arrived at the open door to the building, he stalled so Abdul and Adiba could catch up. They walked in together with the two security guards behind them.

Keisha led them down a hallway and through a door into a laboratory. Fifty feet away, at the center of the lab, four men and two women in lab coats stood in front of a couple tables holding computer equipment and a glove box. Nazar Eudon stood to the right of the group. Quinn turned to Adiba and spoke softly, but loud enough so Abdul would hear.

"I understand how you two feel, but don't do anything about Eudon until I've figured a way out of here." He glanced behind. The two guards stood at the door. Quinn scanned the room for another exit. There wasn't one. They moved across the lab and stopped in front of the glove box. Keisha stood close to Nazar. He stroked her hair as though she were a favorite pet.

"David," Nazar said, a broad smile on his face, "I'm happy to see you again; also Abdul and Adiba. I am delighted you escaped captivity, with your assistance no doubt, Detective Chief Inspector. Thank you. I'm pleased my two young friends are unharmed." Adiba glared at Nazar. Abdul kept a firm grip on her shoulder.

A tall, nervous-looking man in John Lennon spectacles spoke. "David, d . . . d . . . do you have the virginbots?"

"Hello, professor," David said, "Mr. Quinn has them."

All eyes moved to Quinn's face, then down to the plastic carrier in his right hand.

"Mr. Eudon," Quinn said, "my friends and I have some immigration problems to resolve. I would appreciate your help."

Nazar grinned. "Mr. Quinn, if that bag contains what I hope it does, I will help you and my two friends any way I can. But first, we must examine the goods."

The smile stayed, and Quinn saw the steel behind Nazar's eyes. He didn't have much choice. Ironically, they were safer with Eudon than they would be with the authorities, and at least *he* didn't want to murder people with the nanobots. He handed over the carrier. The professor's hand shook as he placed the flask inside the glove box and closed the door.

The professor pushed his hands in the sleeves and used gloves to open the thermos. Wisps of vapor escaped the top. He pulled out a glass tube and put the flask to one side. He positioned the tube in a holder at the center of the box. One of the techs punched some keys on the computer keyboard, and the box flooded with red light.

While everyone focused on the glove box, Quinn scanned the

room again; definitely only one exit, where the guards stood. All the white-coats and Nazar stared at the monitor. David stood back, lips moving in prayer, eyes squeezed shut.

Nazar spun around and glared at David. "Is this a joke? These nanobots are the same as the ones you left here. They have less than a week of life!"

Quinn checked the display, trying to understand the problem:

Target —	C_2H_5OH (Ethanol)
Inhibitor —	$C_2H_5OH*30\%$ (Ethanol)
Feedstock —	Bio
Catalyst —	Photon
Activate —	00secs, 00mins, 00hrs, 00days, 00mnth
Terminate —	59secs, 59mins, 23hrs, 31days, 07mnth

The data didn't mean a damn thing to him, but Nazar was pissed.

David said, "I can reset the parameter."

"You b . . . b . . . built a backdoor, didn't you?"

David smiled at the professor, and he smiled back. The man obviously admired whatever David had done. The group opened a space. Before David stepped forward, he turned to face Abdul and Adiba.

"*Allahu Akbar,*" David said.

"*Allahu Akbar,*" Adiba and Abdul replied simultaneously.

Quinn studied David as he nodded to Abdul and smiled at Adiba. He recognized the expression on David's face.

He'd seen that expression before.

As a police officer, more than once, his life had depended on recognizing that expression.

David had made a decision.

The professor stepped away from the computer keyboard, allowing David access. The technicians followed his every move.

Quinn moved behind Abdul and Adiba and put a hand on each of their shoulders. Adiba turned to say something, but Quinn shook his head and eased them toward a large conference table set against the wall, fifteen feet from the door. Quinn smiled at the security guards, who studied him but didn't smile back.

"I'm beat," Quinn said, loud enough for the guards to hear. He sat on the table, legs swinging. He patted a space next to him, and

Abdul and Adiba joined him.

Quinn spoke in a low whisper. "Abdul, what's going on over there?"

"David has programmed a backdoor. It's like putting a combination lock on the computer. Only someone who knows the code can get in. David is going to pick the lock and reset the termination date on the nanobots."

David punched a series of keys into the computer. After a few seconds, the white-coats started applauding.

Nazar turned, looking for them. He caught Quinn's eye and smiled broadly. Then he put an arm around Keisha's waist, pulled her to him, and kissed the top of her head. She leaned into him and laid her cheek against his shoulder.

While the technicians were clapping and staring at the computer display, David opened the door to the glove box and plucked the tube of nanobots from the induction chamber.

He unscrewed the top, faced Nazar, and raised the tube as if in a toast. *"Allahu Akbar,"* he said.

Then.

Like a man downing a shooter at a redneck bar, David tipped his head back and slid the contents of the tube into his mouth.

He dropped like a rock, screaming and writhing, onto the floor. The professor knelt beside him. "David, what's wrong?"

The technicians, Nazar, and Keisha looked on. It took a few seconds before the group understood what had happened. The professor jerked upright. David had stopped moving, and his head was melting like a block of butter in a hot pan. Already, half his skull was missing. Orange liquid pooled on the floor around his body as if he were bleeding out, except it wasn't blood.

The liquid spread quickly across the floor. The white-coats began hopping, like cowboys in a western movie, dancing while a drunk shoots bullets at their feet.

The professor grabbed his left knee, screamed and stumbled sideways as if he had been tackled; in seconds, his leg was reduced to a stump. The liquid pooled at the technicians' feet. They ran for the door. One by one, they fell as their feet and legs were devoured by nanobots and turned to orange ethanol solution.

Nazar, standing furthest from the group, climbed on the computer table and pulled Keisha up after him.

"The flask. Get me the flask!" Nazar screamed at his assistant and pointed at the empty thermos flask inside the glove box affixed to the table next to theirs.

Keisha clambered across the table. The box's door faced away from her, so she lay on top, swung her arms over the front, and reached through the opening.

"Hold my feet, I can't reach."

Nazar grabbed her legs. She slid forward, bent at the waist over the edge of the box, and grasped the flask. He pulled her back and she held the prize high.

"The liquid contains unlocked nanobots." Nazar pointed to the orange puddle on the floor below them where David had stood a few moments before; a glass test tube was all that remained of the young man. The liquid pooled under and around the front of Nazar's table. The nanobots were consuming the vinyl floor tiles, spreading fast,

"Scoop some into the flask. We only need a small amount. I'll hold your legs." Nazar slid to the far side of the table and braced himself. Keisha, flask in hand, lay on her belly, stretching toward the liquid while Nazar anchored her feet. She touched the open mouth of the flask to the floor and scooped in liquid.

Nanobots reached the front legs of Nazar's table. They began to disassemble the carbon compounds in the steel, and the table tilted and sank to floor. Keisha, flask in hand, slipped forward, dragging Nazar with her. He released her feet and scrambled to the rear of the table saving himself.

As she fell headfirst off the table, Keisha looked in disbelief at her mentor, who had sacrificed her life for his. She landed head-first in the pool of nanobots and emitted a chilling, high-pitched squeal, which lasted only a few seconds before her face and mouth were no longer sufficiently formed to sustain the sound.

Nazar balanced on the edge of the tipping table, but the nanobots had reached the rear legs and the table wobbled. He slid down the tabletop toward the spreading pool of deadly orange liquid and leaped at the last moment onto what was left of Keisha's back. Then, using his loyal assistant as a stepping-stone, he jumped clear of the liquid.

Abdul tightened his grip on Adiba, who glared at Nazar as he stood at the center of the lab scanning the floor, searching for a pathway to the door.

Everything in lab was tipping, falling, melting, like a waking nightmare. Quinn shouted, "Abdul!" and pointed to the exit. The security guards had gone and closed the door behind them. One of the lab technicians had almost escaped. A pool of orange liquid marked where he had fallen, and it blocked their path to the door. A rapacious monster waited for something or someone to feed on.

Quinn pulled at Abdul's arm. "The table. Slide the table. We'll climb along and jump through the doorway."

The conference table was twenty feet long with a polished oak top. He and Abdul braced against the narrow edge, and Adiba jammed in beside them. They pushed, and the table screeched and jerked across the floor until it reached the door.

Abdul clambered up, slid along, and grabbed the door handle, but they'd overshot and table had jammed the door shut. "Pull back!"

Quinn looked behind. The nanobots fed on chairs, tables and equipment, transforming them into more liquid, adding to the spreading orange pool that moved toward him, an incoming tide pushing up the beach. He grabbed Adiba and threw her onto the table.

The table juddered and tipped as the far end, beneath Abdul, dropped two inches. Adiba lost her balance and Abdul grabbed her just before she toppled off. Her eyes remained fixed on Nazar, who had picked his way across the lab and stood close to the center of the table, focused on the pool of liquid swelling behind Quinn's feet.

Quinn pulled with every ounce of every muscle in his body. The table moved, but slower with Abdul and Adiba on top.

"Two more inches!" Abdul screamed.

Quinn yanked again. The deadly liquid pooled six inches behind his feet.

Abdul opened the door.

"That's it. Climb up!"

The table legs nearest the door sunk lower as Adiba grabbed Quinn by the back of his shirt, and he slid and wriggled his belly onto the sloping tabletop, panting and gasping like a landed fish.

Adiba screamed and pointed. "Your shoes!"

Quinn's legs still hung off the end of the table, and orange liquid dripped from the melting soles and splashed to the floor. "Ahhh!" he screamed. A primal sound, born of terror.

Quinn flipped off his shoes, then tore off his socks, threw them down, and turned on his back with arms and legs held high, like an upturned beetle.

For a few seconds, he stopped breathing and stared at his feet, waiting for them to melt.

Then he shouted in a voice tinged with hysteria. "I'm okay . . . I'm okay. Let's go!"

Abdul jumped through the doorway. Adiba pushed Quinn ahead of her. "You next, Mr. Quinn. I'm lighter. I can jump farther."

He didn't argue. She was right. He had more than a hundred pounds on her. The liquid pooled in the doorway and that end of the table had sunk eighteen inches. He crouched low then sprang like a frog through the door. He cleared the orange by two feet and grunted as he landed.

Then he heard a fierce, hate-filled scream from behind him that made the hairs on his arms stand on end. He turned in time to see Adiba, balanced on the crooked table, slam into Nazar, who had slunk up behind her.

The nanobots pooling in the doorway prevented Abdul from reaching her. The table jerked and the movement unbalanced Adiba. She grabbed the doorframe for support. Nazar, disoriented by her blow, staggered backward. When he grabbed for her, she pulled away.

Abdul shouted, "Adiba, jump. Now. Leave him. Jump!"

She stood on the sinking, rocking table, her back to them and feet braced wide apart, knuckles white with their grip on the doorframe. Nazar teetered on the far edge, only twelve inches above the orange floor. His arms whirled as he tried to regain his balance.

Nazar pleaded with her. "Help me!"

The table jerked lower, forcing Nazar to step back off the table onto the floor. The liquid sizzled as it welcomed new feedstock. His legs buckled and he stumbled to his knees, screaming as he was eaten alive from the bottom up. Hands high, reaching, he shrieked at Adiba. "Pull me up. Save me!"

She stood above him, unmoving, and watched as the nanobots devoured his legs, then his pelvis. His body stayed erect as it melted into the floor. The screams were terrible, loud, and desperate.

They stopped when the liquid reached his rib cage and the nanobots disassembled his lungs. His mouth, though, remained stretched open and distorted in a silent scream. As his chest disappeared, he put down his hands to steady himself. They too turned to liquid, and finally, his head toppled, and his eyes turned to glass. Only then did Adiba turn away.

Abdul's eyes locked on the end of the table. The legs sank under the liquid, and orange foam boiled as the nanobots reached the tabletop. The pool of liquid oozed through the doorway, forcing Abdul to retreat until the distance to Adiba had grown to seven feet.

Too far.

Adiba scanned the liquid moat, and her hand came to her mouth. A squeal of fear escaped her fingers. As the nanobots marched up the tabletop toward her, she shuffled her feet away from the end. The stump of the tabletop was a shiny raft in an ocean of orange.

Abdul stared into her eyes, reading the terror but unable to take it away. As the liquid advanced, Adiba stepped along the table and more of her body became hidden by the wall. Soon, only her beautiful face remained visible. One more step and she would be out of sight, just another morsel of feedstock for the rapacious machines. Blood pulsed in Abdul's ears. His stomach churned. He was going to lose her. He moved as close the edge of the liquid as he dared. He wanted to run across and save her. Maybe if he went fast?

Quinn screamed from behind him. "Move!"

Abdul turned and leaped to the side, flattening against the wall as a golf cart roared past him and skidded to a halt inches from the doorframe. The liquid sizzled as it sucked in the rubber of the tires, and the cart rocked wildly as, one by one, they deflated.

Quinn shouted, "Adiba. Climb in. Hurry!"

She grabbed the roof supports, climbed on the cart's nose and swung through the open windshield. Once she was onboard, Quinn reversed, but the cart slewed from side to side unable to gain traction. He stopped driving and slammed on the emergency brake.

"Go. Go!" He pointed frantically to the rear. She clambered over the seat, onto the back bumper and leaped into Abdul's waiting arms.

The golf cart fueled the pool, and the liquid expanded farther into the hallway. For the second time in as many minutes, Abdul thought he might lose someone dear to him. "Hurry, Quinn!"

Quinn followed Adiba's route. He perched on the rear bumper and stared at the five feet of liquid he had to traverse to reach safety. He crouched low, allowed his body to tip forward, and pushed his legs like pistons, launching himself across the deadly pool. Abdul grabbed the big man's shirt before he landed and yanked him backward, adding an extra foot to his leap. Abdul thudded to the ground with Quinn full on top. Sparks flickered across his eyes and pain seared through the back of his neck.

Quinn rolled off him and Adiba grabbed Abdul's cheeks in her hands.

"Abdul, are you okay?"

"I am now." He studied her face. She had risked her life to watch Nazar die in agony. Abdul tried to read her eyes. Not pity or fear or disgust, but something else. Vindication, perhaps.

"Come on," Quinn said. "There's another cart outside. But we have a problem." He led them down the hallway and they burst through the doors into the open. Abdul didn't remember ever feeling so grateful to breathe fresh air.

38

A two-seater golf buggy sat near the entrance. The larger one they had used earlier was three hundred feet away, next to the helicopter, and the two security guards stood beside it. Quinn jumped into the cart and shouted, "Adiba, get in. Abdul, hang on the back." He slammed his foot on the accelerator and Abdul grabbed the cart's roof supports just in time.

Quinn screamed at the cart, "Come on! Come on!"

The guards were in front of the cockpit, waving their arms at Sam. Quinn was still two hundred feet away when they climbed into the chopper and Sam fired up the engine.

Abdul, standing on the rear bumper so his head poked over the cart roof, waved his free hand, screaming, "Wait! Wait for us!"

Sam, head lowered, eyes on the controls, focused on his takeoff procedure. The rotors began their first lazy turns. Quinn pulled the Glock from his jacket and fired into the air. Sam had his headphones on, and didn't react, but the guards' heads snapped around. They stared at Quinn, but made no attempt to signal the pilot.

Quinn muttered under his breath, "Motherfuckers."

The rotors gathered speed. Quinn drove straight up to the front of the helicopter's glass bubble, slammed on the brakes, jumped out, and screamed when his bare feet hit the hot concrete. He adopted a shooting stance, legs braced, Glock held two-handed and pointing directly at Sam's face. The pilot lifted his head, and his eyes went wide. The machine rocked as the blades took its weight. The downdraft thrashed Quinn's face with sand and grit. He didn't falter. He didn't blink.

"Down." He mouthed the word at the pilot and insinuated with the barrel of the gun. The guard riding shotgun was screaming at Sam. The machine lifted off the ground, three feet, four, five. Quinn shifted his aim and fired a single shot into the upper part of the chopper's glass bubble. The guards ducked and a two-foot diameter star appeared in the cockpit glass. He moved the gun back in line with the pilot's face.

"Down! Now!" He knew Sam couldn't hear, but Quinn's message was clear. If he and his friends didn't get away on the chopper, no one would. Sam shouted into his mic, and the guard in the passenger seat shook his head and screamed back at him.

The machine began to descend. Quinn, with a slow, exaggerated nodding of his head, indicated his approval, but he kept the gun locked on the pilot's face.

"Abdul," he shouted, eyes still fixed on the cockpit. "Tell that fat-fuck guard in front to get out."

Abdul jumped from the back of the cart, ran to the helicopter, and yanked open the door.

There was a gunshot, and Abdul dropped like a rock. The guard swung his pistol toward the front. Quinn put four slugs into him before the man's gun was halfway through its arc: two in the chest and two in the head. The plastic bubble splintered into huge, crazy spider webs where the bullets penetrated, then the screen turned red, as blood exploded from the guard's face.

"Abdul!" Adiba ran past Quinn and dropped to her knees, covering her fallen sweetheart—a lioness protecting her cub. Quinn raced around her to get eyes on the second guard. A hand reached out from the rear seat and threw a gun to the ground.

"Get out!" Quinn screamed.

The guard did, with hands held high, and eyes wide and terrified. Quinn checked him for a backup weapon, he didn't have one; he wasn't a threat.

Quinn glanced in the cockpit. Sam was covered in enough blood to give concern until Quinn noticed two thin slits in Sam's cheek. Plastic shards from the cockpit windshield had struck his face, but the cuts seemed superficial. The pilot kept his hands above his head. Quinn glanced at the dead guard slumped in the passenger seat. No threat there. Quinn holstered his Glock, knelt, and put a hand on Abdul's neck—strong pulse.

"Adiba, get up. Let me get a look at him." She remained draped across the boy's chest. Quinn grabbed the back of her blouse and lifted her like a puppy. "You're gonna smother him!"

He flipped Abdul over. Head, chest, belly, all okay. The heaviest blood soaked through his shirt—left forearm.

"Thank God." Quinn turned to the chopper and shouted, "Sam, you got a medical kit onboard?" Sam, hands up, and cans on, didn't hear. Quinn signaled to Sam to take off his headset.

"Bring your medical kit."

Sam killed the engine and climbed from the helicopter. He unclipped a box from beneath his seat and carried it to Abdul. Adiba cradled his head, rocking him and wailing. Quinn moved to help, but Sam put up his hand.

"I got it," he said. He slit Abdul's shirtsleeve with surgical scissors. Quinn glanced at the wound—a through-and-through.

"Make it fast. We need to get outta here." Sam nodded, not looking up.

Quinn pulled the dead guard out of the passenger seat, dragged him clear of the chopper, and dumped him on the hot concrete. "Fuckin' idiot," he said under his breath.

He glanced at the building. The door they'd come from had enlarged to a gaping irregular opening. Orange liquid pooled in front and at the edge of the concrete walkway circling the building.

Orange lines ran vertically up the side of the building as if a cage were painted over the walls. Chunks of concrete fell from between the lines. The building was disintegrating from the bottom up.

Sam had strapped a pressure bandage on Abdul's arm. He sat up and leaned against Adiba while she patted his forehead with a wad of gauze.

"You okay?" Quinn asked him.

"Yeah, fine."

"Sam, let's go," Quinn said. "You!" he shouted to the guard who was on his knees, ten feet from Abdul. He'd been throwing up. "What's your name?"

"Joseph . . . Joseph Dephard."

"Help them up, then get in back."

"Yes, sir." He helped load Abdul into the middle seat. Adiba sat next to him, Joseph behind. Quinn took shotgun. Sam was spraying the inside cockpit glass with Windex and cleaning the blood.

"Abdul, what do you make of that?" Quinn pointed toward the building. Huge semicircular holes had appeared where the concrete, starved of its support beams, had fallen in.

"On the flight over, David told me the nanobots can convert any carbon-based material. That's why the conversion chambers are lined with special concrete. This building's framework must have been built with some kind of carbon fiber, or perhaps steel with carbon reinforcement. They're eating it from the inside out."

"So once they've eaten all the carbon, what then?"

"Dunno. David told me in the refinery they set the nanobots to self-destruct when the ethanol reaches an optimum concentration. I asked him the same question—what if there's not enough carbon to reach the stop-level. He said there's also a termination time set. Who knows what he programmed into these nanobots? If he even did. Maybe they'll stay active."

A shudder ran through Quinn at the thought of the episode in the lab. "That was the scariest shit I've ever seen. People eaten alive, and so fast! I'm sure glad I'm old-fashioned."

"What do you mean?" Abdul said.

"Well, who else do you know wears elastic-sided, slip-on shoes?" Quinn lifted his bare foot and wiggled his toes. Even Adiba managed a laugh.

"That'll do," Sam said. He'd cleaned one-third of the screen. He fired up the engine and they lifted off. As they did, a huge chunk from the upper part of the building crashed down and a plume of dust exploded into the air.

"Sam, get the hell out of here before those bugs splash on us and eat the damned helicopter."

39

Sam angled the blades forward and they headed east, toward the gleaming domes of the refinery. Once he was a thousand feet up, Sam brought the chopper around in a smooth curve, circling the building from which they had so narrowly escaped.

Holes gaped in the roof, and orange liquid covered every exposed area of the floor. A black-tarred pole next to the building tumbled like a felled tree and crashed toward the east, pulled by the lines it supported.

"What's that?" Quinn said, pointing at the pole.

Sam said, "Transmission line. They're off-grid. Power comes from generators at the main plant."

Quinn traced the path of the cables, which drooped and peaked along a parade of poles that ran to the refinery two miles away.

By the time he turned back, the felled pole was half gone, transformed into a black-and-orange smear in the sand.

"Transmission lines are metal," Abdul said. "The nanobots can't process metal, and there must be at least three hundred feet between poles. They won't be able to make the leap."

"Sam. Hang on a sec'," Quinn said. He checked his watch.

Sam eased back on the stick, and they hovered in place. Sam pivoted the cockpit so it faced the transmission lines. In the distance, a heat haze distorted the air above a long line of garbage trucks waiting to deposit feedstock at the refinery.

The next pole toppled.

Quinn checked his watch again. "Two minutes," he said.

"Look." Abdul pointed to a thin orange line in the sand connecting the two fallen poles, which marked the progress of the nanobots. "Maybe the wire has a plastic coating."

The line pointed, like a directional mark on a map, directly at the refinery.

"Sam, fly along the power line. We have to count poles." Sam tilted the machine forward, and Quinn counted aloud as they flew toward the plant—thirty.

Abdul pointed to the large building at the end of the transmission line. "At two minutes each, that's sixty minutes till they reach that."

"Joe, what's in there?" Quinn asked.

"Generators, computer room, the admin offices where we clock in each day."

"How many people?" Quinn said.

"Two hundred."

The parking lot next to the building was crammed with vehicles. Quinn turned in his seat and faced Joseph. "And overall in the complex?"

"Maybe three hundred more."

"Don't forget those." Adiba pointed to a line of trucks waiting to drop their loads. Quinn gazed past the trucks and traced the four-lane road Nazar had built. Two miles to their north, it connected to the I10 Interstate, part of the highway system that spread through every major population center in America.

"Oh. Shit!" Quinn considered having Joe call in the authorities, but unless he could order up an immediate missile strike to take out the power lines, more personnel arriving could only make matters worse. There wasn't time to explain, and no one would believe the urgency anyway.

Looking back along the transmission lines, the prototype building was a pile of rubble. Another pylon crashed into the sand. He was staring at a long, slow-burning fuse, and they were hovering over the bomb.

He had to find a way to cut the power line before the nanobots reached the plant. Underground cables connected the power plant to every part of the complex. The complex connected to the road, and the road connected to the Interstate. If the 'bots made it to the admin building, they would feast on the highway, and once they hit the freeway, there would be no stopping them.

"We have to warn those people. Joseph, what's the protocol for an emergency requiring evacuation?" Quinn said.

"A system of sirens throughout the refinery, but only the head of security can trigger the alarm."

"Call him. Now!"

"I can't."

"What do you mean you can't?" Quinn flipped around and knelt in his seat, leaning hard against the seatback, his finger pointed at Joe's face.

"You shot him," Joseph said.

"So *you* do it!"

"Only Mason had the code, and it's changed daily."

"That's bad practice," Quinn said. "Someone else must have the code."

"Well—" Joseph said.

"What? Well what, Joe!" Quinn came over the back of his seat, between Abdul and Adiba, and got in Joseph's face.

"The Professor had the code," Joseph said. "He was our failsafe if Mason was compromised."

"Quinn," Sam said, his brow furrowed with worry.

"What now?" Quinn barked, his fists clenching and unclenching against the seatback.

"It's . . . we can't stay up here. I need the fuel to return to the airport."

Quinn didn't respond. Sam hadn't been in that building. Sam hadn't seen people melted in seconds into a pool of orange Kool-Aid. Flying back to Phoenix wasn't in their immediate future.

Quinn flipped back into his seat. "Take us over there." He pointed to the nearest conversion chamber, and Sam headed toward the silver-domed building.

Four dump trucks pulled away after dumping garbage on the concrete ribbon skirting the tank. Ten crude piles formed a rough semicircle in front of the loading chute. The scene repeated at each of the chamber's eight loading bays.

A bulldozer, more than twice the truck's height and double its length, moved toward the garbage. Its front blade, lowered flush to the ground, slammed into one pile, scraping and pushing the trash toward the chute that fed the containment vessel below.

"Okay, Sam. Put us down close to that monster." Quinn turned to Joseph. "I'm getting off here. Sam will fly you to the admin building. Get whoever is responsible for the generators to turn off the power to the western building. Can you do that?"

"Yes, sir."

"That's good, because I don't want anyone electrocuted, particularly me."

Quinn passed his cell phone to Abdul. "When you get inside the building, call Scott on a landline, his number's stored in here. Tell him to arrange the exchange at Phoenix airport, but don't tell him anything else, especially don't tell him where we are right now. There are enough people in danger already. Calling in the cavalry will make matters worse. Got it, Abdul?"

"Got it." Abdul slapped Quinn in the shoulder. "Be careful out there, big man."

"Sure."

The pilot landed two hundred feet behind the bulldozer. Quinn underestimated the drop, and a sharp pain shot up his left ankle when it jarred on the hard ground. Baked by the desert sun, the concrete burned his bare feet, and he started hopping in place. Right now, he'd trade his life savings for a pair of sneakers.

The downdraft from the chopper almost flattened him as Sam pulled away. The air was fetid. Carrion birds circled and screeched overhead. Compared with the scale of the building and the machines, Quinn felt insignificant, vulnerable, and exposed.

The dozer was thirty feet long. The operator, in his enclosed cab, sat ten feet in the air, and he wore ear-protectors to block the deafening noise of revving engines, dumping, and scraping. Quinn ran toward the machine, but the ground was littered with scraps of garbage. Quinn's feet were simultaneously burned and cut.

He picked up a large piece of white plastic and waved it over his head, trying to get the driver's attention, but there was no reason for the man to look anywhere except in front. Standing still for a few seconds, he observed the machine to understand the driver's operating pattern: Push trash forward. Reverse and curve counterclockwise toward Quinn before moving clockwise to push the next heap to the chute. Then repeat. The dozer was moving away from him. Sam had dropped him on the wrong side.

Instead of chasing the machine, Quinn set off toward the untouched garbage piles, cutting across the driving pattern.

Reaching the driver was out of the question, climbing over the bulldozer's metal tracks to access the cab, was impossible. Quinn need to get ahead of the driver and attract his attention.

Time was against him. He tried to run head-up, ignoring the pain in his feet. But he stumbled and slipped on the uneven mess, and his eyes were inexorably drawn downward. He gave in to human nature and focused on the ground, picked the least painful path, and glanced up occasionally to be sure he still headed toward the untouched piles.

Instead of completing a full, first pass of the large heaps, the driver doubled back to scrape the remaining trash in the quadrant Quinn had already crossed. With the noise and his focus mostly on the ground Quinn didn't see or hear the dozer circle behind him until a pile of garbage, being pushed along by the dozer, knocked his legs away and flipped him on his back.

The trash shifted and moved below him like a living thing. He couldn't stand, so he rolled onto hands and knees and scrambled over rotting food, plastic cartons, and soggy cardboard. Legs pumping like a running back, he traversed the pile until he reached the hot steel of the blade.

A large tire lay next to him. He straddled it on his knees. Quinn stretched up, but his fingertips fell three feet short of the blade's lip. He judged the dozer's position relative to the chute: two hundred feet from the drop. As the machine gathered more trash, the tire rode the garbage and lifted him closer to the lip, but not fast enough. He'd get one shot; if he missed the top edge and lost his footing he doubted he'd have time to try again before the dozer reached the chute.

Body facing the blade and head turned, eyes fixed on the fast-approaching loading chute, Quinn delayed as long as he dared. Forty feet from the edge, fear overcame logic. With bare feet positioned on either side of the tire, he slammed his knees ramrod straight. The metal blade was a foot thick. He spread his fingers over the width of the blade searching for a grip. Fingernails splintered as he dug into the unyielding, hot metal. Quinn screamed. The sound drowned like a pin drop in a thunderstorm.

He gripped the top edge and heaved himself off the tire. His head cleared the lip, and he wriggled his upper body until the blade lodged in his belly, head and chest on the driver's side, hips and legs dangling over the trash.

Behind him, garbage tumbled and crashed as it cascaded into the chasm below. A strong updraft of hot, stinking air hit his legs as though he were flying. The blade cleared the concrete, and he hung in mid-air, draped over the blade like an old banana skin stubbornly stuck on the lip of a trash can.

The machine stopped. The sudden braking action almost shook him loose. His arms cramped and screamed with the effort of holding on. His legs flailed, useless, treading air on the business side of the blade. He braced himself, anticipating the machine's rough reverse from the chute, but it remained stationary. He peered up. The driver had removed his earmuffs. He stared at Quinn with a look of incredulity.

"Back up slowly," Quinn shouted.

The machine crawled back from the precipice. The engine shut down.

Between the stink and nerves and the strain of keeping his body bent at the stomach over the blade, Quinn wanted to. throw up. He fought the urge, pouring his focus into maintaining balance. It was a long way down. With no garbage below him now, he might break a leg if he fell. The driver climbed from his cab, stood below Quinn and yelled.

"What the fuck you doin'?"

Quinn spoke in gasps. "Help . . . me . . . down." Folded like a pretzel, his body weight squeezed his chest against the hard steel of the upper edge of the dozer's blade. Quinn lost sight of the man, then he felt a tap on his ankle.

The driver shouted from below. "Okay, ease down. It's about two feet to my shoulders. I'm right between your legs."

Quinn edged and slipped his body back. His bare toes pointed, searching for solid contact. Until, at last, the driver grabbed his left foot, then his right, and guided Quinn's feet to his shoulders. As he pushed off the blade, his cheek tore on the metal, and he slid down the driver's back to land in a heap.

"Fuck, buddy, I never saw you. I coulda killed you. What you doin' here?"

Quinn was holding on to consciousness by a thin thread. "Water." It was all he could manage.

The driver gripped him under the arms and spun him around so the curve of the blade cradled his back. He returned a few seconds later with a canteen. The cool liquid helped. After a few deep gulps, the faintness passed.

Quinn signaled the man closer so he didn't have to shout. "There's been an accident at the Western plant. People are dead: Mason from security, Nazar Eudon, Professor Farjohn."

The driver stared at him as if he were crazy.

"What's your name?" Quinn asked.

"PJ. They call me PJ."

"Okay, PJ, here's the deal. If we don't cut the transmission lines between the power plant and the Western facility, this refinery is going to blow, and everyone here, including you and me, will die."

"Look, buddy, I don't know what you're talking about. I'd better get you back to the medics, you're in bad shape." PJ stared at Quinn's feet. "And where the fuck is your shoes?"

Quinn would have liked nothing more than a shot of morphine and a cute nurse to bathe his feet, but he'd already lost ten or fifteen minutes and the nanobots wouldn't be taking a coffee break. He slipped a hand inside his jacket and pulled out his Glock.

"PJ, if you do what I say, I won't hurt you . . . If you don't, I'll shoot you. Doesn't matter to me, because if you don't do what I say you're gonna die anyway."

The driver raised his hands, like in the movies, then he ran around the blade and out of sight.

Quinn tried to stand. First attempt didn't work; his knees gave on him. Then the bulldozer's engine started, and he scrambled on hands and knees away from the blade just before the bulldozer pushed forward toward the loading chute.

"Son of a bitch!" Quinn cleared the blade, glared up at the driver's cab, and leveled the Glock at PJ's chest. PJ saw him, but instead of stopping he turned the dozer, trying to crush Quinn under its twenty-foot-long metal tracks. The machine was big, but not agile.

Quinn put a slug into the side window of the cab, behind PJ's head. The dozer stopped.

Quinn signaled with the Glock for the driver to get down. This time, he obeyed. Quinn kept the gun centered on the driver's chest.

"PJ, I don't want to hurt you," Quinn said, "but I need you to drive this thing over—"

PJ turned and ran toward the admin building.

"Fuck!" Quinn stared at the filthy, serrated metal tracks he'd have to navigate to reach the driver's cab. He winced in anticipation and started climbing.

Sitting in the cab was like perching atop a high building. The series of levers to his right baffled him, but a pedal on the floor gave him hope. He pushed and heard a reassuring hiss of compressed air when he released it—brake. Now he had to figure out the levers.

Because the machine had no steering wheel.

40

Two of the levers were longer than the others. Quinn pulled back on the one to his right. The right-hand tracks reversed, and the dozer rotated clockwise. A screeching sound came from the stationary track. When he pushed forward on the left lever, the noise stopped as the track rolled forward, and the machine swiveled in a zero turn. Once he faced the admin building, half a mile away, Quinn pushed both levers forward.

By experiment, he identified the correct lever to raise the front blade off the ground.

Quinn checked the cab and found what he had hoped for—a radio handset hooked in a pouch on the dash. He depressed the "talk" button.

"This is Steven Quinnborne. I'm a police officer. I need to speak to the person in charge of the facility."

"Quinn. It's Abdul."

"Have you killed the power to the lines?"

"I'm here with the plant manager. He'd isolated the line before we arrived. They'd sent a team out to check what was going on at the western location. Joseph got the crew recalled, they're safe. Where are you?"

"I'm in a bulldozer, heading straight for you."

The dozer covered another forty feet before Abdul said, "Okay, we see you. Damn, that thing's huge."

229

"I hope so. I plan to use it to take out a pole. If I can break the power line, that'll stop the nanobots from reaching the refinery. Ask the plant manager whether it will work."

Quinn was met with silence. A plant manager probably didn't want to hear from someone planning to tear up his facility with a bulldozer.

"Quinn, he doesn't think you can do it. He says ... wait a minute, here he is."

"Mr. Quinn, this is Greg Matteson. The pole might come crashin' down on your head, mate."

"Any suggestions? We only have thirty minutes or so before the nanobots reach your building."

Quinn heard Abdul shouting in the background. "Quinn, they've accelerated. We're looking at the last twelve poles from the viewing gallery and ... wait, eleven left. You've got less than ten minutes."

"Mr. Quinn," Greg said. "Try for the first pole. Lift your blade to maximum and connect as high up as you can. Don't slam into it. Make contact first, then increase power. Make sure you're aligned with the cable, or the tension might tip you sideways. You need to tear the cable from the building. If the line gives before the pole breaks, you should be okay."

Quinn had the levers pushed as far forward as he could. As he rolled through the parking lot beside the admin building, he was relieved that most vehicles had left. On the third floor, five people stood at a large viewing window. He couldn't make out faces, but he assumed they were Abdul, Sam, Adiba, Joseph, and the plant manager.

"You guys need to be ready to get out if this doesn't work," he said.

"I'm gonna watch you from here, mate. Keep your channel open. I built this place, so I should be able to help take it apart," Greg said.

The pole stood dead ahead, less than one hundred feet away. He pulled back on the lever for the blade, which lifted and blocked his view. Suddenly he was driving blind. He eased back on both drive levers, slowing almost to a stop while the blade rose past his line of sight. He moved forward again, slower this time. The bulldozer handled differently with the heavy blade high in the air, less stable, as if he might tip forward.

Quinn maneuvered below the cable, lining up the dozer as Greg had instructed. With twenty feet to go, he slowed to a crawl until the blade contacted the pole. The pole swayed. The cable in front of him, which connected his pole with the next, yawed up and down. His cab rocked in time.

"Okay, you've got her. Make sure you push on both levers equally or you might start her turning."

Quinn eased the levers forward. The engine roared as the machine strained against the resistance of the thick pole and the cable bolted to the wall of the admin building a hundred feet behind him. The tracks dug into the ground, and he heard a high-pitched whine.

"There's a weird noise, sounds like a cat's choir," he said.

"That's the cable straining, mate. Give her more power."

Quinn pushed both levers forward all the way. The whine changed to a scream, then something exploded.

"Get down!" Greg screamed over the radio. Quinn threw himself forward onto the floor. The cab shattered, and dazzling desert sun streamed in and blinded him. Cubes of safety glass peppered the back of his head and neck like buckshot.

Then the world went black.

41

Greg and Joe tore down three flights of stairs and launched themselves into the ATV Greg had parked, ready and waiting, at the entrance to the admin building. Joe stamped the gas pedal, and they sped toward Quinn's bulldozer, careening across the desert at full speed.

Joe caught the monster vehicle and matched speed.

"Closer!" Greg shouted. "Hold her steady." Greg climbed onto the hood of the ATV and leaped over the top of the dozer's tracks, grabbing onto the remnants of the cab's metal frame.

He hoisted himself through the shattered windshield, reached in and pushed back on the drive levers, stopping the big machine. Quinn, crunched fetus-like in the well of the cab where the driver's feet would normally be, didn't move.

Greg heaved Quinn's limp body toward the seat, giving him access to the brake pedal. Calves resting on Quinn's belly, he turned the dozer and headed for admin building. He slowed as he approached the first pole, lying smashed on the ground, surrounded by the cable Quinn had wrenched from the building.

He lowered the blade, picked up the broken pole and pushed it into the desert, dragging the trailing power line behind. Full speed, straight ahead, Greg passed the still-standing number two pylon and deposited the broken pole as far from the plant as the cable allowed.

As he reversed, pole three tumbled. The nanobots would soon

reach the pile he had created, but that was as far as they would get. Once they gobbled poles one and two, they'd be out of food.

He drove the bulldozer back to the parking lot. Quinn, a crumpled, bloody heap beneath Greg's legs, still hadn't moved.

Abdul, Adiba, and Sam waited in the doorway of the building. Joe sat atop the ATV. Sam had the medical kit from the helicopter in his hand. No one spoke as the big machine halted.

The top half of the bulldozer's cab was missing, sliced off by the two-inch-thick power cable when it broke loose from the admin building and whiplashed like a guided missile toward the source of the force that had ripped away its anchor. It had cut through the plate steel of the machine's cab like a blade through paper.

Greg stood on the dozer's tracks, leaned in, and heaved Quinn's body out of the machine. He slid Quinn over his shoulder with a grunt, bore him down, fireman-style, and then ran into the air-conditioned lobby of the admin building. He laid Quinn on the tiles and felt for a pulse.

Sam slammed an EpiPen into Quinn's thigh.

The big man's chest filled with air, and he coughed.

42

"Oh ... Mr. Quinn!" Adiba sat in the rear seat of the helicopter, back against the side of the chopper, Quinn's head cradled on her lap. His right eye opened, and he caught his reflection in the side window. His left cheek had puffed out like a Swiss Roll, closing that eye. His hands throbbed and when he lifted them he understood why—his fingernails were shattered, caked in filth and blood. His swollen, lacerated feet, were numb. Seeing himself through Adiba's shocked face, he began to hurt more.

"It looks worse than it is," he said, without believing one syllable. His voice sounded odd. He ran his tongue around his mouth: one front tooth was chipped to a stub. "Did I reach the pole in time?"

Abdul knelt in the front seat, peering over the seatback. "Yup, once they'd eaten the last poles, they had nowhere else to go. I guess they don't like sand."

Quinn nodded. "Did you give Scott the message?"

"Yeah. He wasn't very pleased about the limited information, though. I might get a lecture in journalistic integrity when I return to London."

"Good job, Abdul. Do you have my phone?"

Abdul passed it over. Quinn hit a speed dial. Scott answered after two rings. "Quinn, is that you?"

"Yes, I'm with Abdul and Adiba, and I'm praying my old friend has sorted out the complications in my life. Because, frankly, Scott, I'm flat out of fixes."

"Your voice sounds strange, are you eating."

"Long story, Scott, and no, but I could."

"Where are you?"

"In a helicopter twenty minutes out from Phoenix airport."

"There'll be a welcoming committee when you land. Quinn, they want to know whether you have the weapon."

"No. But I know where it is, and I can instruct them on safe handling. Look, Scott. I'm all in. Just tell me. When we land, handcuffs or highballs?"

"Well, no handcuffs, but I don't think the FBI is much into liquor," Scott said.

"Thank you . . . thank you, Scott."

And, in front of a disbelieving Abdul and Adiba, hot tears rolled down Detective Chief Inspector Steven Quinnborne's cheeks.

A cordon of white-helmeted military police surrounded the landing pad. Two men in full biological protection gear, looking like astronauts, greeted them at the helicopter. One, with a bullhorn in his white-gloved hand, addressed them over the sound of dying rotors.

"Please follow me."

Adiba's head was on a swivel. "What are they doing? Who are those people? Why are they dressed like that?"

"They're making sure we don't have any nanobots with us," Abdul said.

A violent shiver went through her, and Abdul cupped her cheek in his hand. "It's nearly over. I promise."

The suited men loaded Sam and his passengers into the rear of a plain white van. They sat on uncomfortable metal bench seats. Abdul and Adiba positioned themselves either side of Quinn and supported him as they swayed and tore across the tarmac, past the runways, to two gray temporary buildings set up in a remote corner of the airport.

The white-suits led them into the first building. The men were ushered into one room. Adiba was pointed to a separate door. She panicked and grabbed Abdul's arm. "No. What are you doing? Stop them, Mr. Quinn!"

One of the white-suits spoke. "We need you to remove your

clothing and undergo a sterilization process. You can go together if you wish, we just thought . . ." He nodded toward Adiba.

"How long will it take?" Abdul asked.

"Ten minutes."

He looked at Quinn, who nodded.

Abdul smoothed back her hair. "Adiba, do what they say. We'll get clean, and I'll meet you on the other side."

"Okay." She sounded so meek, so frightened. He'd worry the whole time they were apart.

Quinn handed over his gun, passport, spare magazine, the remainder of Nazar's money, and the phone. They removed their clothes and dropped them in a chute before stepping into a large shower room. Powerful rotating jets blasted them with scalding, disinfectant-laden water from the walls, ceiling and floor. Abdul got a look at Quinn's injuries. It was easier to spot the parts of him that *weren't* bruised and cut. How was the big man not screaming in pain?

They changed into clean, cotton briefs, and one-sized, gray jumpsuits. A decent fit on Quinn and Sam, but Abdul's hung like an empty sack. A uniformed MP led them through an airlock and along a connecting walkway into the next trailer. Adiba waited for them in a large conference room, sipping a soda. She jumped into Abdul's arms, and they kissed as if they had been parted for a month.

"We'll need to get those two a room," Sam said.

Quinn smiled. Then winced because he opened a cut on his lip, but the smile still felt good.

A man wearing a dark suit, straight-backed, clean-shaven, neat hair, in his fifties, came through the door at the opposite end of the room.

"Here we go," Quinn said softly.

The man introduced himself as Patton Armstrong. He didn't say, but Quinn guessed FBI. He confirmed their names and explained that each of them would be separately debriefed. Then they were free to go. Quinn suspected freedom might depend on the results of the debriefing. But, all in all, he felt much better after the shower, and this reception certainly beat the hell out of getting eaten by nanobots, or slapped in prison for illegally entering the US with an unlicensed firearm, or the dozen other offenses they surely were guilty of.

In an interrogation room, Quinn sat at a table across from Patton who questioned him about the weapon. What did it do? How did it work? Where was it? How could he obtain it? Who else had knowledge of it? Quinn spoke for an hour. He held nothing back because he had no way of knowing what part of his story, if any, could put him behind bars. The atmosphere remained cordial, and the longer the questioning lasted, the more confident he became that they were going to be okay.

When Patton finished, he escorted Quinn back to the conference room where the others waited for him. Adiba jumped up, ran to him, hugged him and planted a kiss on his good cheek.

"What was that for?" he said.

"For being the bravest man I'll ever meet, Mr. Quinn. I told them how you saved us, and how you saved those people at the plant."

"Well, not single-handed. I think we shared the load." Quinn's cheeks grew hot.

His cell phone started ringing. An agent passed a bag with his belongings, and he fished the device out and answered. "Quinn here."

Superintendent Porter's voice said, "Quinn. Thank god you're safe. The Yanks briefed me on the refinery. I believe congratulations are in order. You've done a great service for your country."

Quinn had never heard his boss sound so happy. "I don't know about that, but we're all okay and looking forward to coming home."

"From what I hear, you thwarted a major terrorist attack and helped defuse a political crisis. You're a *bona fide* hero, Detective."

Quinn opened his mouth to reply, but no words came out. The last time he'd spoken to his boss he'd gotten reamed out and told to get on the next plane to London. Finally, he managed, "Thanks, Super."

"Quinn, I understand the weather in Phoenix is nice this time of year, well, compared with England. Why not take a few days to recuperate, charge the hotel to the department? I'll sign off on anything within reason."

"Okay." Damn, Scott must have done a fantastic sales job.

237

Abdul and Adiba flew out the next day. Abdul told Quinn that he planned to approach her father as soon as he'd talked to his parents in London. Quinn wished him luck and gave his blessing. The kids' relationship was certainly battle-tested.

Quinn checked into the Phoenician in Scottsdale, on the outskirts of Phoenix. He ate four meals a day and slept, a lot. The FBI found him a dentist and arranged for medical care. No bones broken, just banged-up, the doctor told him—easy for him to say!

On the third evening, Quinn's room phone woke him from a late afternoon nap.

"I heard a rumor you were going to play golf. I had to see that for myself," Scott Shearer said.

"Where are you?" Quinn asked.

"The next room."

Quinn hung up and opened his door. Scott stood in the hallway and offered his hand. Quinn knocked it aside and gave him a crushing bear hug. "Old friend, you saved my nuts."

Scott pushed Quinn off. He was blushing.

"Damned stiff Brit," Quinn said, and they shared a laugh.

After dinner, they retired to the bar and ordered malt whisky.

"The US President's making a primetime announcement tonight," Scott said.

"About?"

"Apparently there's a significant development on the terrorism front." Scott grinned like the cat that got the cream.

At 7:45 p.m., the major networks cleared their programming and talking heads began speculating. Cameras showed a still of the Oval office. Behind the president's empty desk, next to the Stars and Stripes, a British flag was on display.

"A Union Jack?" Quinn said.

"You'll see," Scott said, still with the knowing grin.

At eight, the president walked into the room, took his place at the desk and faced the cameras.

"My fellow Americans, I want to brief you tonight on a significant development in our ongoing battle against the extremists who wish harm on our country.

"Four days ago, agents of the Federal Bureau of Investigation successfully foiled a major terrorist attack on American soil. This attack was carried out by the Islamic-militant group known as

Allah's Revenge. The same terrorists were responsible for the death of two hundred innocents in London, England, and more recently for the massacre at the G20 meeting in Seoul, South Korea, an attack in which the Vice President of the United States lost his life.

"Their target was an ethanol production facility operated by Eudon Alternative Energy near Phoenix, Arizona.

"Thanks to the diligence and enterprise of our intelligence services, the attack was thwarted, and more than five hundred employees at the plant were safely evacuated. However, the refinery was contaminated. The plant has been closed, and a twenty-mile exclusion zone created to ensure the safety of Phoenix residents.

"Mr. Nazar Eudon, the plant owner, and several key staff acted heroically to facilitate our successful intervention. These brave Muslims sacrificed their lives to save the people of Phoenix. Clear proof that the actions of fanatics like Allah's Revenge do not represent the wishes and desires of the many peaceful Muslims living here in America and elsewhere in the world."

The president paused, and smiled.

"You will notice behind me, beside Old Glory, the flag of Great Britain. Without the cooperation of the British Secret Service, we may have discovered this terrorist plot too late to avoid the consequences. Earlier today, I called the British Prime Minister and thanked him for his country's assistance in this matter. Never in recent history has there been a more concrete reason to value the special relationship between our two countries.

"America, and the world, is safer tonight, thanks to the excellent work of our agents in the FBI, the cooperation of the British Secret Service, and a few brave Muslims, equally determined that evil should not prevail. God bless you, and God bless America."

Quinn turned to Scott. "I thought Allah's Revenge was finished with Ghazi's death?"

"According to my sources in the US, rumors of his death are greatly exaggerated," Scott said.

"But I saw the body. So did Abdul."

"A cynic would say that makes him an ideal enemy. Easily manipulated yet posing no real threat. Perception is everything!"

Quinn shook his head. "What about the facility? Do you suppose the Americans will start producing ethanol now?"

"Not unless the Midwest corn producers and the oil companies say they can."

"You really think they'll bury the technology, discard the solution to the world's energy crisis?"

Scott called for another shot of whisky and raised his glass. In a voice dripping with sarcasm, he made a toast.

"Long live Ghazi. And God bless the Oily States of America."

43

Two days later, the Chairman of the Joint Chiefs of Staff sat in his office in Washington with the Director of the CIA. They sipped coffee at his conference table. Two dozen framed photographs chronicling the old soldier's rise through the ranks lined the wall behind his head. They served as a reminder of his seniority.

"I understand the emergency appropriations bill will be fast-tracked," the Chairman said.

"Two or three days in the House, then early next week to the Senate," the CIA man replied.

The Chairman nodded, and then smiled. "You've requested a significant budget increase?"

"We have strong justification. We need to understand this nanotechnology."

"Of course . . . and the weapon?"

"We acquired the residue in Phoenix, but it was inert. The nanobots ceased to function when they ran out of fuel. Our people hope to reverse-engineer what we have."

"What about the Israelis?"

The CIA man spread his hands flat on the table. "They insist the terrorists' lab was empty when they arrived."

"And our SEAL team?"

"Not found."

The chairman raised his eyebrows. "Can we corroborate?"

"We have a visual of them entering. The British police officer, Quinnborne, counted seven bodies in the laboratory, five from the weapon, two from gunshots. But we have no leverage with Tel Aviv. We went in covert, and the Israelis are pissed off."

"Perhaps, in time?"

The CIA man nodded. "Perhaps."

"If they have the weapon, we have a problem," the Chairman said.

"At a minimum they have samples of the residue. So do the Koreans, and every one of the G20 countries, even the damned Saudis."

"It's a race, then."

"Yes, sir."

The old soldier stood and shook the CIA man's hand. "Make sure we win."

. . . THE END . . .

ABOUT THE AUTHOR

Born into a blue-collar family in Liverpool, England, Pete missed The Beatles but did go to The Cavern a few times. He immigrated to the US in the early 90s and became a citizen. After twenty years in the corporate madhouse, he moved to Western North Carolina where he lives with a couple llamas, two spoiled dogs, a brace of cookie-eating goats, one ferocious cat, and a wonderful wife who thankfully understands his obsessive need to write fiction.

For more about Pete, visit www.PeteBarberFiction.com

Made in the USA
San Bernardino, CA
28 August 2014